Shield

A Blackbridge Novel

Claire Boston

BANTILLY
PUBLISHING

About the Author

Claire Boston fell in love with romance and romantic suspense at eleven when she discovered her mother's stash of Nora Roberts novels. Like Nora, she writes series set around families or groups of friends, and always guarantees a happy ending.

Claire loves learning, and exploring new locations, interesting vocations and cultures through her writing.

When Claire's not writing she can be found creating her own handmade journals, swinging on a sidecar, or in the garden attempting to grow something other than weeds.

Claire lives in Western Australia with her husband, who loves even her most annoying quirks and is currently learning how to knit.

You can connect with Claire through Facebook (https://www.facebook.com/clairebostonauthor) and Twitter @clairebauthor, or join her reader group (http://www.claireboston.com/reader-group/).

Also by Claire Boston

The Texan Quartet
What Goes on Tour
All that Sparkles
Under the Covers
Into the Fire

The Flanagan Sisters
Break the Rules
Change of Heart
Blaze a Trail
Place to Belong

The Blackbridge Series
Nothing to Fear
Nothing to Gain
Nothing to Hide
Nothing to Lose
Shelter
Shield
Harbour
Protect

The Beginner Writer's Toolkit
Self-Editing

DEDICATION

To all State Emergency Services personnel who give up
their time to help others. Thank you.

Chapter 1

Jamie Zanetti scanned the bush for signs of the missing boy.

To his left, other State Emergency Service volunteers called Noah's name, their bright orange clothes visible through the straggly gum trees. To his right was more bush. His black steel-capped boots crunched over the damp native grasses.

How far could a four-year-old walk in a few hours? They didn't have enough volunteers to cover the whole national park. The winery had disappeared from sight a long time ago and he couldn't even hear the sound of cars along the highway. At least the ground was relatively flat and it was too cold for the dugites and tiger snakes to be active. The sun sank closer to the horizon, the temperature dropping. It would be dark soon and that would be terrifying for a young kid. Thick grey clouds threatened to make the day even more miserable by dropping rain.

Christ, he hoped they found Noah soon—alive.

Jamie had been back in Blackbridge for six months, and in that time he'd been on far too many searches for missing people. Sometimes they found them alive with only minor injuries, sometimes they didn't. But this time it was a kid. Jamie visualised the photo they'd been shown—wide brown eyes and a cheeky grin. Noah had been wearing a green rain jacket and black jeans, so would blend with the surrounding bush.

Jamie cupped his hands around his mouth. "Noah!" He waited. Only the echo of other searchers calling the boy.

Jamie moved more to the right, still able to see his fellow volunteer, Elijah Johnson, but widening the area of the search. If he were four, what would he do?

He sighed. As soon as he realised he was lost, he would have sat down and waited for someone to find him. His parents had drilled that into him. But that had been *after* he'd decided to visit his friend Kit by himself. Kit had a new puppy and he'd wanted to play with it.

Jamie glanced around. What would have caught Noah's attention? Had he followed something—a bird or a kangaroo? Yeah, he could imagine him running into the bush after an interesting animal, especially because the child was English. Most of Australia's animals would be unusual to him. Perhaps he'd wandered further and further away until he'd lost sight of whatever he was following and then realised he didn't know his way back.

"Noah!"

A sound. A sob?

Jamie froze, straining to hear. "Noah, is that you?" He stepped towards the noise.

A quiet cough, or maybe a hiccough reached him.

Jamie's heart raced as he yelled to Elijah, "Over here." He strode towards the sound. "Wave your arms for me, Noah, so I can find you."

The boy wailed and Jamie pinpointed him sitting next to a tree, his cheeks tear- and dirt-streaked. Relief made him dizzy. "I've found him!" He crashed through the bush. As he reached the boy, his ankle rolled on a rock and he dropped to his knees, pain coursing through him.

Shit.

Noah recoiled.

Jamie gritted back the pain and smiled at the sobbing young boy. "Hey, kiddo. My name's Jamie. I'm with the SES. We've been searching for you."

"I want my Dad!" The boy shook, hugging himself.

Jamie glanced up. The other volunteers were coming. "He's on his way. He's been so worried about you."

Noah bit his lip. "Am I in trouble?"

"Nah. Your parents will be happy to have you back."

Footsteps as Elijah approached. Jamie squeezed the boy's hand and then other members of the Blackbridge SES converged on them. Elijah's wide smile made Jamie's heart stutter. "Hey, Noah. Glad we found you."

Their section leader, Morgan spoke into his radio. "We've found him."

"Noah!" The frantic call of the boy's father as he pushed through the volunteers.

"Dad!" Noah flung himself at his father who picked him up and held him tight, his eyes closed.

"You're all right." The man's voice shook. "Are you hurt?" He examined his son and then hugged him again. "You scared me to death. Don't ever do that again."

The boy buried his head into his father's shoulder and mumbled sorry amidst his cries.

Jamie's heart clenched and he blinked his watery eyes. Reunions like this were the best possible outcome. He swallowed hard and quietly cleared his throat. Elijah squeezed his shoulder and smiled. No judgement.

"It's OK. You're safe. I've got you." The father dried Noah's tears and kissed his cheek. "Why did you wander off?"

"I saw a kangaroo."

His father sighed and glanced at Jamie. "Thank you. Thank all of you."

Morgan nodded. "We're glad he's safe. Let's get him back to the winery. There's an ambulance there to check him." He led the way.

Jamie rotated his ankle and hissed at the fresh pain shooting up his leg. Damn it.

"Need help?" Elijah held out his hand.

They wore identical orange uniforms, but somehow, Elijah wore his with style. His French-tucked shirt drew Jamie's eye to his belt and made him imagine what lay beneath it. He met Elijah's deep green eyes, and hesitated. He'd been avoiding Elijah since he'd moved back, fighting his attraction. But who was he kidding? If he could choose anyone to rescue him, it would be Elijah. "I twisted my ankle."

Concern crossed Elijah's face and he squatted. "How bad is it?"

"Not sure if I can put any weight on it."

Elijah clucked his tongue and examined Jamie's foot, his touch light. "All right, honey. Let's get your shoe off and then I can help you back." He worked quickly on the laces of Jamie's boot and gently pulled it off.

Jamie gritted his teeth at the pain.

Elijah called to one of the other volunteers, holding up the boot. "Can you carry this?"

"What happened?" Brenton asked.

"Twisted it," Jamie said, taking hold of Elijah's hand and bracing his good foot on the ground as Elijah lifted him. Fresh-smelling aftershave tickled Jamie's nose and the firm arm around Jamie's waist revealed the strength below Elijah's slim build. A bolt of desire replaced Jamie's pain.

"I'll tell Siobhan." Brenton walked off. Jamie barely heard him.

Giving in to his attraction to Elijah would complicate his life and the very thought of it made his throat tighten and his pulse race. He swallowed. Don't think about it. He had to get back and have his ankle assessed.

Elijah tucked his shoulder under Jamie's arm, his head so close. "Is this all right?"

It was too nice. Jamie nodded, unable to stop his quick smile in response.

"OK, hop with me."

Jamie was forced to use Elijah's strong body as a crutch, leaning on him every time he hopped. It wasn't how Jamie had imagined having Elijah's body rubbing against his.

"What did you do?" Siobhan, their team leader walked over to them, her bright blue hair clashing with her orange uniform.

"Twisted my ankle."

"Let me help." She wrapped her arm around Jamie's waist on his other side, her body softer and curvier. He blocked the memory of running his hands over her breasts when they'd been in high school. Such a long time ago. He was no longer attracted to her, though she would be the easier choice. No one would bat an eyelid if they dated.

Elijah squeezed Jamie's waist as he tripped, and the flush of desire swept through him again.

OK, so no. Ignoring Elijah wouldn't work.

But he'd think about it later, when he was away from Elijah, when he could think clearly.

Right now, he needed to get back to base.

And it was a long way back to the winery.

The first drop of rain hit the back of his hand. The clouds were full to bursting. Another drop of rain, and then another.

He sighed. What a day.

"What made you move to Blackbridge, Elijah? I don't reckon it was the weather." Siobhan's voice startled Jamie out of his thoughts.

"My parents live here," Elijah said.

"Elijah went to the agricultural college," Jamie added. "He was in our year." He'd first met Elijah at Kit's sixteenth birthday party. That had been a revelation. Elijah had been a little awkward-looking, all arms and legs, but he was already out and proud. The first gay person Jamie had met. "Is that when they moved here?"

Elijah shook his head. "It was after I graduated. They fell in love with the town when they came to pick me up from boarding school, but it took a couple of years for Dad to find a job."

"And you work for Kit van Ross?" Siobhan said.

"Kit Zanetti," Jamie and Elijah corrected at the same time. They grinned at each other. Kit had married Jamie's brother recently and had happily discarded her maiden name. She wanted the world to know Lincoln was hers.

"Yeah," Elijah continued. "She needed a new farmhand just after I moved back. It was perfect timing."

From all reports, Elijah had fitted in perfectly. Kit didn't suffer fools and she was passionate about her farm, so if Elijah hadn't pulled his weight, she would have fired him by now—friend or not. Instead she was always talking about how great Elijah was which made it harder for Jamie to pretend he thought of Elijah as just an acquaintance. He'd stopped himself from asking how Elijah was at their weekly family dinners, but luckily Elijah featured regularly in Kit's stories about the farm.

"How's the ankle?" Elijah asked as they stopped to rest.

"Throbbing." Jamie leaned against a gum tree to get his breath back. They were maybe halfway to the winery and the other volunteers had long since outpaced them, eager to get back before the spits of rain turned into a downpour.

Elijah smirked. "Title of your sex tape."

Jamie laughed. "You watch that show too?"

"It's one of my favourites."

"What are you two talking about?" Siobhan frowned.

"A show on Netflix," Jamie told her. "It's a cop sitcom where the running gag is—" At her bored expression he said, "Never mind."

Elijah placed his arm around Jamie's waist again. "Let's keep moving."

Jamie leaned against him as Siobhan took his other side.

"I've convinced Adam he has to watch it," Elijah said. "You should join us."

"Sounds like fun." With Elijah's roommate there as chaperone, Jamie wouldn't have to worry about how Elijah made him feel.

Siobhan laughed. "Don't tell people you're going to Elijah's to Netflix and chill or they might get the wrong idea."

"No, they won't." Jamie's denial came out a little more forcefully than he meant. His face flamed and he avoided looking at Elijah. "No one thinks Adam and Elijah are partners."

Elijah's fingers tightened on his hip for a second before releasing. He winced. He'd sent the wrong message. Maybe he should say he didn't care, that he was bi, but only his family and closest friends knew. That was part of the problem.

His injured foot brushed the ground and pain pierced him. He'd deal with his attraction to Elijah later.

He checked where they were.

Not too far to go.

***

This was definitely not how Elijah had imagined getting his hands on Jamie Zanetti, but it was a good start. They matched each other's height and Jamie's body rubbed against him with each hop, warming him in more ways than one. Elijah was tempted to go slow, but Jamie's ankle must hurt and it was getting dark. The only problem was Jamie's adamant rejection of Siobhan's statement—as if being accused of being gay was a bad thing. Elijah could have sworn some of Jamie's comments over the past few months had been flirty.

When they finally left the forest and ducked through the fencing into the Vale winery, the only light was from the tower illuminating the car park, and those shining in the windows of the restaurant. The bulk of the rain had held off, spitting regularly, but not showering. Noah, rugged up with a blanket across his shoulders, sat snuggled on his mother's lap in the ambulance, his eyes closed, contentment on his face, while his father chatted to the paramedics and the police. The SES crew packed away their equipment and Elijah's roommate, Constable Adam Marshall spoke to Morgan.

"It's the ambulance for you," Siobhan said to Jamie.

They moved past the playground from where Noah had disappeared, and as if by magic, the fairy lights switched on around the garden. Pretty. As they reached the ambulance, Sergeant Lincoln Zanetti looked up. "What have you done?"

Jamie shrugged. "Twisted my ankle."

"Idiot."

Elijah grinned. Brotherly love at its finest. He helped Jamie to sit and stepped back while the paramedic, Guy, examined him.

"I'm going to take your sock off," Guy said. "It might hurt."

Jamie nodded.

Elijah clenched his fists to resist reaching out to Jamie when he winced. Instead he said, "I'll report to Morgan."

He hadn't quite figured out his section leader. Whenever Morgan spoke to him, he was brusque and kind of distracted. He reminded Elijah of his father—a man's man. There'd always been something more important on his mind when Elijah had wanted to talk to him. Perhaps Elijah had made his relationship with Morgan worse by turning up to his first training session wearing thick dark eyeliner and a rainbow tie-died shirt. He'd discovered it was best everyone was clear about who he was from the beginning.

There'd been some sideways glances and raised eyebrows, but no one had confronted him and, over the past few months, he'd established a strong camaraderie with his fellow volunteers. Except for Morgan. He always felt he had to prove himself. His major freak out the first time he'd done roof-safety training probably hadn't helped. Turned out heights and he were not the best of friends. Another issue his ex had left him with.

Morgan spoke with Kay Patton, whose family

owned the winery. Kay looked distinctly unhappy, and Morgan appeared none too pleased either. At least Elijah wasn't the only one Kay scowled at. As he walked towards them, Kay said, "You'll do what you're told." She glared at Elijah and stalked off.

"What was that about?" Elijah asked.

Morgan let out a shaky breath as if trying to control his anger. "She didn't appreciate us taking up most of her car park with equipment."

Elijah shook his head. Way to have empathy for a missing child.

"What happened to Jamie?" Morgan asked.

"He twisted his ankle."

Morgan grunted. "Get him to fill out an incident report." He dug through his folder and handed Elijah one.

"Anything else you need me to do?"

"Nah. Just get the form filled out." He stared after Kay, effectively dismissing Elijah.

Elijah wandered back to the ambulance. Noah's parents were thanking Jamie and the paramedics again. "Come on," the father said. "Let's go get ice cream." Noah perked up and held out his arms to his dad.

Jamie lay on the stretcher, an ice pack on his elevated foot.

"What did Guy say?" Elijah asked.

"It's just a sprain. I've got to keep it rested for a day or so." He grimaced.

"Can you drive?"

Guy answered for him. "Not today."

Jamie frowned. "Hopefully I can by Monday, otherwise I'll have to get Mum to take me into work."

And there was the downside to crushing on Jamie— he still lived with his parents.

"I can give you a lift home from the depot," Elijah

said.

Jamie hesitated. "That would be great."

Why the hesitation? They'd laughed together on the walk back. Was he really that upset about Siobhan's suggestion people might think he was gay? Jamie didn't strike him as someone who was insecure about his reputation. He handed Jamie the form. "Morgan wants you to fill this out."

Jamie groaned. "You got a pen?"

Lincoln walked over, took one out of his shirt pocket. "Here. Want a lift home?"

"Elijah's taking me," Jamie said.

Elijah grinned. At least Jamie wasn't fobbing him off when he got another offer.

"All right. Take care of yourself. I'll see you Sunday night." Lincoln went to talk to Morgan.

Jamie filled out the form, his forehead rumpled as he concentrated. Cute. Everything about Jamie Zanetti was attractive, from his luscious dark brown eyes, to his eyelashes which went on and on, and the designer stubble, always trimmed to perfection. His short brown hair wasn't quite styled to Elijah's level, but it was always neat and even though the bright orange clothing wasn't subtle, somehow Jamie managed to look damn fine in it.

He'd been lusting after Jamie since February when he'd seen him for the first time after moving back to town. OK, so that wasn't quite true. Jamie had starred in a number of his teenage fantasies as well, even though he'd been certain Jamie was straight. Besides, Elijah hadn't been confident enough in those days to even consider asking someone out.

"Done." Jamie handed Elijah the form. "Can you give it to Morgan?"

"Sure." Their fingers brushed as he took the paper

and a thrill ran through Elijah's body. Yeah, he was seriously smitten. And it wasn't just Jamie's hotness, he was a nice guy as well. Seeing him reassure Noah and blink back tears at the reunion had warmed Elijah's heart.

He had to get to the bottom of Jamie's sexuality. He snorted at his pun, shaking his head. He'd organise the Netflix binge session soon.

As Elijah returned to the ambulance, his gaze caught two people at the base of the stairs to the restaurant. The owner, Richard Patton and his daughter, Kay.

"Dad, it's time to go home." Kay tugged on her father's arm, but he didn't move. Instead he stared at the ambulance.

"What's going on?" Richard asked.

Kay's sigh was audible. "I told you, Dad. A boy went missing, but they've found him." Kay glared at Elijah, pulling Richard towards the car.

Kay hadn't been particularly friendly to him when he'd worked at the winery, but since Richard had been diagnosed with early onset dementia, she was a lot more gruff. Not that he blamed her. Suddenly she was in charge of the whole winery as well as dealing with a father who was losing more and more of his memory.

The sheds beyond the playground caught Elijah's attention. He'd spent a couple of months working there, mostly picking grapes and helping around the property. The buildings where the wine was made had been strictly off limits to plebs like him. Richard had always been paranoid about people wanting to steal his secrets.

Not that it mattered. He now had a dream job.

He strolled to the ambulance where Guy was giving Jamie clearance to leave.

Jamie shuffled to the edge of the stretcher.

"Let me help." Again, Elijah tucked his shoulder under Jamie's arm and wrapped a hand around his waist. Maybe he was a sad little panda for feeling this damn good having Jamie so close to him.

They moved to the SES land cruiser waiting for them and Elijah opened the door.

"Bit unco were you?" Brenton teased as Jamie got in.

"Had an argument with a rock," Jamie said, flashing him a grin.

"You just wanted to get out of the depot audit Morgan threatened us with," someone else said.

"Hey, at least he found the boy." Elijah's arm brushed Jamie's as he got in next to him.

"Thank God for that," Brenton said. "I was getting worried."

"We all were," Jamie said.

"Three cheers for Jamie," Siobhan called from the front seat.

At the rousing cheers, Elijah grinned. A successful outing was always cause for celebration.

At the depot, Morgan asked, "How are you getting home?"

"Elijah's giving me a lift," Jamie said.

Morgan nodded. "The two of you can go. The rest of us will pack up."

"Thanks."

Elijah smiled. Finally a chance to have Jamie to himself. They got into his blue hatchback and Elijah said, "I might need directions. It's not the same road as Kit's is it?"

"Take a left out of here."

His car seemed incredibly small with Jamie in the passenger seat, the hint of his spicy aftershave wafting between them. He needed to say something. "What have you got planned for the weekend?"

"I was going to play football on Sunday, but that's a bust."

"Good point." Nerves swelled in his stomach. He should just ask Jamie out for coffee, something totally casual and figure out where Jamie's interests lay. Jamie wasn't the type of guy who would be offended by the offer of a date. It shouldn't ruin the casual friendship they had.

OK, not so much a friendship, more of a small-town thing where Elijah's friends were friends with Jamie's friends. They only really saw each other at SES training, though occasionally bumped into each other if Elijah watched the football or the motocross. And usually he went because he hoped to run into Jamie.

He was pathetic.

In Europe, he'd had no problems asking guys out. Though he had hung out in gay bars most of the time.

"What about you?"

Jamie's voice startled Elijah from his thoughts. "I'll be milking at Kit's place both afternoons." She had asked him to work a weekend shift because she was helping Fleur with wedding preparations on Saturday and had dinner with Lincoln's parents on Sunday. He didn't mind. Kit was one of his best friends and he was thankful she'd given him a job doing what he loved.

Silence fell. It shouldn't be so hard. Normally people couldn't shut him up. "I'm glad Noah was all right."

Jamie sighed, ran a hand through his luscious hair. "I was getting worried. The kid wandered further than I thought he would."

"I'm glad you heard him. He was well camouflaged."

"Yeah. I hate the search and rescues," he said. "Not knowing what we'll find. My stomach gets tied in knots each time we're called out." His voice was gruff.

Elijah's heart went out to him. "You've been on a few?"

Jamie nodded. "The last one wasn't great—suicide." His voice was dull.

Elijah reached out and squeezed his hand. "That must have been tough."

Jamie twisted his hand and squeezed him back before letting go. "It was, but it's not uncommon. Searches usually involve kids, the elderly or the mentally ill. Only occasionally is it a hiker who's lost."

When he'd joined the SES, Elijah had expected to be doing things like helping with storm damage more than any real rescue missions. Though now winter had arrived, there'd probably be more storm work.

"Turn right here." Jamie's voice made him jump.

Get a grip. He noted the cheese factory sign on the turn-off and something clicked. "Your parents own the cheese factory, don't they?"

"Yeah."

"Do you help out much?"

"If they need it."

It was nice he helped, though they were back to the downer of him living with his parents. Still he'd only been back in Blackbridge since the beginning of the year and it was hard to find a place to rent. Elijah had got lucky when he'd moved back.

Elijah turned into the cheese factory driveway and Jamie directed him to the cute little farmhouse surrounded by beautiful lush gardens. A black Labrador ran out barking.

"Sasha's friendly," Jamie said, reaching for the door handle.

"Let me help you inside."

Elijah hurried around to Jamie's side. The porch light was on and Jamie used the stair bannister to hop up the steps onto the wooden verandah that encircled the house.

"We'll go around the back," Jamie said.

That suited Elijah fine. More time with his arm around Jamie. Light spilled through the glass window in the back door. As Elijah opened it, a rich garlicky smell wafted towards him from the kitchen. "Smells like someone has been cooking."

"Mum," Jamie said.

They shuffled into the kitchen where Jamie's mother, a small dark-haired woman, stirred a pot on the stove. "Hey, Mum."

She gasped and hurried over. "What happened?" She pulled out a chair at the table for Jamie.

"Twisted my ankle. It's nothing serious. This is Elijah."

Elijah held out his hand. "Nice to see you again, Mrs Zanetti." He'd met her briefly at Kit and Lincoln's wedding a couple of months back.

She pushed it aside and hugged him with a grin. "Call me Rosa." She squatted to inspect Jamie's ankle and whistled. "Have you had an x-ray? Do you need any painkillers?" She pulled out another chair for him to put his ankle on.

"It's fine, Mum. The paramedics gave me something."

"Oh, did you find the boy?"

"Yeah. Just before dark."

"Good. His parents must have been frantic. I remember when you were in kindy and visited Kit on your own." She put a hand to her chest. "Scared the life out of me for a good ten minutes until we found you climbing over the gate between our properties."

Jamie flushed. "Elijah doesn't need to hear stories of what I did as a kid."

Elijah chuckled. "Sure he does. I need something to prove Jamie Zanetti isn't perfect." He grinned at Rosa. "No one has a bad word to say about him."

"I should hope not," Rosa said. "He's perfect." She kissed Jamie's cheek. "Except when he's not doing what his mother tells him."

Jamie groaned.

"What's all the noise?" Jamie's father walked into the kitchen and glanced at Jamie's ankle. "What have you done?"

"It's just a sprain."

"Damn. I was hoping to get your help in the shop tomorrow. Elsie called in sick and your mum and I have plans for our anniversary."

Jamie hesitated. "I should be able to put some weight on it."

What was he thinking? "Guy told you to stay off it all weekend, he ordered elevation and ice."

Jamie scowled at him. "It's their thirty-fifth wedding anniversary."

How beautiful. They shouldn't miss out. Elijah hesitated. Though maybe it would seem strange. Never mind, they could always say no. "I have the morning free," he said. "If you can show me what to do, I can help out."

Mr Zanetti frowned. "Sorry, who are you?"

Oh, right. He held out his hand. "Elijah Johnson. We met at Kit and Lincoln's wedding."

Mr Zanetti shook it. "Right. I thought you looked familiar. Harold."

How could Elijah convince him, he was reliable? "Jamie could even stay seated and supervise, tell me what to do. I just need to be gone by three so I can milk Kit's cows."

"You're Kit's farmhand!" Harold made the

connection. "She's always praising you."

Elijah flushed. "The feeling's mutual."

Harold glanced at his son. "What do you think?"

Jamie nodded. "We'll manage. Joy will be there as well, won't she?"

"Yeah." He turned to Elijah. "Thanks so much. We'll pay you going rates. It's been a while since we've had a Saturday off, and I've got something special planned."

"Which he won't tell me about," Rosa added.

"It wouldn't be a surprise if I did." The affectionate smile and the way his gaze tracked his wife's movements in the kitchen showed Elijah how much they still loved each other after all these years. It was sweet, the kind of love he wanted in his life.

"Why don't you stay for dinner?" Rosa asked. "It's just about ready and Harold can fill you in on what's required." She went back to the stove.

Did Jamie want him to stay?

Jamie smiled and gave a small nod. "Go on. Mum's food tastes as good as it smells."

Elijah's heart squeezed. "All right. Thanks. I'd love to."

Maybe the attraction wasn't one-sided after all.

Chapter 2

Jamie barely tasted his mother's carbonara. He was too focused on Elijah sitting next to him, looking completely at home while he chatted to Jamie's parents.

Jamie shouldn't be surprised. The man was comfortable wherever he was.

He wasn't certain how he felt about Elijah's offer to help at the cheese factory. Spending the whole day in public with Elijah and hiding his attraction would be hard. What if someone noticed? Maybe he should call Lincoln and ask him to help instead. Or ask Lincoln to do it instead of him. Jamie still had a mountain of end of semester reports to write. No, he'd deal with them later. He couldn't let his parents down.

Besides, asking Lincoln would make Elijah feel as if Jamie didn't trust him. And it wasn't that. Jamie didn't trust himself with Elijah. It was easy to hide his attraction when their interactions were brief or they were surrounded by people, but a whole day in the shop together would be hard.

"I hope your ankle is better for Fleur's wedding next weekend," his mum said.

He was the MC for the reception. "I'm sure it will

be." He flexed his foot, biting back a wince at the pain. He still had a week for it to heal.

Elijah clapped his hands. "I can't wait. I'm Will's best man." He positively beamed.

Jamie smiled. Fleur was one of his closest friends and Elijah had shared a house with Fleur's fiancé, Will. Fleur and Will made a cute couple.

In fact almost all of his friends were marrying this year. Funny how he'd never considered marriage during the two years he'd been with Sandra. Perhaps he should have ended the relationship, but things had been comfortable enough.

He glanced at Elijah who was talking about the bucks' night. Elijah would never settle for comfortable. Jamie wasn't sure why he had.

"When do Will's parents arrive?" his mum asked.

"Thursday, I think. Will told them they'll need warm clothing, but they'll get the clothes in Albany."

"Blackbridge will be a shock to them after Goldwyer." His father cleared the table.

"Yeah, going from twenty-five to sixteen degrees will take some getting used to." Elijah grinned, his eyes lighting up, making him shine and the conversation faded into the background.

Jamie took a breath. It was impossible not to be drawn in as Elijah excitedly talked about the upcoming wedding almost as if he was the one getting married.

Jamie wanted to be the one who excited him.

He wanted to see how Elijah's expression changed when it went from happy to aroused. Jamie shifted as he grew hard. Not a thought he should be having sitting at his parents' dinner table.

"Is your foot hurting you?" His mother watched him with concern.

He cleared his throat. "It's fine, Mum." If he didn't

say anything else, she'd fuss around him. "I could do with a cup of tea though."

"Of course. Would you like one, Elijah?"

He sighed as she got up to fill the kettle.

Elijah raised an eyebrow and Jamie smiled. Yeah, he wanted Elijah to stay longer. It was nice to be near him.

"Yes please, Rosa."

It was stupid to think he could ignore his attraction to Elijah. His gut clenched and his pulse became thready. Quietly he focused on his breathing. Was he ready for the assessing looks, the whispers, the rumours?

Could he handle it this time?

Would it be as bad as it had been before he'd become the town's golden boy? He clearly remembered those days as a child when he'd been the butt of everyone's jokes. His favourite teacher sneering down from the pedestal Jamie had placed him on, telling him he should be ashamed, he was odd. When he couldn't go anywhere without some kid calling him names. At the time he hadn't understood what he'd done wrong, but in later years he'd recognised it had been because he hadn't fit the gender stereotypes.

Just like now.

He'd fought hard to earn back their respect and admiration. People liked him and he liked being liked.

How much disdain would he have to endure again?

His mother placed a steaming mug of tea in front of him.

"Thanks." He wrapped his hands around it, letting the warmth seep into him, calming him.

"Do I have to wear anything in particular tomorrow?" Elijah asked.

The image of Elijah naked sprung to mind and Jamie swallowed his smile as his father answered. "We'll give you an apron, so jeans and T-shirt are fine. We're always busy in the morning and it gets hot with all the running around."

"Great. What time?"

"Eight-thirty. I'll come and open. Help you get set up."

Jamie shook his head. "Don't worry about it," he said. "Elijah and I can manage. You wanted to get an early start."

His mother glanced at him. "You can't even walk."

"But I can talk and Elijah can take instruction." He didn't want his parents to miss out on the full romantic pamper package his father had organised. "Can you pick me up from here?" he asked Elijah.

"Sure."

He sipped his tea.

"Have you had any experience in retail?" his father asked Elijah.

Elijah's laugh was full of mirth. "Absolutely. I spent eight years working around Europe. I've tended bar, made coffees, sold clothing and, at my lowest point, I did door-to-door sales." He grinned. "Sometimes I was lucky and got work on farms, but most of the time I found whatever I could."

"Sounds like you'll be fine tomorrow," Jamie's mother said.

Eight years travelling around Europe. Part of Jamie longed for the adventure. He hadn't gone any further than Bali. He dreamed of going to England, following the footsteps of Shakespeare and Chaucer, visiting Ireland and seeing the places where Oscar Wilde had written. He couldn't imagine doing it alone though. That took guts.

Far more than Jamie had.

"I should go." Elijah pushed back his chair. "Thanks

for dinner."

Jamie went to stand and bashed his ankle on the table leg. He swore.

"Don't get up." Elijah's hand on Jamie's shoulder warmed him. "I'll pick you up at eight-thirty." He hugged Jamie's mother. "Dinner was lovely."

"You're welcome any time," she said.

Elijah smiled. "Enjoy your day tomorrow."

Jamie's dad walked Elijah out and some of the energy left the room. Jamie watched them go.

His mother sat next to him. "So, Elijah, huh?"

He shifted in his seat and frowned. "What do you mean?"

She raised her eyebrows. "You couldn't keep your eyes off him."

Jamie glanced towards the door to make certain Elijah had gone. "He talked a lot. I was being polite."

She shook her head. "That's not all it was."

"I'm not talking to you about my love life." He grimaced.

She grinned.

"Or lack thereof," he added.

Her hand covered his. "We'll love you no matter what. We don't care who you choose."

"Who's choosing?" his father asked as he walked back in.

Jamie's face flamed. "No one."

"We're talking about his sexuality," his mother said. "I told Jamie we don't care which gender he dates." She quickly added, "Or if they're non-binary."

He loved that his mother had educated herself about the queer community.

His father cleared his throat and looked a little pained. "That's right." He glanced at his wife. "No child wants to talk to their parents about their sex life."

"Dad's right." He struggled to his feet. Their acceptance had never wavered, even when he'd first told them. He was fortunate, but it didn't mean he had to talk to them about it.

"Well, just so you know, I like Elijah," his mother said.

His father's eyes widened, and he nodded. "He seems like a good sort."

Jamie shook his head. "I'm going to have a shower."

"Let your father help you to the bathroom." She gestured and Jamie's father came to help.

When Jamie finally closed the bathroom door behind himself, he let out a deep breath. Their approval meant a lot to him. No matter what, they'd always support him.

So why did he care so much about what others thought? Why was he clinging to his reputation as if it was the most important thing in the world?

Poofter. Faggot.

The words echoed in his head. Far worse was the disgust and derision that had accompanied them. At eight he hadn't understood what the words meant, but he'd known they meant he was unacceptable. Different.

His chest tightened and he panted for breath as he considered facing the disgust again. It hadn't mattered in Perth. The city gave him anonymity, gave him the space to hide.

But Blackbridge was a different matter.

Blackbridge was home.

And he couldn't run away.

***

Elijah loved Jamie's parents. They were so incredibly welcoming and he wanted to adopt them as his own. Not that his mum wasn't great, she was just a little flighty. His father was another story… Elijah would never be masculine enough for him. He and his sister had long ago accepted they wouldn't live up to their father's expectations. Not that it mattered. He was happy with who he was.

Right now he had bigger things to worry about—like what to wear today. He was about to spend the day with the delectable Jamie Zanetti and he wanted to get his look just right. Stylish, but not effeminate.

He checked the time and swore. Half an hour spent in front of the mirror trying on different combinations of jeans and T-shirts was plenty. The dark blue skinny jeans and superhero T-shirt clung in all the right places. No point ruining the look with a jumper, particularly if he would be running around all day. But his hair definitely needed work.

He spent another twenty minutes in the tiny retro orange bathroom blow-drying it and adding enough product to ensure it didn't move a millimetre throughout the day. Retail always played havoc with his hair.

When he was ready, he headed to the kitchen. Adam was at the kitchen table with a bowl of cereal. He scowled. "You finished, finally?"

Elijah blew him a kiss. "Bathroom's all yours."

"I don't want the bathroom, I want quiet," he grumbled.

"Someone got up on the wrong side of the bed this morning." Elijah snagged the box of cereal from the table and poured himself a bowl. It was freezing this morning, the walls of the fibro shack not thick enough to keep the cold out. "What did you do last night?"

"Bought some take-away after I finished writing the search report," Adam said. "Watched a movie."

Elijah sat across from him. Adam stared at his bowl,

his expression glum. It had been his default emotion since he'd moved in about a month ago. "Why so sad?"

Adam glanced up, shrugged. "I'm fine."

"No, you're not." The only time Elijah had seen the friendly, light-hearted Adam was when they were out amongst people. He tried to fake it with Elijah, but Elijah was an expert at seeing through fakers. "Honey, I know something's bothering you. Is it the illegal migrant case?" A couple of weeks ago the police and Border Force had arrested someone for an illegal migrant racket. They were still looking for at least two accomplices.

"Border Force are dealing with it."

If not that, then one other work-related event was a possibility, and the last time Elijah had mentioned it, Adam had shut him down in no uncertain terms. Still, he wasn't one to avoid conflict, especially if his friend needed to talk. "Is it the Foley case?"

The glum expression turned downright stony. "Shut it, Elijah."

"When you're ready to talk about it, I'll be here."

Despair flashed through Adam's eyes so quickly Elijah almost missed it. "Any time," he added.

Adam nodded once and pushed back his chair, took his bowl to the sink. He stood there a long time, his shoulders hunched, staring out the window into the backyard.

"What are you doing on the weekend?" Elijah asked.

"Ah, not much. Working today and Lincoln's taking me out to the shooting range for practice tomorrow."

Elijah put down his spoon. "That's good." He winced. At least he guessed practising his shot was good for someone who'd killed in the line of duty.

Adam cleared his throat. "What about you? Who are you primping for?"

It was Elijah's turn to glance down. "Just because I like to look fabulous, doesn't mean I'm doing it for anyone." At least no one he wanted to admit to yet. "When I took Jamie home yesterday, his parents mentioned they needed help in the cheese factory today. I offered to help."

"You're working?"

"Yeah. When I'm finished there, I'll be milking at Kit's." Which reminded him he should pack a change of clothes. Adam stared at his bowl again. "How about we get take-away tonight, watch Brooklyn Nine-Nine? Jamie's a big fan too and we can see if we can get you hooked."

Adam let out a deep breath. "Sounds good." He headed for the hallway.

Elijah would keep a close eye on his friend, maybe talk to Lincoln about how he could help. He wouldn't let Adam spiral into depression.

Checking the time, he leapt to his feet.

He'd call Lincoln after work. He grabbed his keys and rushed out the door.

***

Jamie was waiting on the couch on the verandah as Elijah pulled up in front of the Zanetti farmhouse. The eaves shaded him, and the black jeans and T-shirt he wore made him look dark and mysterious in the dim light. Did Jamie have a dark side? Either way, it was sexy as all hell.

Elijah swallowed hard and lifted a hand in a wave. "Morning." The chill bit into his arms as he jogged up the front steps. "I hope I'm not late."

"No. Mum and Dad just left so Dad helped me out here."

"How's your ankle?" He helped Jamie to stand,

inhaling his scent.

"Getting better. I can put some weight on it."

They walked to the car, Elijah's arm firmly around Jamie's waist. A whole day to have Jamie to himself, to really get to know him. "Is your car still at the depot?"

"Yeah. Lincoln and Kit are going to pick it up for me later."

Once they were settled, Elijah started the engine. "How's school going? It must be the end of term soon."

"One week to go and the kids are hanging out for it." Jamie laughed. "The last place they want to be is English class."

It would be twice as bad as normal schools because Jamie worked at the ag college and the kids wanted to be out on the school farm rather than indoors in mandatory classes. "I remember those days."

"Were you a good student?"

Elijah shrugged. "I guess. Dad shipped me off to the ag college in the hope it would toughen me." School hadn't really interested him—he'd just wanted out of the many small towns they'd lived in. "Turns out farming suited me, and Kit took me under her wing." Finally, he'd found somewhere he'd belonged.

"Kit's pretty protective of the people she likes," Jamie said.

Elijah smiled. "A big heart hidden under her 'don't-give-a-shit-about-what-you-think' attitude."

Jamie laughed. "You've described her perfectly."

They shared a smile and Elijah's heart pitter-pattered. "I'm surprised we didn't run into each other much," he said. "You went to the district high school, didn't you?"

"Yeah, but I played a lot of sport and Kit spent most of her free time working at the dairy, so we didn't hang out as much in high school."

Elijah pulled up outside the cheese factory. As they got out, he said, "I've convinced Adam to watch Brooklyn Nine-Nine tonight. Do you want to come over?"

"I'd love to." Jamie's face fell. "Actually, I don't think I'll be able to drive there." He gestured to his foot.

"I can pick you up on my way home from Kit's," Elijah said, helping him inside.

"All right. Thanks."

A long line of refrigerated cabinets full of cheeses formed a counter separating the public space from the work space. Shelves lined the walls, filled with assorted paraphernalia: cheese boards and knives, chutneys, spreads and biscuits. Half a dozen tables for patrons were scattered in a small space to his left.

"This way." Jamie pointed and Elijah helped him behind the cash register.

"What do I need to do?"

"We need to cut up tasting portions of the cheese and put it on top of the cabinets," Jamie said, pulling out a cutting board from the shelf behind him. "There're a couple of stools out the back. Can you bring one in for me?"

"Sure."

He pushed through the double doors which separated the retail area from the actual factory. A large glass window gave visitors a peek through to what was happening, but today it was quiet. He'd have to ask Jamie about the factory hours. The black vinyl chair was a bit grubby so he cleaned it before wheeling it out to Jamie.

"Thanks." Jamie balanced mostly on one foot, counting out the float while the coffee machine warmed up. "We usually do tastings of a soft cheese, a cheddar and one of the speciality cheeses." He handed Elijah some disposable gloves. "You can choose."

Elijah perused the choices and took three from the cabinet. "These all right?"

"Yeah." Jamie's eyes crinkled at the sides when he smiled and it momentarily entranced Elijah.

Oh, he would be in trouble if Jamie kept smiling at him. It frazzled his brain. Quickly he shifted the cutting board and knife down the bench away from Jamie. "How big?"

"About a centimetre."

It didn't take long before the cheese and float were ready. "Can you check that the shelves are fully stocked?" Jamie asked. "Elsie should have done it last night, but I always double-check."

Elijah did as asked and discovered a single bare spot on one of the shelves. "Is something supposed to be here?"

Jamie glanced up. "A cook book I think. The stock is in the cupboard here." He shifted to get off his stool and Elijah held out a hand.

"I'll get it."

"I'm not an invalid."

Elijah raised an eyebrow, looked at Jamie's swollen ankle. "Yes, you are, honey." He opened the cupboard Jamie had indicated and bent down. "This one?" He held up a book.

No answer.

He glanced back and found Jamie staring at his butt. Well, hello. He cleared his throat.

Jamie blinked and his face turned red. "Yeah, that's the one. Let me check the price." He fumbled on the shelf underneath the cash register and pulled out a folder.

Elijah grinned as he retrieved a dozen books from the cupboard. Price tags were on the same shelf.

"They're twenty-five dollars each."

"Got it." Elijah tagged the books and arranged them nicely on the shelf. When he turned back, Jamie was watching him. A thrill went through him. "What's next?"

"The drinks fridge, but first let me take you through the logistics."

Elijah wandered over. Jamie explained the cheese packages they offered. "We also make milkshakes, coffees, cheese platters and ice creams if people want to sit and have a break." He hobbled to the ice cream cabinet and showed Elijah the options. "Cheese platter stuff is here." He opened a door under the refrigerated cabinets and then scribbled some cheese names on a piece of paper. "A quarter block of each one, half a packet of biscuits and a couple of tablespoons of each spread."

Elijah nodded. It was all fairly straightforward.

Jamie winced as he put weight on his ankle.

"You should stay seated." Elijah wrapped his arm around Jamie's waist and helped him back to his stool. He was close enough to kiss Jamie's luscious, full lips.

Jamie cleared his throat and shifted back. "I can ah, wheel around on this thing, but it might be better if I take the money and do the drinks. Speaking of which, can I make you a coffee?" He scooted to the coffee machine, not looking at Elijah.

"A latte would be great. Your dad mentioned something about an apron?"

"Under there." He pointed to a cupboard and Elijah drew out two black aprons bearing the company logo. He handed one to Jamie as a car parked in front of the building.

"That's Joy. Can you unlock the front door and turn the sign to open?"

Joy had P plates on her car, the badge of a teenager's independence. She already wore the black apron and had pulled her blonde hair back in a ponytail. Her footsteps slowed and she frowned at Elijah. She glanced towards her car.

"Hey, I'm Elijah. I'm helping out today because Elsie is sick." He held the door open for her and she walked in, her eyes widening when she saw Jamie behind the counter. Her face went bright red. "Jamie." His name was a breathless sigh on her lips.

Elijah totally understood.

"Hi, Joy. Elsie called in sick last night, so you'll have to put up with Elijah and me today." Jamie smiled at her and Joy's face flushed even redder.

"Oh, right. OK." Her hands knotted around themselves as she shuffled forward.

"Do you want a coffee?" Jamie asked.

"Oh, sure. I mean, yes, please."

Jamie didn't notice how flustered she was. It was probably an everyday reaction for him. "Jamie will be seated for most of the day because he twisted his ankle," Elijah said, walking to her. "So you and I are going to do the heavy lifting. If I do something wrong, you tell me. I hear you're the expert."

She tucked a non-existent hair behind her ears and blinked as if she'd forgotten he was there. "Right. Sure."

"Can you check the drinks fridge for me, Joy?" Jamie called.

"Of course." She hurried to do his bidding.

Elijah chuckled. He felt for the girl. He was definitely caught in Jamie's spell as well.

Another car rumbled into the car park, this time

with a hire car logo on the side and Elijah moved back around the counter. A few minutes later, an older woman, her hair curled like a halo around her face, walked in. Elijah recognised her from the motocross.

Jamie grinned. "Hey, Barbara. How are you today?"

She scowled. "Some low-life stole my car yesterday so I've been better. If you see a little yellow Toyota Corolla around, let me know."

"I'm sorry," Jamie said. "I heard a few cars have been stolen recently. Let me make you a coffee on the house."

Her face softened. "You're sweet. A flat white would be lovely. It might give me the energy to deal with Mum today. Her favourite book was in the car and she's ready to go on a rampage looking for the thief."

Jamie laughed. "Then we'll throw in some of Gladys's favourite ice cream as well."

Barbara sighed. "Thank you."

Elijah made the coffee while Jamie chatted to Barbara, persuading her to try a new cheese they had. By the time Elijah had made the coffee, Jamie was ringing up almost a hundred dollars in sales.

"I shouldn't come in here when you're working." Barbara tittered. "I always buy far more than I should."

Jamie grinned. "Think of all the new delights which await you."

Elijah handed Barbara her coffee and lowered his voice. "He's got a golden tongue, hasn't he?"

Barbara laughed. "He does. You're Elijah Johnson, aren't you? Shelby's boy."

"Yes."

"She was so happy when you moved back. Did you enjoy your time overseas?"

"Very much."

She checked the time and gasped. "I need to get

going. I'll see you boys later." She struggled to get her keys out with her hands full of her purchases.

"Let me help," Jamie said, wincing as he got to his feet.

Elijah placed a hand on his chest. Jamie never thought of his own welfare. "You sit. I'll help." He hurried around the counter and took Barbara's purchases from her. Then he held the door open and carried them to the car.

"I'll tell your mum what a gentleman you are. Thank you." With a wave she left.

Elijah shook his head as he walked back inside. "I'd forgotten what it was like to have everyone know who you are."

Jamie laughed. "Barbara knows everything there is to know in town. I hope she gets her car back."

Another car pulled in starting a never-ending stream of customers. It had been a while since Elijah had been so busy in a back and forth kind of way, but he quickly found his rhythm, using the same techniques as Jamie to upsell customers.

By midday Elijah was glad he hadn't worn a jumper.

"Joy, take a lunch break," Jamie said when they had a moment's lull.

Elijah cleared the tables. After he'd put the dishes on to wash, he asked, "Is it always this busy?"

"Not usually at this time of year," Jamie answered. "Next week when school holidays start it will be busier, but today's a bit of an anomaly." He rotated his ankle and winced.

"Do you need more painkillers?"

"Yes, please. There's a first aid kit out the back. Joy can show you where it is."

Elijah got him the tablets and then served the few customers who came in.

When Joy came off her break, Jamie told Elijah it was his turn. "There's food in the fridge out back. Help yourself to whatever's there. It's for the staff."

"Do you want anything?"

Jamie's intense look put a shiver up Elijah's spine. "A sandwich with the lot would be great."

Ho, mama. Elijah resisted the urge to fan himself. Instead he made the sandwiches, took Jamie's out to him and then sat at the little table out the back. He sighed as the weight left his feet. Through the window he watched Jamie unhindered as he served another customer. The look had sealed it. He was definitely asking Jamie out after they finished today.

A commotion at the door before a whirlwind shaped like Kit Zanetti burst into the kitchen. "I'm busting you out."

Elijah grinned. Kit liked a good entrance as much as he did. "I'm not imprisoned here." He bit into his sandwich.

"Doesn't matter. Lincoln and I dropped off Jamie's car and we're taking over. You're due at my farm in a couple of hours, and you deserve some time off."

No. What he deserved was time with her brother-in-law. He was tempted to tell her to butt out. "You finished with the wedding stuff?"

"Yeah. Hurry and finish your sandwich. Jamie's ready to go home." She waggled her eyebrows.

He took back all his negative thoughts about her. "Jamie's finished too?"

"Of course. He needs to rest his ankle. Now scoot." She made shooing motions with her hands.

Elijah finished his sandwich and gave her a hug. "Have I told you lately how much I love you?"

She laughed. "You can show it by making a move already," she murmured, hugging him back.

He gaped at her. "What?"

"I've seen the way you look at him," she said.

He didn't comment. Instead he handed his apron to her and walked back into the retail section. Jamie was already on his feet.

"I hear we've been busted out," Elijah said.

"Yeah. Let's go."

"See you, Jamie." Joy's hopeful smile was a little sad.

"'Bye, Joy. Good work today."

Elijah helped him out of the building before he said, "You realise she has a massive crush on you, right?"

Jamie frowned. "She's a kid."

"She's a teenager who looks at you as if you're some kind of hero."

He snorted as he got into the car. "She's a little nervous around me at first."

"Because she desperately wants you to notice her." Like all of us do.

He swore. "That's awkward. Should I say something to her?"

"God no. Do you want to humiliate her?" Elijah shook his head. "Surely this is a common occurrence. Don't your students crush on you?"

"No!"

"What's wrong with teenagers these days? If I'd had a teacher as hot as you, I would have totally failed English because of my inability to concentrate." He pulled up outside the Zanetti farmhouse and as he got out he realised what he'd said. Jamie grinned at him over the roof of his car.

"You think I'm hot?"

This was his chance. Don't ruin it. "Scalding." He kept eye contact as he made his way around to Jamie. "Don't pretend you don't know how good-looking you are."

Again he wrapped his arm around Jamie's waist, this time letting his fingers caress Jamie's side briefly.

"Let's get inside," Jamie said.

Elijah couldn't read his expression. Jamie met his gaze, but he didn't smile. Had Elijah completely stuffed up?

It was a very long walk up the stairs and around the verandah to the back door. Nerves partied in Elijah's stomach. No matter what, he'd get an answer before he left. If Jamie wasn't interested, Elijah would avoid him until the hurt faded. "Which way?" Elijah asked as they entered the house.

"Lounge room would be good. Down this way."

Elijah followed his directions into a room with comfortable-looking blue couches and a large television. As he lowered Jamie to the couch, Jamie wobbled, squeezing Elijah's arms and pulling him off balance. Awkwardly he fell forward, twisting so as not to land on top of Jamie but ended up chest to chest, his mouth only centimetres from Jamie's.

Time froze.

This was it—the perfect opportunity for Jamie to show he was interested. All he had to do was close the gap between them.

Elijah waited, not moving.

Jamie pulled back, cleared his throat and Elijah shifted away, the rejection sharp. "Sorry." He had to get out of here. "Is there anything you need before I go?"

"I'll be fine." Jamie hesitated. "Are we still on for tonight?"

It took a second for Elijah to remember what he was talking about. Netflix. He forced a smile. "Sure. I'll pick you up about six."

Hoping his cheeks weren't as red as they felt, he waved and walked out.

Chapter 3

Jamie had seriously messed that up. He swore, his chest tight and his skin crawling. He wanted to walk off the anxiety coursing through him. Damn ankle.

Instead he shook out his arms, ran a hand through his hair.

He'd been so close, could have easily kissed Elijah. He groaned. He'd never wanted anything more in his life. But as he'd stared at Elijah's lips, the voice of his third-grade teacher had echoed in his head. *Poofter.*

He closed his eyes.

He was one word, one action away from being ostracised again. All the years he'd spent trying to be perfect, trying to be everything to everyone would be obliterated by one kiss.

Damn it.

If only he didn't care so much about what people thought, but it was difficult to change a habit of a lifetime. A habit that led to major anxiety if he even considered breaking it.

Jamie counted backwards starting from one hundred and by the time he reached thirty the tightness in his chest eased.

Maybe he wasn't giving people in town enough credit.

No one had said a bad thing about Elijah. Not even about his sexuality. Barbara had been nice to him, had called him a gentleman. So perhaps the town had changed. Maybe no one would care he was attracted to both men and women.

His skin flushed hot and his chest tightened again. Yeah, he wasn't ready to test his theory yet.

He groaned. But he wanted to. That moment of indecision had been laden with desire. He hadn't been that hard that fast in, well… ever. And it wasn't just the physical attraction. He liked Elijah. The man had offered to help his parents without hesitation, and it had been entertaining trying to out-schmooze each customer. Being with Elijah was fun.

Then there was Kit. She never stopped raving about how wonderful Elijah was, and for Kit to rave, he had to be pretty damned special.

Still, the image of people like Barbara glaring at him with the same disdain as his teacher gave him chills. And he couldn't forget the whispers about the attractive, new, openly bi teacher at his last school. Someone in the staff room had commented they'd have to watch her with both boys and girls. It was as if being bi meant a person was more promiscuous, had fewer morals. Some people in both communities thought bisexuals simply hadn't made up their mind yet.

Ignorant asses.

He squeezed his eyes closed. Teaching was his one true passion. He loved sharing his joy of literature with students and finding ways to help them appreciate it. And he enjoyed being the teacher kids came to for help, wanted to nurture them into becoming adults. Life was hard without support. For anyone to cast a shadow over that…

Outside, Elijah's car started. He wasn't coming back. Disappointment and relief mixed in equal parts.

Jamie grimaced. He had more important things to do than mope and stress about his love life.

He limped into the kitchen to put the kettle on. His ankle wasn't too bad, but he'd enjoyed Elijah's arm around his waist, liked being so close to him, so he hadn't mentioned it. Another day of rest and he should be fine for work on Monday.

He set the mug on the table and limped to his room to get his bag. The reports he had to write before the end of the week would keep him busy for the rest of the afternoon.

He paused at the entrance to his bedroom. Not much had changed since he'd been a teenager. The posters of Jessica Mauboy and Goyte above his single bed had been removed, and his small white desk was clear of any text books, but aside from that, it was the same furniture but with a new navy blue bedspread. He was twenty-six years old and back to living with his parents. His eighteen-year-old self would be horrified.

What did Elijah see in him?

In his defence, his visit to Blackbridge last Christmas was going to be temporary until Sandra broke up with him and he got the job at the agricultural college. He'd searched for a rental, but the owners hadn't liked the fact he'd been in his current job for less than three months. So he'd stayed at home, all his belongings stored in his parents' shed.

It was easy. His parents were chill and busy with their own lives. They didn't demand to know where he was or when he'd be home. Free rent and good food made him less inclined to search hard for an alternative. It wasn't all one-sided though. He helped at the cheese factory, did his own laundry and cooked a couple of times a week.

Still, it was pathetic. He had plenty of savings, enough for a deposit on a house.

He grabbed his bag and returned to the kitchen and fired up his laptop. Were any new rentals available? He clicked a few buttons. Only a beautiful place on the beach totally out of his price range. So, no.

He hovered the mouse over the link for properties to buy and his chest tightened again. It seemed like such a big step, such a big risk. Some people couldn't afford the repayments and lost everything.

Maybe Hannah could rent him one of her cabins at Hideaway Retreat on a long-term basis. No, it wouldn't be fair to her. She was at full capacity almost all the time.

Though there was her shed. She'd lived there while she'd been building the cabins, before she'd moved in with Ryan and his boy. He could rent it from her. He couldn't bring anyone he dated back here, with his parents at home and only a single bed. He wasn't that sad.

The shed was a solid option. A small step in the right direction. He called Hannah.

"Hey, JJ. How's your ankle?" Hannah's cheerful voice made him smile.

"Getting better, Hannah Banana. How's things with you?"

"Wonderful. My final cabin at the retreat is almost finished and already booked for the school holidays."

"Great." This was his chance. "Speaking of which, what are you doing with your shed? Is it empty?"

"I'm storing equipment in it, but it's mostly empty. Why?"

"Would you rent it to me?"

"Oh. Of course," she said. "I should have thought to offer it. No need to pay rent, as long as you don't mind me getting my equipment out from time to time."

She was too nice. "I'll pay you rent," Jamie said. "I'm not taking advantage of you."

"Suit yourself, JJ. I don't mind. It probably needs a good clean, though."

"Thanks, Hannah. I appreciate it."

"Getting tired of the folks?"

He hesitated. "Something like that. I need my own space."

"All right. When do you want to move in?"

He took a deep breath. It shouldn't feel like such a big deal. He'd lived out of home before. "I can pick up the key Monday after work."

"How about I meet you out there at four?" she suggested. "You can check it out and decide if you're still interested."

"All right. See you then." He was about to hang up when Hannah said, "Oh, wait a second."

"Yeah?"

"Are you coming to Fleur's hens' night on Friday or are you going to Will's bucks' party?"

Good question. Fleur, Hannah, Kit and Mai had been his best friends growing up. He was an honorary musketeer and still went to their *girls'* nights. He wanted to celebrate Fleur's upcoming marriage, but he'd also be the only male going. And Elijah would be at Will's bucks' night. "I don't know."

"Well make up your mind and let me know. Kit's driving, but if you're coming, we'll take my car."

He frowned. "Kit's giving up the opportunity to drink?"

"Yeah, I thought it weird as well. I wondered whether she and Lincoln might have some news. Have you heard anything?"

His eyes widened. "You think she might be pregnant?" He couldn't imagine Kit being a mum. That was something people much older than him did. And he'd be an uncle—that blew his mind.

"Maybe." He heard the smile in her voice. "If you don't know about it, I could be wrong. Married life might have matured her."

He laughed. Kit was the same as ever. "I'll ask Lincoln."

"Don't you dare! If she's pregnant, she'll want to tell us herself."

"Yeah, all right. Listen, I'll go to the bucks' party so parking is easier."

"Jamie Zanetti, you're always welcome."

"Yeah, I know. Still, boys are better." Before she could retort he added, "See you Monday," and hung up.

His smile faded. His connection with the musketeers wasn't as strong as it had been. Living in Perth for eight years had seen to that. It was his own fault. He'd stayed away from them at school, hanging with the boys to avoid being called names. The only time he'd spent with them was on the safety of Kit's farm, on weekends or school holidays, away from anyone who could tease him. He'd had his reputation to protect. Stupid really. The guys he went to school with were casual acquaintances now. Not like the musketeers. They'd been the first people to whom he'd confessed he liked boys and girls, and they'd kept his secret and told him they didn't care.

With friends so solid, why was he so afraid of what the rest of the town thought?

The familiar anxious flutter of his pulse started again. In front of him, his laptop screen turned black, into energy saving mode.

He sighed, pushing away all thoughts of Elijah and the town's people. The end of semester reports wouldn't write themselves.

And they were currently preferable to thinking about his love life.

***

Elijah drove away from the Zanetti place, his heart racing, his breath fast. He glanced in his rear-view mirror. How mortifying.

It was clear Jamie wasn't interested and now Elijah had to hang out with him tonight, pretending like the moment never happened.

It had been a long time since Elijah had got things so wrong. Not since Alex.

He gritted his teeth, the pain no longer as sharp. He'd been so stupid, but it had been his first relationship and he'd been blissfully happy. Hiding the relationship so Alex's work didn't find out and fire him made it that much more exciting—illicit even. Even Alex's refusal to introduce Elijah to his friends hadn't raised any red flags because Alex had wanted to keep Elijah to himself for a while. It had been glorious for three months until they'd run into each other at the theatre. Elijah had been with friends who knew the big, hairy masculine man Alex was with—his husband.

Elijah's throat closed just thinking about it. Alex looked at him as if he'd been a stranger, not an ounce of regret or apology in his eyes.

Elijah tapped on the steering wheel. He wished he could go back to that day. With his new-found confidence he would have handled it better, would have confronted Alex, and told his husband about the lying bastard he'd married. But back then he'd been young, and deep down he'd questioned his own masculinity.

Ugh. What a mess. He was never taking Kit's advice again.

He checked the time. Might as well head out to her farm now. There was always work to be done and the physical work would help release some of his frustration.

He'd been too busy fantasising about all the ways they could get together to recognise that if Jamie had wanted to date him, he would have asked him out by now.

Unless he was scared. People's expectations were a bitch to deal with.

No, Elijah was probably too effeminate for him. He swallowed hard past the lump in his throat. Jamie's loss.

A road sign flashed past. Shit. Elijah pounded the steering wheel with his palm. He'd gone the wrong way out of the Zanetti place. He turned off the highway and drove along the road between Kit's property and her neighbour's. Foley's place was still on the market, vacant since he'd died a few months back.

He might as well check Kit's fence line while he was here. No one used the road anymore, but it used to be how Foley transported his sheep. Elijah slowed his car and kept his gaze on Kit's property, scanning the fence through the sparse trees lining the road. The fence sagged in a couple of places. He'd have time to fix the posts before the cows arrived at the dairy for milking. At the end of the road he did a U-turn and noticed the open gate into Foley's property.

Elijah stopped his car. He was pretty sure no one had bought the place so the gate shouldn't be open. Getting out, he scanned the area. Little blue wrens fluttered through the grevillea which lined this side of the road, and the burnt shell of Foley's old shearing shed still managed to hold some of its shape, though the roof had partially caved in. A few insects hummed, but otherwise it was silent.

He shivered. This place always creeped him out. It was too close to where his predecessor had been murdered. Swallowing hard, he hurried to the gate. A flash of yellow through a hole in the shed wall caught his eye.

He touched his phone in his pocket. When he'd last been there, the shed had stood alone, but something was definitely behind it today. He rubbed the scar from his bullet wound, debating whether he should go any closer. He'd feel foolish if he called the police and it was nothing but an old barrel. Steeling himself, he moved around the side of the shed. A little yellow Toyota Corolla was parked next to two other cars, its bonnet raised. All the cars were missing their tyres and some were also missing doors or bonnets. The engines had been taken apart as well.

A car graveyard.

If the Toyota was Barbara's, they were probably all stolen and had been chopped up for parts.

Elijah lifted his gaze, scanning the surrounding area, but nothing moved. Hopefully the thief was already far away.

He called the police.

About half an hour later, Adam and Senior Constable Ryan Kilpatrick arrived. The tension in Elijah's shoulders relaxed as he got out of his car to greet them.

"Hey, Elijah." Ryan withdrew his notebook from his pocket. "What brought you out this way?"

Damn, Ryan had a jawline to envy—strong and masculine.

"Checking fences." He still had another hour before he needed to milk the cows. "I was going to close the gate when I noticed the Corolla. Barbara mentioned her car had been stolen, so I gave you a call."

Ryan nodded. "When was the last time you were out here?"

"I haven't been this way since we helped Foley's ex sell the sheep—I guess a couple of months." At Foley's name, Adam flinched. "Usually when I check the fences I do it from Kit's property."

"Have you touched anything?" Ryan asked.

"No."

"All right. Thanks. You can go and we'll deal with this."

Adam stared at the ground, his fists clenched.

Being here must bring up bad memories of the shooting. "I'll see you tonight, Adam," Elijah said.

Adam blinked and looked up, pain on his face. "What? Right. Yeah. See you later." He walked to the stolen vehicles.

Elijah lowered his voice. "Keep an eye on him."

Ryan's expression was grim. "Will do."

With a last look at his roommate, Elijah went to work.

***

Jamie waited on the sofa on the verandah, his uninjured foot tapping on the wood. Maybe going to Elijah's wasn't a great idea. Not after their near kiss. Would things be totally uncomfortable?

But he wanted to get to know Elijah better, work through his fear of coming out to the town and the only way to do that was to hang out with him.

Elijah's blue hatchback rumbled up the driveway and Jamie hauled himself to his feet, using the stair rail to hop down the stairs to the car. He could put a bit of weight on his toes and was at the passenger door before

Elijah could get out.

"Hey, I hope I didn't keep you waiting." Elijah's cheery greeting dissolved some of Jamie's tension.

"Not at all." He plucked off the bit of hay clinging to Elijah's plaid shirt and threw it out the window. "How was the milking?"

"Easy. The cows know what to do. All we're needed for is to put the milking cups on and off."

"Did you know the ag college has an automatic dairy?"

Elijah nodded. "I've been meaning to go check it out."

Jamie smiled. "It's pretty impressive. I can arrange a visit for you." The guy in charge of the dairy loved to show it off.

"Thanks. That would be great." Elijah turned on to the main road. "Are you fine with Vietnamese for dinner?"

Jamie nodded. "Will we pick it up on the way?"

"Yeah. Adam ordered."

Silence fell. Should he mention the near kiss? Should he explain to Elijah that he liked him, but wasn't quite ready?

"Have you got a run sheet for the wedding?" Elijah asked.

Relief filled Jamie at the change of topic. "I think Kit's bringing it around tomorrow night." He shrugged. "I don't imagine it will be more than introducing people for speeches and directing people where to go. I do that kind of thing all day at school."

Elijah's hands twisted around the steering wheel. "I don't know how you do it. Getting up in front of people is my worst nightmare."

Jamie frowned. "But you're so confident."

Elijah shook his head. "In small groups maybe. But

everyone will be watching me, waiting to see if I completely stuff up the best man speech."

"You'll be fine. Have you written it yet?"

Elijah laughed. "Written and rewritten it, and then rewritten it again for good measure."

"Want to practise it?"

Elijah glanced at him. "Now?"

"If you want."

"I don't have my notes." The slightly panicked tone to Elijah's voice made Jamie smile. So like his students.

"You can practise when we get to your place," he said. "What are you talking about?"

He listened as Elijah spoke about how he met Will and about Will and Fleur's relationship and how happy he was for them. Elijah finished speaking as he pulled up outside the Vietnamese restaurant.

"Your speech sounds great." Jamie grinned at him.

Elijah's mouth dropped open. "How did you do that? I didn't think I knew it at all."

"I didn't do a thing. You were relaxed and you know what you want to talk about. You don't need your notes."

"Thanks."

A knock on the window made Jamie jump. Kim stood there with a bag of food. Elijah wound down the window. "Thanks, honey."

"You two looked as if you were going to stay there all night," Kim said with a grin.

"Quiet night?" Jamie asked.

"Lots of take-aways, but it's too cold for people to go out." He rubbed his arms. "I'll see you later." Kim jogged inside as Elijah handed the food to Jamie.

He inhaled deeply. "Smells great."

"I'd marry Kim just for his cooking," Elijah said. "Pity he's not gay."

"Maybe he's bi." Jamie bit his lip. He shouldn't have said that.

"Is he?" Elijah asked.

Jamie shrugged. "I don't know." Thankfully Elijah parked in front of his fibro shack and Jamie fumbled with the doorhandle in his rush to get out of the car.

"Let me help." Elijah hurried around to the passenger side and took the food from Jamie. Then he slipped his hand around Jamie's waist and helped him inside.

"Finally." Adam strode over and took the food from Elijah. "I'm starved." He nodded at Jamie. "Hey, mate. How's the foot?"

"Getting better."

In the kitchen, Adam got out bowls and plates. Elijah let go of Jamie. "I'm going to take a quick shower. Don't let Adam eat it all." He disappeared down the hallway.

Adam laughed. "I don't think he knows the meaning of quick."

"He likes to look good." Jamie piled some rice onto his plate. "Is he hard to live with?"

Adam shook his head, offering Jamie a beer from the fridge. "Nothing fazes him. The only problem is the time he takes in the bathroom and if I'm working, I make sure I get first dibs."

They carried their food and drinks to the living area and sat on the long grey couch in front of the TV. Adam turned it on and switched to Netflix, finding the show they wanted to watch.

A couple of minutes later Elijah strode out wearing baggy grey tracksuit pants and a thick red puffer jacket, his hair still damp and tousled.

Something about his casual attire sent a shot of lust through Jamie. Elijah was hot.

"That's got to be a record," Adam said. "Is it the food, or the fact Jamie's here?"

Elijah waved his hand. "I didn't want to keep you waiting." He dished up his own food and sat between them on the couch, his leg brushing Jamie's.

Desire shot through Jamie and he subtly shifted so they weren't touching. He wouldn't be able to concentrate on the show if his brain shifted between his legs.

Elijah reached for the remote. "Shall we get started?"

Chapter 4

By Monday morning Jamie's ankle had healed enough for him to drive to school. Teenagers milled about the grounds of the agricultural college, hanging out, some playing basketball on the courts; others would be at the dairy milking cows. He parked in his usual spot and got out, swinging his backpack on and taking his grandfather's walking stick from the back seat. The less weight he put on his ankle the better.

"Hey, Grandpa," one of the kids yelled as he walked up the path to the staff room.

Jamie laughed. "Be nice to me, Tyler," he called back. "You've got English first period."

Tyler groaned. Not many of the students enjoyed the compulsory classes, they'd much rather be out on the farm, doing hands on learning. It was a constant challenge to interest them, but Jamie enjoyed it.

A couple of female students hurried up. "What did you do, Mr Z?"

"Twisted my ankle Friday afternoon. It's getting better."

"Do you need a hand?" One of the girls batted her eyelashes at him.

Elijah's words about Joy having a crush on him, popped into his head. Crap. "Nope. I'm fine. I'll see you in class later." He continued to the staff room and was relieved when he got inside.

"What happened to you?" Patricia asked, placing a hand on his arm, her long, perfectly manicured nails painted a demure pink today, which matched the skirt suit she wore. Far too formal for the kids they taught, but being strictly professional was her motto.

The staff room wasn't the sanctuary he'd hoped for. "It's just a sprain." He headed for the coffee machine away from her. Patricia was nice enough, but her conservative views rubbed him the wrong way and he got the feeling she was interested in more than a business relationship.

"You going to be OK taking the kids to Kit Zanetti's farm on Wednesday?" Henry asked.

"Yeah, it'll be fine by then." He enjoyed the excursions as much as the kids did, especially to Kit's farm... though would that mean he'd run into Elijah too?

He'd enjoyed spending Saturday night with him and Adam. They'd laughed a lot and on the drive home Elijah had chatted nonstop about what he loved about the show. Jamie enjoyed hearing him talk, enjoyed his enthusiasm about everything.

He carried his coffee up the corridor to his classroom. Patricia hurried to catch up with him. "So how did you twist it?"

"I had a search with the SES and rolled it on a rock."

"Oh, I'd forgotten you volunteered. Did you find the person?"

He nodded as the bell rang and students flooded the hallway, their conversations echoing loudly.

"Here come the great unwashed." Patricia screwed up her nose. "I don't know why I bother. They're not going to amount to much." She waved and strode into her classroom.

Jamie stared after her. What a horrific attitude. Sure, the kids weren't here because they wanted to become academics, but they were smart and enthusiastic and deserved better from their teachers.

He'd have to share some stories about his students with her, show her how amazing they could be.

He entered his classroom and raised his voice over the babble. "All right, listen up."

The conversation faded away and the kids turned their attention, more or less, to him. "Today we're going to talk about story structure."

The students groaned.

It was his challenge to make what he taught relevant and interesting to the kids. "Anyone heard of the X-Men?"

A couple of kids perked up.

He grinned and picked up the graphic novel. "Let's get started."

****

During Jamie's last class of the day, Don Patton stared out the window. His gaze was distant, his forehead rumpled and a deep frown on his face. "Don, what do you think about the father's reaction?" Jamie called.

Don blinked as if he'd just woken up. He glanced at his classmates and shrugged. "I don't know."

Jamie frowned. Don wasn't the best student, but he normally paid attention at least. "What about his obligation to his family versus breaking the law?"

"Family comes first, right?"

Jamie was about to probe deeper as the bell rang.

The kids shot to their feet as if they were horses out of a gate, packing their things. He sighed. "Don, can I see you for a minute?"

One student sing-songed, "You're in trouble," but eventually all the kids left except Don.

He slung his backpack over his shoulder. "Yeah?"

Jamie smiled. "Is everything all right?"

"Yeah. Why wouldn't it be?"

"I know your grandfather is living with you now. It must be hard with his dementia."

Don stiffened. "It's fine." He crossed his arms and stared at the floor.

"If you need someone to talk to, my door's always open."

The boy gave a tiny nod, barely looking at Jamie as he walked out the door.

Jamie sighed and tidied his desk. He couldn't help everyone, particularly if they didn't want to be helped, but he'd keep an eye on Don. Right now though, he had to hurry if he was going to meet Hannah on time. He grinned. By the end of the day he could have his own place.

Someone knocked on the door. "Mr Z?"

One of his Year Twelve students, a tall skinny kid, stood at the door, clasping his hands together.

"Hey, Lewis. What's up?" Jamie tucked his things into his bag.

Lewis checked over his shoulder as he stepped into the room. "Can I ask you something?"

"Sure."

"It's not about school."

Jamie stopped what he was doing and gave Lewis his full attention. Hannah wouldn't mind if he was late. "Go ahead."

"I was wondering, is it possible... do I have to go

home this school holidays? Is it possible to stay here?" Like many of the students, Lewis boarded at the school.

Concern lodged in Jamie's stomach. "Why don't you want to go home?"

Tears welled in Lewis's eyes and he furiously blinked them back. "It's my dad," he said. "See, the thing is, well… promise you won't tell anyone?"

The hope and trust in Lewis's eyes cut straight through Jamie. He remembered feeling that way about a teacher—but his trust had been betrayed. "Of course."

Lewis glanced over his shoulder again and stepped closer, lowered his voice. "I, ah, told him last holidays I was gay, and he said I shouldn't come home next holidays if I still believed it." Lewis's face flamed red.

Christ. Jamie ran a hand through his hair. "Have you spoken to him or your mum in the past ten weeks?"

"He won't speak to me. Mum said I should pretend to be straight when I come home." Lewis shuffled his feet, staring at the ground. "She said he threatened to stop paying for school if I'm gay."

Anger stirred, but Jamie kept his tone mild. "What do you want to do?"

Lewis brushed away a tear from his cheek. "Shouldn't he love me no matter what?" he mumbled. "I can't help being gay. It's who I am."

The words resonated with Jamie, but he had to consider options for his student. "Sometimes it takes people longer to understand than others," Jamie said. "You don't want to pretend to be straight?" It's what he would have done.

Lewis shook his head violently. "It's taken me three years to tell them. I don't want to go through it again."

He was braver and stronger than Jamie. Jamie had to help somehow. "Do you have your mum's number?"

Lewis rattled it off.

"All right. I'll give her a call and I'll talk to Ms Simons about whether the college will be open over the holidays. Come and see me tomorrow afternoon."

Lewis nodded. "Thanks, Mr Z. I didn't know who else to talk to." He hurried out of the room.

Jamie's chest filled with joy. This was one of the reasons he was a teacher. To help them when they had no one else, to offer another support pillar to a child.

"You're not terrorising our students, are you?" Patricia walked in, not a hair out of place from her French knot, and no wrinkles in her suit. He didn't know how she managed it.

He frowned. "No."

"Lewis was in tears."

"He's having family issues," Jamie said. "What can I do for you?"

"Thought you might need a hand getting back to the staff room." She gestured to the walking stick.

"No, I'm good. Thanks." His ankle was a lot better.

They walked side-by-side back to the office. "Listen, a bunch of us are going for a drink after work on Friday to celebrate the end of term," Patricia said. "Do you want to come?"

His muscles tightened. He hated saying no to anyone. "I'd love to, but I'm going to a bucks' party."

"Maybe we can catch up during the holidays then," she said.

Jamie glanced at her. No thanks. Not after her comment this morning. "I'm going to be pretty busy. I've got a friend's wedding and Mum and Dad always need help in the cheese factory."

"Oh, I forgot your parents owned it." She smiled. "It's nice of you to help."

Jamie held the staff room door open for her. "I need to make a couple of phone calls. I'll see you tomorrow." He continued to his office. Perhaps he should have made it clear he wasn't interested, but Patricia could get a little spiteful when she was embarrassed. She'd get the hint eventually and hopefully it wouldn't sour their relationship.

He shut his office door behind him and sat, then quickly sent Hannah a text to say he was running late. He then dialled the college coordinator's number. "Hey Bec, it's Jamie. One of the students asked if it's possible to stay at the college during the holidays. He's not certain he'll be welcome at home."

Bec sighed. "No one's going to be there. I booked a trip to Bali after I confirmed we'd have no boarders."

Damn. "All right. Thanks." Jamie hung up. With that option off the table, hopefully he could talk some sense into Lewis's mother. He dialled the number and introduced himself to Mrs Cross.

"Is Lewis in trouble?" she asked, concern in her voice.

"Not at all," Jamie assured her. "He was a little upset when he came to see me this afternoon. He mentioned the last time he was home, he told you and your husband about his sexuality and Mr Cross didn't take it so well."

"He's still saying he's gay?" she asked.

Annoyance stiffened his shoulders. "It's not something which will change, Mrs Cross," he said. "Coming out to the people you love can be very stressful and people are generally certain about it before they do."

She sighed. "My husband isn't going to take this well."

He took a breath to calm his anger. "What about you, Mrs Cross? Do you still love your son?"

"Yes. I do, but my husband is in charge of the

money." She sounded resigned. "He'll cut Lewis off, stop paying for his schooling."

Lewis still had six months before he graduated. "Mrs Cross, Lewis is a very smart young man. It would be a shame for him not to finish school." He hesitated. What other options did they have?

An idea struck him. It would only delay the inevitable but if it saw him through school... "Lewis suggested not going home this holidays."

"Can he stay at the college?"

"No. It's closing for the break. I might be able to find him somewhere to stay though. If you agree to it."

"Where?"

"My parents have a spare room and I can probably get him some work experience at my friend's dairy." He'd owe his parents big time.

"That would be fantastic," she breathed. "If he's got work experience, my husband would completely understand Lewis not coming home."

"All right. I'll make some more phone calls and call you tomorrow with details."

"Thank you, Jamie. My son is lucky to have you as a teacher."

Jamie's heart squeezed. "You're welcome." He hung up. Time to call in those favours.

Half an hour later, he'd spoken to his mum, Kit and the college principal and received approvals from all of them. Lewis would stay in Lincoln's old room, work at Kit's dairy through the holidays and return to the boarding college when school resumed.

Jamie stood. He was so late. Hopefully Hannah had some work to do out at her retreat. He picked up his backpack and headed to his car.

On the way out to Hannah's place, a car was parked at the side of the road, a man peering under its raised bonnet. Not many people came out this way, and while it wasn't raining yet, the heavy clouds indicated it would start soon. Jamie pulled up and wound down his window. "Need a hand?"

The man waved. "No, I'm right." Morgan.

Jamie grinned. If anyone could fix the car, it was the local mechanic. "See you later." He continued to Hannah's retreat, winding through her property past little turn offs to the various cabins, and eventually pulled up next to a large silver shed. Hannah's white four-wheel-drive was already there and her large bull mastiff, Joe, bounded across to greet him.

Jamie ruffled Joe's head and walked over the concrete verandah to the shed door. "Hannah?"

"Come in."

He walked into the dusty-smelling shed and found her cleaning the little kitchenette. She turned, a bright smile on her face, small tufts of blonde hair peeking out from her blue beanie. "Hi, JJ."

"Sorry I'm so late."

"No worries. I figured I'd do a bit of cleaning while I waited. It's dustier than I realised."

"You didn't have to," he said.

"I don't mind." She put down the cloth. "The fridge is still running. I've been leaving drinks in there, but I'll take them out."

"Keep them there," Jamie said, touching her arm. "I appreciate you helping me, Hannah. If you need to use the place for work, go ahead. I'll be at the college most days anyway."

"All right." She gestured him to follow her. "The bathroom has to be cleaned still, but I tested the hot water and everything seems to be working fine. The water tank outside is full."

The bathroom was a small room next to the kitchen

with a shower, toilet and basin, but he didn't need more. The main room was partitioned from the shed portion by a row of bookcases and there was plenty of space for his bed and furniture. It would be a little draughty, and probably a bitch to heat, but at least it was his own space. A place he could bring Elijah if it got that far.

"The air con is reverse cycle," Hannah continued. "But I generally piled on the quilts rather than leaving it running all the time."

He nodded. "I'll add more to my rent to pay for electricity." His phone signal was strong.

"I used a dongle for internet when I lived here," Hannah said. "It was good for surfing the net, but I didn't bother with streaming services. You're stuck with normal TV."

He chuckled. "I'll manage." His e-reader was full of books he hadn't got around to reading.

She handed him a key. "When are you going to move in?"

The sooner the better. "I'll ask if I can borrow Dad's ute tomorrow."

"I can help you move and Mai's probably free."

He grinned. "That'd be great."

"We'll meet you at your parents' at four-thirty."

"Thanks, Hannah Banana." He hugged her.

She stiffened slightly and then relaxed. "You're most welcome."

He walked her out and watched Joe leap into the back seat of the car. When they'd driven off, he went back into the shed.

A big airy space, all of his own.

Jamie huffed out a breath, calmed the anxiety jiggling in his stomach. If he was moving in tomorrow, he should clean tonight.

He grabbed the bucket Hannah had been using and got to work.

***

Elijah rubbed the ache in his shoulder from where he'd been shot a few months ago and then hunched forward to check the sky as he drove home from work. The deep grey-purple clouds hung low and the wind whipped the trees back and forth. Night was falling rapidly and a storm was coming. He'd review the bureau of meteorology website when he got home. Chances were high the SES would be called out tonight if the storm was bad.

He turned up the heating, wishing he'd put on his red puffer jacket before he left Kit's instead of leaving it on the backseat.

He pulled into the dirt driveway of his little fibro shack. The wind pushed him towards his door. Yeah, definitely needed to prepare for a call out. He flicked on the lights, put the kettle on to boil and pulled his tablet towards him. A quick search confirmed wild weather on its way. He got out the torch and some candles and left them on the kitchen bench. Then he made sure his SES gear was ready to go.

Dinner next while he still had electricity. Adam would be at work until late so Elijah made himself a pizza and curled up on the couch. The wind outside buffeted the house and the branches of the overhanging eucalyptus scratched the tin roof. Elijah winced. He should have trimmed it back. As he reached for the remote, the heavens opened and rain hit the roof like gunshots, so loud he couldn't hear the television.

A flash of light illuminated the street outside and it was quickly followed by a boom of thunder.

Not the kind of night you wanted to go out in.

Why had he joined the SES?

As if reading his thoughts, his phone beeped. Call out.

Adrenaline surged through him as he scoffed the slice of pizza, switched off the television, and hurried into his room to dress in his orange uniform and steel-capped boots. Ugh. Orange was so not his colour.

He swiped another slice of pizza on his way out the door and pulled up the hood of his jacket. The rain was coming in sheets. He'd be soaked before he got to his car.

Shrugging, Elijah clicked his car unlocked and dashed to it, the rain blowing in his face and down his collar. He slammed the door shut and sat for a moment breathing heavily. This was not going to be a fun night.

With a sigh, he drove the short distance to the headquarters and headed inside where a half dozen other people gathered in the briefing room. No Jamie. His ankle was probably still injured and he had further to drive to get into town.

Not that Elijah wanted to see him.

Siobhan raised her voice over the rain on the roof. "Morgan's not here, because it's his place that's been hit. The roof has lifted and rain's flooding in." A loud clap of thunder and Siobhan looked skywards with a grimace. "We need to be careful on this one, people. The wind's strong and the lightning is dangerous. You listen and you take precautions." She scanned them, her eyes resting on Elijah. "This your first roof?"

He nodded.

"You stay on the ground. Let's go."

Relief filled him as he climbed into the land cruiser and drove the short distance to Morgan's house. Morgan was already outside, tying a ladder to the eaves. Elijah carried the big tarps which would cover the gap in the roof closer to the house. It was hard to see with the wind blowing the rain into his face and the temperature had dropped. Around him, volunteers shouted to each other.

"Elijah!" Morgan called.

He hurried over and took the plastic tubs Morgan shoved at him. "Come with me."

He jogged after Morgan and into the house, stopping at the entrance to shake off the water before he continued.

"Mary!" Morgan called.

A middle-aged woman hurried down the hallway. "Good. You've got more buckets. This way."

Morgan stopped her at the kitchen. Water rained down the walls and the whole ceiling sagged with the weight. He swore. "Get the kids. Move the car onto the street and sit in there. The ceiling's not going to last long."

Mary twisted her hands together. "Julia's scared. She's hiding under her bed."

Morgan sighed. "Put buckets under as many leaks as you can," he said to Elijah.

"It's worse in the bathroom and the office is leaking too," Mary said.

Elijah nodded. "I'll see to it. You get the kids out." He placed several buckets against the wall and then went along the hallway. In one of the bedrooms, Morgan was on his hands and knees peering under the bed.

"Come on, sweetheart, we need to get out. You can watch what the guys are doing on the roof."

Elijah smiled at his gentle tone. Perhaps Morgan wasn't as brusque as his father. Julia was crying, babbling in fear. Mary saw him at the door and said, "She doesn't like changes to her routine."

Oh. That could be hard. He continued to the bathroom, wanting to help as much as he could.

The rain had let up and his fellow volunteers yelled to each other and there was the thud of someone on the roof. The bathroom ceiling was also bowing dangerously low. He placed a bucket in the centre and as he left the room, Morgan and his family hurried down the corridor.

"Don't be long," Morgan told him.

"I'll just do the office." Elijah walked inside and took stock of the situation. The room was small with a desk in the middle covered in greasy spare parts. He grinned. Morgan obviously brought his work home with him. A few lines of water ran down the walls and a damp spot spread on the ceiling, but at least it wasn't bowing.

"Elijah!"

His heart jumped as he turned. That sounded like Jamie. "This way," he yelled back peeking out the door and moments later Jamie strode down the hallway towards him carrying a couple of tarps, looking totally hero-worthy. Damn.

"What are you doing?"

"Waterproofing the office."

"Take the other end of this." Jamie handed him a corner of the tarp and together they draped it over the furniture.

Working quickly, they positioned the other tarp and the buckets to catch the worst of the leaks. Elijah grimaced. The carpet was already soaked. It wouldn't be fun to clean.

"What now?" Elijah asked.

An almighty crash. Jamie glanced at the ceiling. "That isn't good."

They both hurried along the corridor where dust

floated out of the kitchen. A pile of ceiling rubble and insulation was in the centre of the room on top of the kitchen table. Elijah winced. The hole in the roof was covered by an orange tarp, but the weight of the wet insulation had been too much. "Do we clean it?"

"We need to shut the power off first."

Elijah followed Jamie outside to the mains box and flicked a switch. Morgan strode over to them. "What's the damage?"

"Kitchen ceiling collapsed," Jamie told him. "Want us to clean it?"

"No, I'll do it later. We've got another call."

"We're finished here?" Elijah asked.

"Yeah. The guys are packing up."

"Where are we going?" Jamie asked. "I've got my car."

"Alyse Wilson's place."

"She lives down the road from Jeremy, doesn't she?" Jamie said.

Morgan nodded. "I'll meet you out there. I need to assess the damage and check my family's OK."

"Stay here," Elijah said. "I'm sure we can handle it." He glanced at Jamie for confirmation.

"Yeah. You've got more important things to worry about tonight."

Siobhan ran up. "We're ready to go."

Elijah jogged to the land cruiser.

The wind was still wild, but the rain came in fits and starts and the thunder was a rumble in the distance. Elijah was squashed against the side of the car next to two very broad and wet men. With the heating on, the cab was beginning to steam.

"What are we facing?" one of the guys asked.

"Tree branch has fallen on the roof, cracked the tiles," Siobhan replied.

It was a ten-minute drive out to the Wilson place. "Elijah, how are you with a chainsaw?" Siobhan asked.

"I manage. You should see my sculptures." He grinned.

"Great. You can get on the roof this time."

His smile vanished and his stomach churned. Maybe he should tell her he wasn't good with heights. No, the first time was probably an anomaly. Now he knew what to expect, he'd be fine. He dealt with chainsaws and bad weather as part of his normal job. This was the same, only higher.

He let out a shaky breath.

The land cruiser's headlights illuminated the white karri branch covering half the roof. A man was already up there and a woman with gloriously red hair was on the ground staring at him.

Someone swore. "Mark doesn't know shit about what he's doing."

"Yeah, but don't tell him that," Siobhan said. "Otherwise he'll never get down. Leave him to me."

As Elijah jumped out of the car someone yelled. He spun around as Mark's arms flailed and almost in slow motion, he fell. Memory transported Elijah to a different night, a different location. Sitting on the theatre balcony balustrade, trying to pretend his heart wasn't breaking with Alex standing there, his arm wrapped around his husband's waist.

"Hey, you shouldn't be sitting there." Alex had reached out to him and Elijah flinched, overbalancing, and suddenly it was him falling, flailing to the ground.

The thud as Mark hit the ground brought Elijah back to the present, as did the roar of pain that quickly followed.

Mark was still alive. They both were.

The redhead reached him first and as she squatted

next to Mark, he backhanded her and she flew back into the mud.

Bastard!

Elijah ran to her, ignoring the screaming, cursing man and squatted. "Are you all right?"

The woman looked at him, blood coming from her nose, tears and a flash of anger in her eyes. She nodded.

"What the hell, Mark?" At the angry shout, Elijah glanced behind. Jamie stood over Mark, hands on his hips, fury radiating from him.

"I've broken my leg," Mark growled.

"Good." The woman muttered it so softly, Elijah almost missed it.

"It doesn't give you the right to hit Alyse."

Elijah warmed at Jamie's outrage and turned back to Alyse, holding out his hand. "Let's get you inside and cleaned up."

Her grip on his hand was light and he hauled her to her feet. When she swayed, he wrapped his arm around her waist. "I've got you, honey."

She flinched and then leaned into him as he helped her inside.

The small brick farmhouse had high ceilings, with those corner air vents common to old houses. Elijah wiped his feet on the door mat and said, "Which way to the first aid kit?"

Alyse stepped away from him. "I'll be fine." She wiped the blood still dripping from her nose with the back of her hand, not looking at him. In the light of the hallway, he noticed bruising around her eye. It was too dark to have been caused by Mark's backhander.

"Honey, that was a fair whack he gave you." He moved forward down the hall.

"Not really," she muttered as she passed him to lead the way into the bathroom and get a first aid kit out of the cupboard.

"I'm Elijah, by the way." He took a bit of gauze, wet it and wiped her nose.

She took it from him. "Alyse." Quickly she cleaned the blood, holding her nose like someone who'd done it multiple times before.

Elijah hoped Mark's broken leg really, really hurt. "Hey, you're the one who has beehives out at Kit Zanetti's."

She frowned and nodded.

"I'm Kit's farmhand. I've been fascinated by them. Let me know next time you're out there, I'd love to see what you do."

Her smile was genuine. "I will."

An awkward silence filled the room.

"I'm fine," Alyse said. "You can go."

He didn't want to leave her alone. "Has any rain got inside?"

"Yeah. I've got buckets out."

"Where? Do you need some tarps?" He moved into the hallway and glanced into the nearest room. An office. The ceiling was free of water stains and as he scanned the room his eyes caught on the piles of money on the desk. Far more cash than an apiary should have. What did Mark do for a living? His family owned the Vale winery, but he only worked there when they required extra hands.

Alyse pushed him out, her hands shaking, and closed the door behind them. "It's fine. I've got it covered in here. Just get the tree off the roof." She nudged him back towards the front door.

Something wasn't right here, and it wasn't just the fact Mark beat his partner.

Still, Elijah walked back outside. At the door he said, "You stay inside, out of the weather until the ambulance arrives. We'll take care of Mark."

She nodded.

He strode to Siobhan who was directing efforts. "Where do you need me?"

"On the roof. We've set up the safety line, so you're good to clip on. The chainsaw's up there."

Damn it. He'd hoped they would have sent someone else by now. Gritting his teeth, he nodded. He always faced his fears. Though the wind was still fierce, the rain had stopped for the moment.

"Don't step on any of the broken tiles," Siobhan said. "We don't want you to go through the roof."

His skin crawled. Not what he wanted either.

Jamie held the ladder for him as he climbed. Elijah ensured each grip was firm and his feet were correctly positioned on each rung before he moved to the next one. He took long, slow breaths. As long as he didn't look down, he should be fine.

Someone had set up the large flood lights to illuminate the area better. The tree branch had made a hell of a mess, tiles broken and leaves and smaller twigs all over the place. Piles of leaf litter made the surface slippery. Gritting his teeth, he clipped onto the safety rope and hefted himself onto the roof, crawling away from the edge.

He was up.

Pulse racing, he gingerly got to his feet, squatting low for balance as he examined the branch, being careful not to shift his gaze past it to the ground below. He'd cut it into small pieces in order to lift it off the roof. Any attempts to roll it would damage the tiles or gutters further.

He double-checked his connection to the safety line and started the chainsaw, the high-pitched whine loud even over the wind. The first few branches higher on the roof were easy. He cut them close to the main branch, leaving a long trunk behind.

Jamie joined him on the roof. "How's it going?" he yelled.

Some of the pressure in Elijah's chest eased as he switched off the chainsaw, placing it out of the way. Having someone else up here—having *Jamie* with him—made him instantly feel safer.

He pointed, not looking at the edge. "Can you throw these bits down while I focus on the main branch?"

Jamie went to work as Elijah took a moment to prepare himself for moving closer to the edge.

The wind buffeted him as he picked up the chainsaw again. Nausea swirled and he braced his feet firmly on the tiles. The whine of the chainsaw was loud as he cut through the branch, once, twice, three times. Jamie shuffled around him and threw the blocks of wood to the ground. The rain started again, cold, stinging drops that blew sideways in the wind. Elijah shifted along the branch, careful not to step too close to the cracked tiles.

Suddenly his foot slipped, and he fell back, the whirring chainsaw raising above his head. Shit. He couldn't regain his balance, not without dropping the chainsaw which would be deadlier than a fall. He was screwed. Hands gripped his waist, and a body pressed into his back, giving him the support to find his feet.

Heart racing, he leaned against Jamie for a moment to get his breath back and then carefully switched off the chainsaw and placed it on the roof.

"You OK?" Jamie asked.

He nodded, bending over, hands on his knees, breathing deeply to control his rapid heartbeat, his legs like jelly. "Thanks." And he'd thought the worst thing that could happen was falling off the roof. Not even close. His gaze lifted to the ground below him. Vertigo spun his head and he wobbled.

Jamie grabbed him again. "Sit." He rubbed Elijah's back and the slow up and down motion made his body flush for a whole different reason. He swallowed hard. The sooner he got this done, the faster he could go home. He shifted away and almost slipped again on the slick roof. With a curse, he scraped away some of the leaf litter on the tiles. Jamie squatted next to him, helping. They worked in silence until they had cleared enough for Elijah to start work again. This time he made certain his footing was secure before he bent to cut the rest of the branch.

While they worked, the ambulance arrived and Mark was loaded into the back. Alyse didn't go with him.

"I don't know why she stays with him," Jamie said.

"Love makes people stupid sometimes," Elijah replied and continued cutting the branch. When the roof was clear, he examined the tiles. They were cracked and broken in places but it shouldn't take too much to repair the roof if they had replacements. In the meantime, they needed to get it watertight.

Jamie passed down the chainsaw and Siobhan handed him a huge tarp. Together Elijah and Jamie covered the affected area and the crew tied the tarp in place. When they were done, Elijah hovered near the ladder, the nausea swirling in his stomach again. Now to get down.

"Do you want to go first?" Jamie called.

Elijah squeezed his eyes shut. He had to do this. He couldn't stay here all night.

"Elijah?" Jamie touched his arm. "Are you all right?"

He swallowed hard. "You go. I'll follow."

Jamie hesitated and then said, "Take your time."

Elijah noted where Jamie put his hands and feet in order to get back onto the ladder. Right. He could do this. Slowly he shifted, crawling backwards to the edge of the roof, then slipping a foot off to find the first rung.

Someone gripped his foot and steered it to the rung. He let out a breath as he made sure he had a firm purchase before he moved his other foot. When his hand gripped the ladder, relief rushed through him and he moved quickly down the rungs, wanting to be on the ground.

He let go, his head light. Made it. He turned to find Jamie frowning at him. "You don't like heights."

"They're not my favourite." Elijah swallowed hard and then unable to resist, he flung his arms around Jamie.

Jamie jolted and then hugged him back. "Hey, it's all right. You're safe." Gently he pushed Elijah back, brushed the hair off his face. "You need to tell Siobhan and Morgan. There's plenty of other things you can do to help without you having to go onto roofs."

Elijah hated to be weak. "It's fine. I've got to face my fear some time." Having Jamie holding him, even just his hands gave him a sense of security. Not good. He let go and stepped back. Time to get over his crush. If he let himself get too involved, he'd have his heart broken again. He headed to Siobhan.

"Good job," she said, slapping him on the back.

The smile came easily now he was on solid ground. "Thanks." The wind had died and the others packed up the lighting. They'd already neatly stacked the blocks of wood to the side. "Any more calls?"

"Not yet," she said. "When we're done here, we should be good to go."

"Mind if I check on Alyse?"

Siobhan nodded. "At least Mark won't be as mobile for the next six weeks."

It appeared as if the whole town knew Mark beat Alyse. So why hadn't anyone helped her?

She answered his knock on the front door, pulling her jacket tighter around her. "Are you finished?"

"Yeah. The tarp should keep out any more rain. Do you need help in here?"

She shook her head violently. "No. Everything's fine."

It was far from fine, but now wasn't the time. "You'll have to replace a couple of dozen tiles," he told her. "But the gutters are OK. If you go up there, be careful, it's slippery with all the leaf litter."

She scowled. "I asked Mark to clear the roof and the gutters before winter."

Elijah gave her a small smile. "How's your nose?"

"Fine." Her voice was dull.

He cleared his throat. "If you need anyone to talk to, or if you need help—"

"I'm *fine*." Anger lit her face. "Thank you. I'm sure you have lots to pack up." She pushed him towards the door.

Elijah nodded. "Take care, Alyse."

All he could do was hope she would get help before it was too late.

He stuck his hands in his pockets and returned to his team.

<h1 style="text-align:center">Chapter 5</h1>

Elijah stared out at the darkness as they drove back to the SES depot, his mind replaying the moment he had slipped on the roof. His pulse fluttered and his head spun even now. He gritted his teeth and pushed back his hair, wincing as water ran down the back of his shirt.

What a night.

He wanted a hot shower and bed. In the morning when he could think clearly, he'd decide whether to tell Morgan he hated heights. But the fear reminded him he hadn't been masculine enough for Alex, and was weak like his father said. He couldn't let either of them win.

"You did good, newbie." Siobhan nudged his shoulder.

Elijah straightened, forcing a smile. "Thanks."

They pulled into the depot and he cleaned the chainsaw while the others returned equipment to its place. After Siobhan dismissed them, he wandered out to where he'd parked his car.

The space was empty.

He frowned. He would have sworn he'd parked it there. But that might have been last week. He waved goodbye to his colleagues as he scanned the car park.

"You OK?" Jamie asked.

Nope. His car definitely wasn't here. "My car's missing." Maybe he'd parked behind the depot… He wandered around the back, glanced towards the wire mesh that fenced the yard and separated it from the banks of the river below.

Still no car.

He groaned. Not what he needed. All he wanted to do was crawl into bed. Without his car, he couldn't get to work in the morning. He'd be reliant on others. He could already hear his father's voice asking him if he'd locked it properly, as if getting his car stolen was his own fault.

Jamie followed him. "Has it been stolen?"

Elijah shrugged and walked back into the depot where Siobhan was locking up. "Siobhan, I think my car's been stolen."

She whirled around. "What?"

"I left it in the car park and it's not there anymore."

"Oh no," she said. "You should call the police. Do you want a lift home?"

"I'll take him."

Elijah's shoulders tensed at Jamie's offer. "Thanks."

"I'll write an incident report on Wednesday," Siobhan said.

It was too late for the police station to be manned so Elijah looked up the number to report a car theft.

The call connected as Jamie left the depot. Elijah answered the questions, his eyes closed as heat blasted through the front vents in the dashboard. Jamie's car was small, and Elijah smelled the rain on Jamie's jacket, felt his presence next to him. He shifted the phone to his right hand to resist the urge to hold Jamie's hand.

The car came to a stop and Elijah opened his eyes.

Home.

"We've got all your details and we'll be in touch," the person on the phone said.

"Thanks." Elijah hung up and reached for the door handle.

"Elijah, wait."

Elijah glanced at him. "Can it wait?" He didn't have the energy to deal with Jamie tonight.

Jamie grabbed his hand. "How are you coping? What happened on the roof was scary."

Elijah sucked in a breath and closed his eyes as the memory flowed over him. "It was."

"Hey, it's all right. You're safe." Jamie's fingers caressed Elijah's cheek and Elijah opened his eyes, his heart racing.

The light from the front porch illuminated the intensity in Jamie's eyes. Elijah couldn't breathe.

"It was so brave of you to go up there." Jamie's thumb continued to brush Elijah's face, almost an unconscious movement.

"You don't think it was stupid?"

Jamie flashed him a smile. "Maybe a little unwise, but you don't shy away from difficult things. I like that about you."

Hope and desire circled Elijah slowly. "You like me, huh?" He tried to keep the question casual, but failed.

Jamie sighed. "I do. A lot."

There was no mistaking what Jamie meant, not with the way he still cupped Elijah's cheek and leaned forward so their heads were close together.

"But here's the thing…"

OK. Nothing good ever started with *but*. He shifted away and Jamie dropped his hand. "Go on."

"Well, see… I'm bi."

Elijah waited for him to continue and when he

didn't he said, "So?"

"Some people have a problem with that."

"I don't, but if we got involved, I wouldn't accept any cheating, no matter the gender."

Jamie nodded. "Of course. I don't sleep around."

Elijah smiled. "Glad we got that sorted." He shifted forward ready for Jamie to kiss him, but Jamie glanced out of the windscreen, concern on his face.

"What else?" Elijah asked, unease stirring in his stomach.

"Not many people in Blackbridge know I'm bi."

He read between the lines. "You've only dated women while you've been here?"

He nodded. "I didn't have my first experience with a man until I moved to Perth."

"So you're saying anything we have is a hook up?" Disappointment filled him. He was after more.

"I don't know. I like you, Elijah. I'm just not ready for everyone in town to know."

Oh. The admission lodged a weight in Elijah's gut. "Why would it matter? Everyone loves you."

Jamie shook his head. "It might change. Don't tell me you never get any side-glances or comments from people."

Sure. It was part and parcel of being gay. "I've learnt not to care what people say."

"You're more advanced than I am," Jamie said. "You said it yourself, I've always been the town golden boy. I'll be disappointing so many people."

Oh, no he didn't. Elijah reached for the door handle. "You think being bi is a disappointment?" Anger raged through him. "So what's being gay—some kind of abomination?"

"No. I didn't mean it like that. You don't understand."

He never thought Jamie would be so short-sighted. "I understand plenty. I had to deal with bullying and abuse by a few people in this town when I came out ten years ago. Those people don't matter." His chest tightened, his breathing fast. He'd come to expect this kind of attitude from those outside his community, but inside it was another thing.

"I won't hide who I am, Jamie. I won't hide any relationship I'm in." Not anymore. The scars still hurt from that mistake. "So when you're ready to be open with who you are, give me a call."

He fumbled with the door handle and slammed the door behind him.

Head held high, he walked back to his house.

***

Lewis knocked on Jamie's office door at four o'clock the next day. He clenched his hands together and lifted his eyebrows as he asked, "Did you talk to my mum?"

Jamie smiled, gestured for him to come in. "Have a seat."

Lewis sat but fidgeted.

"I have a potential solution, but you don't have to accept it." He'd spoken to Lewis's mother earlier in the day, confirmed the details he'd put together and received her approval.

The teenager nodded, eyes wide.

"Your mum is happy for you to stay in Blackbridge during the holidays if you have somewhere to stay."

"So I can stay at the college?" His eyes lit up.

"No, Ms Simons is going away and can't supervise you." As Lewis slumped in the chair Jamie hurried on. "I have an alternative. Kit Zanetti is happy to have you do work experience with her. You're going to her farm tomorrow with class, so you can talk to her and see if you like her."

"Can I stay with her?"

"She's a newly-wed, so I didn't want to ask," Jamie said. "How would you feel about staying at my parents' place? They live right next door to Kit and they have a spare room if you want it."

Lewis leaned back. "Why would they want me?"

"I explained the situation and they're more than happy to host you for the fortnight."

Hope filled Lewis's face. "So I don't have to go home?"

Jamie shook his head. "Not if you agree to it."

"I'll get to finish school?"

"Yeah."

Lewis burst into tears and threw his arms around Jamie. "Thank you. Thank you so much."

Jamie's heart filled and he patted the boy on the back. "You're welcome."

A movement at the door caught his eyes as Patricia walked past. Teachers weren't supposed to touch students, even to comfort them. Jamie gently pushed Lewis back. "You're going to be fine."

Lewis wiped his tears on the back of his hand. "Are you sure your parents don't mind?"

"Yeah, I'm certain. Mum likes having someone to fuss around." He handed Lewis a tissue. "I'll take you out there after school on Friday if you're happy with the proposal."

"I'll stay anywhere if it means I get to finish school," he said. "You're the best, Mr Z." He wiped his eyes and with another sniff, he walked out.

Jamie let out a breath. Lewis would be all right.

If only sorting out his own life was as easy.

***

By the time Jamie arrived at his parents' place, Kit and his father had already loaded his bed onto one ute and his sofas on the other. Hannah and Mai were filling Hannah's four-wheel-drive full of the boxes he hadn't unpacked when he'd moved back to Blackbridge.

A warm glow filled him. He loved his friends.

He walked to them. "Keen to see me gone?" he asked his father.

Harold laughed. "Just helping out. Didn't want the girls lifting your stuff by themselves."

"I reckon the boxes are heavier than the bed," Mai complained. "What have you got in them?"

"Books." Jamie took the box from her and added it to the pile in the four-wheel drive.

"That's the last of it," Hannah said.

They drove in convoy out to the shed and after his father helped get the sofas and bed off the utes, he said, "I'm off. Thought I'd make your mum dinner for a change."

Kit smiled. "Just as sweet as his sons."

"Go on with you." Jamie's father blushed and kissed her cheek.

After he'd driven off, Jamie helped his friends carry the remaining boxes inside. "Thanks for your help."

Hannah got some soft drinks out of the fridge and passed them around as they sat on the sofas. "Fleur's sorry she couldn't make it, but she's working."

"There's barely anything for her to do."

"You don't have a lot of stuff for living in Perth eight years," Mai commented.

He shrugged. "I left most of it with Sandra." He'd felt guilty about the breakup, even though she'd been the one to end things. He hadn't wanted her to struggle.

"Always the nice guy. She didn't deserve you." Kit leaned forward. "So now we've got you alone, tell us, what's happening with Elijah?"

Jamie's hand froze with the can to his lips. Slowly he lowered it. "What do you mean?"

Mai rolled her eyes. "Come on, JJ. This is us. You don't have to hide."

Kit nodded. "I didn't work half a day in the cheese factory for you to chicken out."

He glanced at her. "That's why you took over on Saturday?"

"Of course. You and Elijah have been making goo-goo eyes at each other for months."

His face flamed. "No, we haven't."

Hannah patted his hand. "It's not overt, but we know you, JJ. We can see it."

Mai nodded. "So what's the latest?"

He groaned, giving in. "I stuffed up."

"Tell us how, so we can help you fix it," Hannah said.

Briefly he told them about the night before.

"What are you so worried about?" Mai asked. "No one in town will care."

He shook his head. "You weren't here when they did."

"Are you still going on about the hairdresser incident?" Kit demanded, her tone incredulous.

He scowled at her. "It took almost a year for that to die down."

Hannah held up her hands. "Let's not get angry." She glanced at Kit. "The kids were still teasing him when I moved here."

"Kids are stupid and cruel," Kit said. "Your other friends won't care, and if they do, good riddance to them."

"It's not that easy, Kit. I've got to think about my reputation, think how students' parents might react."

"JJ, you can't be discriminated against because of your sexuality," Mai said. "Society has got better in the past eighteen years."

Better, but still not great. His chest compressed thinking about it. "I've pissed Elijah off, so it doesn't matter."

"He'll forgive you if you explain," Kit said. "He doesn't hold a grudge."

The walls felt as if they were closing in on him. He had to get out of here. A quick look at the time gave him his escape route. He leapt to his feet. "Shit. I'm late for footy training."

He dug his clothes out of the suitcase he'd borrowed from his parents and dashed into the bathroom to change. By the time he came out, his friends were by the door.

He hugged them. "Thanks for your help."

"You're welcome," Mai said.

"We're here any time you need us," Hannah said.

"Want me to talk to Elijah for you?" Kit asked.

"No!" He sighed. "I'll sort it out in my own time." He locked the shed behind him and drove into town.

He pulled into the town oval about ten minutes late. The huge lights lit the field, bathing it in a bright white light which made it a mecca for moths. The rest of his team were already on the field, kicking the ball to each other. He dumped his bag with the gear and did a couple of gentle laps of the oval to warm his ankle before he jogged over to them.

"Forgot how to tell the time?" Kim asked with a grin.

Jamie rolled his eyes. "I was moving."

"Not very fast," Jeremy joked.

"Moving *house*."

"Where to?" Adam asked.

"Hannah's shed at Hideaway Retreat."

He partnered with Jeremy and marked the ball Jeremy sent his way. The evening's bite was soon a nice respite as Kim kept them moving, kicking, marking and tackling. Jamie loved the burn in his chest, the slight shortness of breath as he ran hard. He could forget about everything else in his life for an hour. By the time Kim ended the session, Jamie was sweating. He joined the others in the change rooms to shower.

"We going to the pub?" Kim asked.

The four of them usually did. Others in their team had families they had to get home to. "I'm up for it," Jamie said. "I want to hear about Jeremy's trip to Melbourne."

Jeremy chuckled. "Yeah, all right. Adam, you coming?"

Adam hesitated like he did more often than not these days. "I promised Elijah I'd hang with him."

"Tell him to meet us there," Kim said.

Jamie's muscles tightened. Great idea.

"All right."

Jamie went into the shower while Adam made the call. He wouldn't ask if Elijah was coming. It would seem too eager.

The pub wasn't too busy on a Tuesday night, maybe half the tables were full, and Dee was clearing their usual booth in the corner. The juke box played Aussie rock but not loud enough to be deafening, and the scent of beer and chips was strong. After Dee had taken their orders, Kim said, "So, how was meeting the in-laws, Jeremy?"

Jeremy had fallen in love with Zamira a month ago. She was from Melbourne and was moving to Blackbridge, but Jeremy had gone to visit her and meet her parents on the weekend.

Jeremy's smile was so wide it almost swallowed his face. "It was great. Her parents are nice and her sisters are sweet. We packed most of her apartment together."

Jamie's heart twinged. How would it feel to be so in love with someone? Over the past six months he'd seen all his friends get that dopey look on their face when they talked about their significant other. Everyone was pairing up, settling down.

And he was living in a shed—but at least he wasn't living at home anymore.

"Hey. Have you guys already ordered?" Elijah pinched a chair from a nearby table and put it at the end of the booth.

Jamie's heart skipped a beat. Elijah's hair was always perfection and tonight he wore a royal blue hoodie which fitted his body, showing off his sleek lines. The skinny jeans showed off his lush arse.

"Yeah, just now," Adam said. "Tell Dee what you want."

Elijah hurried to the counter. Damn he looked fine.

"I guess the SES kept you busy last night," Jeremy said.

Jamie nodded. "The storm was pretty fierce. Morgan lost part of his roof and a branch landed on Alyse Wilson's house."

Kim leaned forward. "Was Alyse all right?"

"From the branch she was," Jamie said. "Mark Patton fell off the roof and broke his leg as we arrived. Alyse went to help him and he backhanded her."

Elijah sat with his pint. "I thought you were going to punch him." His knee brushed Jamie's and he shifted his chair back a little.

He deserved that. "I was tempted."

"You should have," Kim growled. "Was she hurt?"

"A bloody nose," Elijah said. "I took her inside,

helped her clean up."

"Did she say anything about it?" Jeremy asked.

Elijah scowled. "Told me she was fine, which was bollocks. She was scared."

"Zamira was worried about her," Jeremy said. "She invited her for coffee before she left, but Alyse refused. It's obvious she doesn't do anything without Mark's approval."

"Isn't there anything the police can do?" Kim asked Adam.

"It depends on the situation."

"So what's the situation there?" Elijah asked. "How long has she been with him?"

"Since just after high school," Kim answered immediately. "Mark was considered a catch. One of my sisters crushed on him even though he was much older." He grimaced. "He was rich, good-looking, a star athlete and an older man. No one could compete." He slugged back his beer, expression grim.

Jamie had never heard Kim bitter. Had he had a crush on Alyse?

"Zamira will keep trying when she moves here," Jeremy said.

"When's that?" Elijah asked.

"Eleven days."

"Not like you're counting," Jamie said. They all laughed.

He shifted and his knee brushed Elijah's again. Hot thrills shot through him. Elijah raised an eyebrow.

Yeah, not cool. He needed to keep his distance from Elijah until he had made a decision. He wasn't that much of a douche-bag.

Dee arrived with their food and it gave him the opportunity to shift closer to Kim and away from Elijah.

His body knew what he wanted.
But his heart wouldn't make up its mind.

Chapter 6

Elijah grunted as he hefted the roll of wire into the back of the ute and double-checked that he had everything. If he was lucky, he'd be gone before Kit noticed. He glanced out of the machinery shed to the dairy where Kit had her office and winced as Kit strode towards him.

"Elijah, where are you off to?" she called.

Elijah put on an air of nonchalance. "Heading out to fix those back fences."

She frowned, her blonde ponytail swinging behind her. "The kids from the ag college will be here any minute."

He was well aware. He inched towards the ute. "I figured you would deal with them." And he wouldn't chance running into Jamie again.

She shook her head. "There's a kid I want you to meet. He'll be doing work experience with us during the school holidays."

Elijah paused. "The kids get plenty of work experience on the school farm."

Kit sighed. "Lewis needed an excuse not to go home. Jamie called me about him on Monday."

Elijah's heart jumped at Jamie's name. Idiot. "So what's Lewis's story?"

"He told his parents he was gay the last time he was home and his father flipped out. Told him not to come home next holiday if he still believed it." She positively glowered. "When Jamie called Lewis's mother to get the story, she said her husband would stop funding Lewis's education and he only has six months to go. Jamie arranged for him to work with me and stay with his parents over the holidays."

Elijah's heart expanded. What a wonderful thing to do. It made it so much harder to stay mad at Jamie.

The rumble of an engine announced the arrival of the school kids. An orange school bus drove along the long tree-lined drive towards the dairy. Elijah sighed. "All right. What do you want me to do?"

"I'll get Jamie to introduce you to Lewis and you two can get to know each other. I figure we'd take turns getting him to shadow us each day."

Great, Jamie would be there. Elijah nodded, nerves doing gymnastics in his stomach as the bus pulled up between the machinery shed and the dairy. Maybe he shouldn't have worn his fluoro pink safety shirt today. Would it seem too effeminate?

No, he wasn't going to change who he was to make someone else happy.

The first person off the bus was Mr Browne, a teacher Elijah had had when he'd been at the school. He strolled over to Kit. "Thanks for having us, Kit."

"It's no problem, Henry." She gestured to Elijah. "You remember Elijah Johnson?"

He nodded. "Good to see you."

"Likewise, Mr Browne."

He laughed. "You can call me Henry." He directed the mix of teenaged boys and girls into a group.

Jamie stepped off the bus and Elijah couldn't take his eyes off him. Jamie wore dark blue pants which clung to his thighs and a white short-sleeved shirt with the top button undone. Casual but professional. Delicious.

Jamie met his gaze and smiled.

Elijah's heart skipped a beat. He really was pathetic.

"Hi, everyone," Kit called. "I'm Kit, that's Elijah and this is my place. I know you're more interested in the dairy than me, so let's go." She moved towards the big silver shed. Elijah remembered farm tours when he was at the college where the farmer had droned on endlessly about his farm or some new method he was testing. He'd bet Kit remembered them too.

He followed the kids, watching as a couple of the boys shoved each other playfully, and one of the girls whispered something to her friend, her eyes glued on Kit like she was some kind of superhero. Elijah smiled. The ag college hadn't had many female role models when he'd been there.

A hand touched Elijah's shoulder, strong and warm. The spicy aftershave and the spark that went through him told him it was Jamie.

"Hey, Elijah, can I introduce you to someone?"

He pasted on a smile and turned, taking in the tall skinny kid next to Jamie. It was like looking at a younger version of himself. He'd had no muscle or meat on his bones when he'd been in high school. Hadn't filled out until his early twenties. "You must be Lewis."

The kid nodded, shaking his hand, eyes a little wide.

Elijah swallowed a grin. He'd been nervous around strangers too. "Kit tells me you'll be hanging out with us on the school holidays."

Lewis nodded again.

"That's great. It's always good to have more hands around."

Lewis's eyes darted towards Elijah's hands and blushed.

Oh. Awkward. He had to distract him. "Kit told me about your parents. It takes guts to be true to yourself," he said, not looking at Jamie.

Lewis glanced at Jamie and then at his feet. "I couldn't have done it without Mr Z."

Elijah's heart softened. Jamie was a hero to others, why couldn't he be one for himself?

"Why don't you catch up with the group?" Jamie said and the boy hurried away.

Jamie grinned. "Lewis isn't chatty at the best of times, but that was a new level of silent."

Do not be lured by his smile. "Perhaps the pink was too much for him." Elijah moved after the group of kids.

"Maybe." Jamie fell into step beside him. "It looks good on you."

Elijah inhaled, warmth filling him, unable to help the small smile before he focused on business. "You spoke to his parents?"

"His mother. She said her husband isn't ready to accept that Lewis is gay."

It said a lot about Jamie that Lewis was comfortable going to him for help. And for Jamie to instantly help him said even more. He was the kind of teacher every student should have. "So they're going to ignore the issue until he graduates?"

Jamie shrugged. "He's only got a semester left and his father has threatened not to pay his school fees. I want him to graduate."

"What about afterwards? He'll be a newly graduated kid with no home to go to."

Jamie sighed. "We'll cross that bridge when we come to it. Lewis's mum might convince his dad to accept him."

Elijah hoped so. They walked into the shed and Kit spoke about her dairy plan, talked about the number of cows currently pregnant and how much milk they got from the remaining cows.

"How long do you keep the calves with their mothers?" a girl asked.

Kit pressed her lips together. "Only a week. It's longer than some dairies, not long enough for others, but I've got a business to run."

Elijah grinned. "What she's not telling you is the calves get treated like her own babies. She makes sure they're well cared for."

Kit's cheeks tinged pink. "I treat all my animals well." She glared at Elijah and moved through to the milking section.

"She's good with the kids," Jamie commented.

Elijah nodded. "We've both been there and aside from Lincoln and the musketeers, there's nothing Kit loves more than farming."

Jamie's chuckle warmed Elijah's insides. "Yeah, she and Lincoln are good together. I can't believe I didn't see it sooner."

"For all her bluster, she's good at hiding her true emotions."

The ping of rain on the metal roof echoed loudly. Kit glanced up. "All right. Let's get you back on the bus for the farm tour before it buckets down."

The students rushed past Jamie and Elijah and suddenly they were alone in the shed. "You'd better hurry or you'll be left behind."

Jamie's lips curled up. "Might be worth it."

Elijah's body stirred. No. He wasn't going there. Not

with someone who wanted to hide who he was. "No." He scowled and strode away.

He didn't stop until he reached the machinery shed and then he let out a long breath as the bus's engine roared to life. He shook the tension from his shoulders and checked the equipment in the ute's tray.

The forecast was for constant rain, but the work still had to be done, and he wanted to check whether his car had been dumped at Foley's. He threw on his Driza-bone coat and drove out to the border of Kit's property. The school bus was nowhere in sight which meant Kit wouldn't spot him. She wouldn't want him going to Foley's by himself.

He kept his distance from Alyse's beehives in the paddock, parking instead close to the fence line. He ducked between the wires and walked out to the road which ran between Kit's place and Foley's. It was a long shot. Only an idiot would continue to leave stolen cars in a place the police had already discovered.

The gate into Foley's was closed and padlocked shut. Elijah climbed over it and rounded the burnt out shell of the shed.

Clear.

Shame. He needed his car.

Pulling his jacket closer, he lifted his face towards the buildings in the distance. The roar of a motorbike reached him. Elijah glanced to the road. No, it was definitely coming from the direction of Foley's shed.

He ducked inside the burnt shell to get shelter from the rain and rang the police. Adam answered.

"We haven't found your car yet," he said.

"It's not at Foley's place either," Elijah told him.

"How do you know?"

"Because I'm standing there right now."

An exasperated hiss and then Adam said, "Elijah,

you're trespassing. You shouldn't be there."

Elijah shrugged. "I was in the neighbourhood. That's not why I'm ringing. I heard a motorbike near Foley's sheds. Has someone moved in?"

Silence stretched between them.

"Adam. Are you still there?"

Adam cleared his throat. "Yeah. I'll tell Lincoln. He might want to check it out. You should get back to Kit's."

The roar of the motorbike was getting closer. Elijah's shoulders tensed. "Yeah. I'll do that as soon as I can."

"Now, Elijah." Adam had his authoritative police tone working.

"About that…" The roar echoed through the structure. Elijah hunched behind a bit of roof metal.

"Is that a motorbike?"

"Yep."

Adam swore.

Elijah breathed deeply. The last time he'd confronted a man on a motorbike, he'd been shot. It wasn't an experience he wanted to repeat. His skin prickled and his chest tightened.

The engine settled into an idle, but it wasn't too close. Elijah peered out from behind the metal. The red and white farm bike was at the gate and the rider wore a black dirt bike helmet and a thick black puffer jacket, his back to Elijah as he cut the padlock. Even with the jacket on, he was broad-shouldered with thick legs, built like a rugby player, but tall as well, over six-foot. He'd bench-press Elijah with no problems.

No number plate on the rear of the bike so it wasn't licensed for the road, not that it would stop the rider. Still Elijah snapped a photo as the man opened the gate and pushed the bike through. As the man turned to close the gate, he looked towards the shed and Elijah ducked back behind the roof panel and held his breath, heart thumping. With shaking fingers he sent the photo to Adam.

The bike continued to idle.

"Elijah, what's going on?" Adam's voice was faint.

He didn't dare answer him.

"Elijah, if you can hear me, we're on our way." Then Senior Constable Sue Wintie came on the line. "I'm staying on the phone. Talk to me when you can."

Elijah winced. He strained for any sound aside from the bike's engine; the crunch of footsteps, a cough, the snick of a gun.

Sweat beaded on his brow.

It would take at least twenty minutes for the police to get here. A lot could happen in that time. A man could bleed out. The trespasser could get away. He didn't dare peek out. Any movement might attract attention.

The engine revved and Elijah flinched. Then a roar, and it slowly faded.

Elijah stayed where he was for a good few minutes before he lifted the phone to his ear and said, "He's gone."

Sue immediately responded. "What did he look like? What motorbike was he on?"

"I sent a photo to Adam." Elijah slowly crept to the entrance of the shed. He scanned the road. It was empty. Still there was a chance he might come back. "I'm going to Kit's."

"Stay where you are. Adam and Lincoln are almost there."

Would they drive past the rider on the way?

He shifted his feet, the urge to run to safety strong. But he should listen to Sue. She knew what she was talking about.

He moved towards the back of the shed, undercover and stayed still. It was hard to hear anything past the rain pelting what was left of the roof. Hopefully the rider had decided any motion he'd seen was a bird or imagined.

He rubbed his arms. How was it that he was messed up in this stuff again? It had been a case of wrong place, wrong time when he'd been shot and today could have been the same. He had to learn to not stick his nose into other people's business. Had to leave things to the experts.

Finally the growl of an engine reached his ears. "I can hear a car," Elijah said to Sue.

"It's Lincoln and Adam," she said.

The police car pulled up outside the gate. "Thanks, Sue." He hung up, stuck his phone into his pocket and quickly vaulted the gate the rider had shut behind himself. He shook away the remnant unease. "Did you see him?" he called to Lincoln who wound down the car window.

Lincoln shook his head. "Get in the car."

Shaking out his jacket, he climbed in.

"Why the hell were you there?" Lincoln demanded.

Immediately his spine stiffened. "My car was stolen. They might have dumped it here."

"I should charge you with trespass," Lincoln muttered. "Tell us what you saw."

Elijah shuffled into the middle of the seat. Adam stared towards Foley's property. Shit. He should have called the Albany police rather than subjecting Adam to this place again. "Should we go back to Kit's?"

Lincoln glanced at Adam and shook his head. "Be quick about it. Adam, you take notes."

At his name, Adam flinched and reached for a

notebook in his top pocket.

Nice work distracting him. Elijah explained again what he'd seen. "I sent you a photo."

Adam pulled out his phone. "Same build as Henk's guy."

He was one of the two guys the police were still searching for after they'd raided Henk's property for being involved in an illegal migrant ring. He was bad news.

"He must have headed into the bush," Lincoln said. "An unlicensed bike would have caught someone's attention."

"Not necessarily," Elijah disagreed. "There aren't many people in this area."

Lincoln sighed. "You're right. Do you need a lift somewhere?"

"No. The ute's through the trees." Elijah reached for the door handle.

"Elijah, don't investigate this," Lincoln said. "These guys aren't messing around. I don't want you hurt again."

He didn't want that either. He met Lincoln's gaze in the rear-view mirror. "I won't. Let me know if you find my car."

"Will do."

Elijah waved goodbye and jogged across the road and through the thin bush to Kit's property. When he got into the ute, the tension in his shoulders fully released. He definitely wouldn't be looking for trouble in the future. He fully believed in the police's ability to do the job properly.

Now he needed to get those fences fixed.

Otherwise he'd be in trouble with Kit.

And *that* was a scary thought.

Chapter 7

Elijah briefly considered not going to SES training on Wednesday evening. He'd seen quite enough of Jamie Zanetti over the past few days and it was becoming harder and harder to ignore his attraction to him. He was seriously thinking about ignoring his own rule about being in a secret relationship.

But he wasn't a teenager, he wasn't going to avoid a commitment because of a crush. So he put on his big boy's panties and walked to the depot. Only Morgan was there when he arrived and he was setting out harnesses while talking on the phone. "I'm not doing any more," he growled. "I've had enough."

Elijah placed his kit bag in the change room and by the time he returned to the main room, Morgan had hung up. "What are we doing today?"

Morgan jumped. "Shit. I didn't hear your car."

"Still missing," Elijah answered. "I walked."

"Oh, right. Siobhan told me." He looked up from the harness he was examining. "Police have any leads?"

He shook his head. "No, it wasn't dumped in the same place as the others."

Morgan frowned. "Others?"

Lincoln hadn't said it was a secret. "I found Barbara's car at Foley's place."

Morgan's eyes widened. "Really? What were you doing there?"

Elijah shrugged. "Checking Kit's fences. Foley's gate was open so I went to close it and saw the car." Time to change the subject. "So, what's happening today?"

"Roof safety systems and rescue," Morgan answered. "We'll have a lot of roof work coming up in the next few months and I want to confirm everyone knows the correct procedures. You were lucky not to injure yourself the other night."

Elijah's stomach clenched. "I should have taken the time to clear the tiles."

Morgan scowled. "You shouldn't have had to, but don't get me started on people's inability to do simple maintenance on their homes."

Elijah bit his lip. Had he cleared out his gutters yet? "What do you need me to do?" He gestured at the harnesses and swallowed hard. If he exposed himself to heights regularly, the vertigo might disappear. He hated the idea something Alex had done could have such a hold over him.

"I'm about done."

Siobhan walked in chatting to Jamie. Scratch that, flirting with Jamie. The smile, the way her body was turned towards him, not much distance between them, her hand brushing through her short blue hair. And Jamie was being just as friendly back.

His spirits fell and a different type of vulnerability hit him. Yeah, Jamie would date a woman before he dated Elijah. It was easier. He turned back to Morgan. "Want me to go first?" At least getting on a roof would work on one area of vulnerability.

"Sure." Morgan handed him a harness and Elijah

moved across the room away from Jamie to get ready while the others arrived. During the toolbox meeting, Morgan explained the exercise, and then they moved outside where it was icy cold.

No clouds in the sky tonight and the wind blew right through him. Elijah rubbed his hands together and slipped on his gloves. He stood back while a couple of volunteers set up the safety ropes over the top of the roof. He was going up there. His shiver had nothing to do with the cold. The depot building had high walls and the roof was further off the ground than Alyse's had been.

"Are you sure you want to do this?"

He jumped at Jamie's voice, but kept his gaze on the crew. "Of course."

"Aren't you afraid?"

Elijah ignored the concern in Jamie's voice. "I've got to face it someday." He gave Jamie a pointed look. "I won't let it rule my life."

Jamie winced.

"Elijah, you're up," Morgan called.

Without another word, Elijah strode to the ladder and examined his harness again before he stepped on the first rung. Nausea swirled in his stomach, and his skin flushed as he moved up the ladder. He squeezed his eyes shut as the vertigo danced in his head. Funny how anger could only carry you so far.

He could do this. One step after the other. Three points of contact at all times.

Releasing his grip on the rung got harder and harder the further he climbed. As he reached the edge of the roof, he stopped. This was definitely the worst bit. He clipped onto the safety rope and hauled himself onto the aluminium roof, then crawled away from the edge. Swallowing hard, he gave the people on the ground the thumbs up. Another volunteer joined him on the roof and clipped in. He would supervise the exercise from up here.

"All right, Elijah," Morgan called. "Time for you to fall."

He gritted his teeth. The point of the exercise was to practise how to rescue someone who had fallen off the roof, but was clipped on to the safety system. He breathed deeply again and tugged on the rope holding him to the roof to make sure it was secure, then checked the connection on his harness. It all looked good. But it was a long way down.

His team waited below, watching, and Elijah swayed with dizziness. Volunteering for this had to be one of his dumbest ideas. Sweat broke out on his forehead and panic welled in his chest. He caught Jamie's eye and Jamie gave him a little nod.

Elijah breathed out, refusing to let panic take hold. All he had to do was abseil off the roof. He shuffled backwards closer to the edge, his stomach doing its best impression of a cement mixer. His heels found the edge of the roof and his grip tightened on the rope. The safety line was still connected on both ends. He only had to lean backwards like he'd been taught. The rope held and he lowered himself over the roof, legs braced against the side of the shed.

"Hang there for us, Elijah," Morgan yelled. "We'll get you down in a jiffy."

Elijah didn't look down. Very slowly he lifted his legs away from the wall and let himself hang. The rope jerked at the extra weight and he clung to it, squeezing his eyes closed. It was fine. He would be fine.

Below him, the team called to each other as they ran through the scenario. Already someone was climbing the ladder onto the roof.

Rip.

He jolted and his breath froze in his lungs.

What the hell was that? The tension under one of his butt cheeks wasn't as tight as it had been. He felt under his butt, but the harness strap was gone. Hot fear swept through him and his hands sweated in their gloves. The rope swung in the wind and there was another rip. He gripped the rope as one leg dropped. He was going to fall. He swallowed hard to get some moisture back in his mouth.

"Morgan!" he yelped. "My harness ripped."

The only thing holding him was the strap around his waist and one thigh. His fingers hurt from clenching the rope. "This isn't a drill," he added in case they thought he was playing the part.

"Hold on, Elijah. We'll get you down." Jamie's voice.

Some of his panic receded momentarily until the fabric ripped again.

Not good.

"Hurry!" he squeaked. The harness was still attached at the front. If he braced his feet back against the shed wall and kept a tight grip on the rope, he could stay there until they got him down.

Lifting both legs he stretched them towards the metal wall and used his arms to take some of the weight off the harness. His muscles burned.

He risked a glance below and wished he hadn't as his head spun. A long way to fall. Jamie stood beneath him while Siobhan set the ladder back in place.

He panted as his arms shook at the effort of holding on. The ladder appeared next to him. Would the harness hold while he reached for safety? He was too scared to try, but his arms burned. He couldn't hold on for much longer.

"Grab the ladder, E," Jamie called.

Legs first. He lifted his right leg, felt around until it connected with the ladder and found a rung. Hooking his foot on the strut, he pulled himself closer, placed both legs on a rung. He had to let go of the rope, but his centre of gravity was back, away from the ladder. If he let go, he'd fall. Using core muscles he hadn't realised he had, he leaned forward, shifting towards the ladder. He grabbed the rung nearest to him, his grip like a vice, and released the rope with his other hand and held on to the ladder. He stood there a moment, legs trembling, arms numb and a death grip on the rung. One of the crew called out from above. "Are you secure, Elijah?"

Secure wasn't the word he'd use. He wanted to hug the ladder and never let go. In fact they might have to pry him off it with a crowbar. Still, he glanced up. "Yeah." He swallowed hard so he could speak. "You want to release the rope so I can get down?"

"Doing it now."

A few moments later, the rope looped through his harness slackened. Time to get on firm ground. But it meant letting go of the rung and his fingers were curled around it like chicken claws. He closed his eyes. He couldn't stay here all night.

When he opened his eyes, another ladder was next to him and Jamie appeared.

"You can do this, E," Jamie said. "One rung at a time."

Elijah's chest was too tight to breathe. Jamie touched his hand and the contact thawed a small portion of his fear. "I've got you. Start with your right foot, OK?"

He gingerly lowered one foot until it reached the next rung.

"Good, now your left foot."

Focusing on Jamie's instructions, slowly, rung by rung he climbed down the ladder. His breath whooshed out of him as his boots hit the concrete. "Smashed it."

"Title of your sex tape," Jamie joked.

It surprised a laugh out of him, as he tried to make his jelly legs hold him. "That was a little more excitement than I was expecting." Jamie clapped a hand on his shoulder and Elijah desperately wanted to fling his arms around him. Instead, he stepped away.

Morgan's frown would have frightened a child at ten paces. "Take off the harness. I want to know what went wrong."

With pleasure. He loosened the buckles, stepped out of the harness and handed it to Morgan.

The blood drained from Morgan's face. "Shit. I gave you the harness I was about to bin," he said. "I'm so sorry."

Elijah fought control of the spike of anger. He was still riding on the edge of fear, but yelling wouldn't make anyone feel better in the long term. He swallowed hard and shrugged. "It's fine. I'm in one piece." He was safe. That's what mattered.

"I'll write the report. Siobhan, take over." Morgan stalked away, head down.

Elijah's anger washed away in a sea of compassion. Morgan obviously blamed himself. Elijah would have a word to him when he was done.

Jamie looked him in the eye. "Are you really all right?"

He took off his helmet, ran a shaky hand through his hair. "I'll probably have some gorgeous bruising around my groin in the morning."

"Listen up, folks," Siobhan called. "Let's pack up and do a full equipment audit. We want to prevent this from happening again."

A couple of people grumbled, but not too loudly. No one liked auditing the equipment, but after tonight they couldn't complain.

"Jamie, you and Elijah can start."

Damn it. He wanted a few minutes to calm himself and being with Jamie wouldn't help. "I'll meet you there. I'm going to the loo." He strode off.

Once inside the bathroom, he pulled off his gloves and splashed cold water on his face. The temperature cut through the jitters. He had to tell Morgan about his fear of heights, but he wouldn't do it today, not when Morgan was already upset about the harness. The man felt guilty enough. He'd tell him next training session. Screw facing his fear. Screw Alex. He wasn't ever going on a roof again.

The door opened and Jamie walked in. Elijah straightened from the sink and dried his face on some paper towel. Was this nauseous, weak, light-headed sensation how Jamie felt about telling the town about his sexuality?

"You handled it well," Jamie said.

"Thanks." He still wanted to throw himself into Jamie's arms. He stepped back. He'd give Jamie the space he wanted.

"Do you want to get a drink after we've finished?"

Elijah raised his eyebrows, as a fluttering of another kind started in his chest. "What kind of drink?"

"Ah, we could go to the pub."

Elijah lowered his voice. "That's not what I meant."

Jamie pursed his lips. After a long pause he said, "A can-we-talk-about-things drink."

Elijah refused to let the fluttering turn into hope. He shrugged. "Sure." The bathroom was suddenly too confining. He pushed past Jamie and headed for the equipment room.

"Elijah—"

A volunteer walked towards them.

Elijah raised his eyebrows, waiting for Jamie to continue.

"Never mind."

The fluttering stopped. Right. Can't have anyone overhear them.

Elijah sighed. The talk had better be good. He couldn't continue pining after Jamie.

He wasn't that desperate.

***

Jamie tapped his steering wheel as he drove to the pub after training ended. He wasn't convinced Elijah would meet him there. He hadn't seemed enthusiastic when Jamie had asked him out and had refused the offer of a lift to the pub, said he wanted to walk to clear his head.

Not that Jamie blamed him, but before he could try to persuade Elijah, Siobhan had asked for his help putting back some tarps and by the time Jamie had finished, Elijah had already left.

He pulled into the car park and exhaled. Was he actually going to do this?

His fear was nothing compared to what Elijah had just faced. Seeing him dangling off the ground, clinging to the rope had terrified Jamie. The accident could have been a lot worse and Jamie would have regretted not being brave enough to explore things between them.

He'd only had eyes for Elijah when he'd walked into the depot, despite Siobhan flirting with him. And afterwards, when Elijah was safe on the ground, he'd wanted to drag him into his arms and hug him, comfort him when Elijah had clearly still been scared.

All of that told him what he had to do.

And he wasn't doing it sitting in the dark in his car.

Grow some balls, Zanetti.

He got out and strode towards the pub on the corner. Nerves tumble-dried in his stomach as he pushed open the wooden door. The jukebox played country music today and about a dozen tables were full. He scanned the room, inhaling the stale smell of beer and lifted his hand in greeting at Mr Corson at the bar and his principal, Noel, who was with his family. Elijah sat in the corner booth facing him. Jamie let out a sigh of relief and walked over to him.

"Can I get you a drink?"

"A shot of tequila would be good."

Jamie studied him. His skin was still a little paler than normal. Without thinking, he squeezed Elijah's hand. "I'll be right back."

He walked up to the bar and Dee grinned at him. "Two days in a row, Jamie?"

"Yeah," he agreed. "I'll get a shot of tequila and a midi of the local beer."

She raised her eyebrows. "Tough night?"

It would be all over town by tomorrow anyway. "Elijah had a near miss at training."

She glanced at the booth. "I thought he wasn't as chirpy as normal. What happened?"

Jamie explained and Dee said, "Well in that case, the tequila's on the house."

He handed her his card. "Thanks."

He scooted into the booth next to Elijah. "Dee said the drink's on the house."

Elijah made more room for him. "That's nice of her." He downed the drink in one mouthful and slammed the shot glass onto the table. He closed his eyes and sighed. "I needed that."

Jamie itched to offer some physical comfort. He

clenched his hands. "Must have been pretty scary, dangling like that."

Elijah shuddered. "Please don't remind me."

"You should tell Morgan."

"After tonight, I definitely will."

Jamie hesitated. Elijah's determination to face his fear had inspired Jamie, but now he was backing down… No. Stop making excuses. Jamie cleared his throat. "I'm sorry about the other day."

"Hey, guys. Mind if I join you?"

Jamie jumped and turned to Jeremy standing next to the table, beer in his hand. He froze. What was he supposed to say?

"Not today, honey," Elijah said. "Jamie and I have some SES business to discuss."

"Oh, right. Sure." Jeremy raised his glass in farewell and went to the bar.

Jamie relaxed. Thankfully Elijah was a quicker thinker than him.

Elijah raised one eyebrow. "Monday?"

Jamie nodded. He needed Elijah to understand where he was coming from. "I, ah, had something happen when I was a kid, and it's kind of stuck with me."

Elijah covered his hand, concern in his eyes. "Want to talk about it?"

His instant attempt to comfort warmed Jamie, but he removed his hand on the pretence of drinking more of his beer and checked the room to make sure no one had noticed. "The more I think about it, the more stupid it seems to be so hung up on it."

"Childhood trauma can stick, especially if you've never dealt with it." Elijah took Jamie's beer and sipped.

His skin prickled. Hopefully talking about it would

help. "I was in Year Three and I worshipped my teacher." He shook his head. He'd been such a teacher's pet. "He had all these travel stories to exotic sounding places. The way he described them he sounded like a superhero." These days he'd probably see through the boasting. "I tried to be the perfect student, so he would praise me."

Elijah frowned. "I don't think I'm going to like where this is going."

Jamie shook his head. "It's nothing sexual." He sipped his drink. "About halfway through the year we had an assignment about what we wanted to be when we grew up. We had to research it and do a presentation at the end."

"Did you choose teacher?"

Jamie's laugh was bitter. "If only. I wanted to be a hairdresser." Elijah's jaw dropped and he continued. "I used to love going to the hairdresser's with Mum, listening to the gossip and I loved how good everyone felt when they left. It was a happy place."

Elijah smiled. "I take it others didn't agree?"

Jamie's chest still tightened at the memory. "I was the last to do my presentation." He closed his eyes, still able to picture it with such clarity. The shuffles and whispers of his classmates who were bored after sitting still for so long, the damp, fusty smell from clothes that had got wet during recess and were slowly drying. "I didn't get halfway through it before my teacher started mocking me."

He lowered his voice to mimic him. "What are you—a girl? Hairdressing's for poofters." The same feeling of shame washed over him. "I was devastated the man I idolised was being so cruel." Elijah's face screwed up in outrage, but Jamie kept talking. "The kids teased me mercilessly for months. Kit and Fleur stood up for me, but it only made things worse because they were girls."

"So what did you do?"

"I worked harder at sport, training after school. I went fishing with Dad and Lincoln and took in photos of the fish I'd caught." He still hated fishing. "I begged Lincoln to teach me to surf and hung out with some of his friends at school. Having older high school guys talking to me added to my cred."

"So you became the perfect man's man?"

Jamie nodded. "Eventually the names and the teasing stopped and girls took interest again. Everyone picked me first on their sporting teams and they forgot about me ever wanting to be a hairdresser."

"Did you forget about it?"

"Absolutely." He cringed at the way he'd behaved. "I made Mum's life hell any time she spoke about taking me for a haircut. Eventually she agreed to take me into Albany whenever I needed a trim. That way no one would see me and remember."

"Didn't your parents speak to the school about your teacher?"

"I never told them about it. Looking back I guess they knew something was wrong, but I pretended everything was fine. I'd tell them I was going to Kit's place and instead I'd hang out by the river by myself."

"So realising you were bi must have been pretty traumatic for you."

"Initially." The idea of going through it all again… "I figured I'd choose girls not guys." He glanced at Elijah. "It wasn't hard until I met you one weekend at Kit's place."

Elijah's eyes widened. "At her sixteenth birthday party?"

Jamie smiled. "You remember?"

"Oh, honey I almost combusted when you walked into the room." He grinned.

"I could only focus on you, and because you were already openly gay, you fascinated me. I wanted to be like you."

"No way!"

Jamie chuckled. "Yeah. You became the centre of my fantasies for quite a while afterwards. Part of me kept hoping Kit would invite me over again while you were there, or I'd run into you in town, but it never happened. I worked most weekends, and you didn't play sport."

Elijah sat back and studied him. "Would you have dated me?"

Jamie sighed. "No, but the fantasies kept me going until I got to Perth, away from all the expectations."

"And then you went wild?"

"Not wild, but I enjoyed being single and went to some gay bars. Then I met Sandra and I was with her for a couple of years."

"Have you had a long-term relationship with a man?"

His muscles tightened. "Not yet."

"Do you want one?"

He looked deep into Elijah's eyes. "With you I do, but I need to take things slow, work through my issues. I shouldn't give a damn if someone doesn't like it, but I've spent most of my life trying to please everyone." He paused. "And I get this real anxiety, like I can't breathe when I imagine their reactions."

Empathy crossed Elijah's face, but he leaned back. "What's your definition of slow?"

Jamie cleared his throat. Elijah wouldn't like his proposal. "No public displays of affection at first. Not openly telling people we're dating."

Elijah shuffled away from him, a deep frown on his face.

Panic jiggled in Jamie's chest. He was losing him. He couldn't blame him. He was essentially asking Elijah to hide their relationship until Jamie got over himself. "We'll tell the musketeers," he blurted. "I just need a few weeks to prepare myself for the town's reaction."

"You really think they'll care?" Elijah raised an eyebrow.

He sighed. "They probably don't give a damn, but I need it. I should probably tell work as well…" He glanced at Noel. The principal wouldn't have a problem with it, but Patricia's smile and frequent touches popped into his mind. He could only imagine what she'd say. But he'd do it.

"How long?" Elijah demanded.

Jamie shifted away, his chest tightening. "What do you mean?"

"If I agree to this, how long do I have to wait—a week, two, a month?"

Shit. He wanted a time limit. It made it so real. He longed to say a couple of months, but he wasn't a complete wuss and he'd always have his family's support. Better to do it quickly like ripping off a Bandaid. "Two weeks?"

Elijah studied him for a long moment. "The last time I hid a relationship, I discovered it was because the lying bastard was married, and not because he was worried about his reputation."

Jamie cringed. No wonder Elijah was so against it. "I can promise you I'm not married."

"Yeah, I know. No way Kit would set us up if you were."

Jamie grinned. "No, she wouldn't."

"All right. You've got two weeks." Elijah's smile was

small, a little uncertain.

Jamie hated having made him feel that way. "Absolutely. I promise I'll get my shit together by then."

"Adam has a late shift tomorrow night. Do you want to come for dinner?"

"I'd love to."

Elijah brightened a little. "OK. I'm heading home before I decide it's a good idea to drink all the tequila in the bar."

Jamie brushed Elijah's arm. He'd been so focused on himself he'd forgotten about Elijah's trauma. "Want to talk about it? I can drive you home."

"I'll be fine." He made shooing motions with his hand. "If you'll let me up."

Jamie wanted to insist on helping him, but he hadn't earned that yet. He slid out of the booth instead and walked Elijah out of the pub.

"Can I bring anything tomorrow night?" he asked.

"Just yourself—six-thirty all right?"

He nodded and glanced around the car park. Streetlights illuminated the family nearby getting into their car. No way could he kiss Elijah goodbye. "Can I drive you home?"

"No, I could do with the fresh air." Elijah stepped forward, bent his head and followed Jamie's gaze to the family. His shoulders slumped. "Right, no PDA. I'll see you tomorrow." He walked off.

Jamie gritted his teeth. The family weren't the least bit interested in him, the children arguing, the parents trying to wrangle them into the seatbelts.

But Elijah was interested. So Jamie had to get over his fear before he messed it up.

Chapter 8

"What the hell, Elijah?" Kit's outrage spun Elijah around. He slipped, almost crashing into the cow he was about to milk.

His boss strode towards him, her scowl sharp enough to strip paint. Crap. What had he done? He hadn't seen her this morning when he'd arrived, and had been working all day at the back of the property fixing water troughs. "Hey, Kit. What's up?"

"Don't you 'what's up' me. What's this crap about you going to Foley's place yesterday?"

He frowned. It wasn't like Lincoln to be a tell-tale. "Where'd you hear that?"

She glared at him as if he was an imbecile, a hand on one hip, her head tilted. "Where do you think?"

Lincoln probably hoped Kit would stop him doing something stupid. "I thought my car might have been dumped there. I wasn't expecting to see anyone."

"You should know better after all the shit that happened a few months ago."

Yeah. She was right. "I'm sorry. I didn't think of that." How to distract her before she gave him a shit job as punishment? "Did I mention Jamie's coming to dinner tonight?"

Her whole demeanour changed instantly. She straightened, a huge grin splitting her face. "Seriously? Tell me everything."

Elijah smiled and continued placing the cups on the udders. "We had a drink last night and I invited him to dinner."

"Great! Wait until I tell the musketeers."

Elijah winced. "You can't tell anyone."

"Why not?"

"Jamie doesn't want it public knowledge yet."

She scowled. "What?"

"He's not had a same-sex relationship in Blackbridge and he's worried about what people will say."

"That's bullshit! I told him no one will care."

Her outrage soothed him. "I gave him two weeks."

"Good." She prepped the cows across from him. "So what are you making for dinner?"

"Not sure yet. I'll have to stop at the supermarket on the way home."

Kit checked her watch. "What time is he coming?"

"Six-thirty."

"Why don't I finish milking tonight and you go now?"

"It's fine. This is my job."

"No. I insist. Go and give yourself time to primp. I can handle things here. Lincoln's working late tonight anyway." She took his arm and led him to the dairy entrance. "Go home."

Elijah hesitated. "Are you sure?"

"Of course. Have fun." She opened Adam's car door and before Elijah knew it he was behind the wheel.

He wasn't going to look a gift horse in the mouth. With a grin, he waved and drove away. He'd managed to distract her from Foley's place and got off work early—win, win. He frowned as he reached the main road. Kit often griped about Lincoln not telling her police business, so why had he told her about this? Wasn't it a big deal, or was he seriously worried and hoping Kit would keep him under control?

Not that he would search for his car again. He wanted to stay out of trouble too.

He pushed his concern aside. His biggest issue currently was what to make Jamie for dinner. He should have asked Kit for a recommendation.

Clouds blotted out the sun, darkening the evening and he flicked on the headlights, but they did little to add additional light. As he passed a car coming in the opposite direction, he discovered one of the headlights wasn't working. The least he could do for Adam was replace the globe. The clock ticked over to five as he drove into town. Lights were still on in Morgan's workshop, and a car was in the car park. He pulled in, left the lights on and checked. Yep, he'd blown a globe. He flicked off the lights and headed for the office. There was a 'closed' sign on the door and it was locked.

"Morgan?" he called, moving around the side of the building into the scrap yard. He heard voices towards the back, so he headed in that direction.

A black ute was parked around the side. Morgan spoke with a big man with rugby-sized arms and legs who had his back to Elijah. It was getting dark, and Elijah lifted his hand to get Morgan's attention. Then the man raised the gun in his hand.

Elijah's gut turned to water and his breath caught in his throat. Not again. He froze, staring, unable to move, flashing back to a few months ago when someone else had waved a gun at him, felt the pain as the bullet had sliced through his shoulder.

Time to get out of here. But Morgan was in danger. He had to call the police.

"Don't you threaten me," Morgan shouted. "I'm doing what you asked."

Elijah shifted backwards, moving to hide behind a pile of scrap. The man with the gun spoke, but too quietly for Elijah to hear.

Elijah reached for his phone, turned towards his car and came face to face with another man, another gun.

He froze.

A balaclava covered the man's face, but Elijah's focus was on the gun. His heart pounded so hard it was audible.

"You didn't see anything, right?" the man growled.

Elijah's throat was too dry to speak.

"You didn't stop here, you saw nothing, and all your family will sleep soundly tonight."

Fear rushed over Elijah's skin, turning it hot and then ice cold. He swallowed hard. "Nothing," he agreed. "I won't even notice the globe is broken until tomorrow."

The man nodded. "Good. Get out of here."

Elijah didn't need any further prompting. He raced to his car, muscles tight, expecting a gunshot at any second. His hand shook as he turned the key and put the car into gear. He sped out of the car park, glancing in his rear-view mirror, but the man with the gun was gone. He let out an explosive breath and gripped the steering wheel tighter as his arms weakened.

The police station's white and blue sign illuminated the street ahead. No, he couldn't stop. It was too close to Morgan's place. He'd be seen driving in.

Maybe he shouldn't report it. The man had threatened his family. He frowned. How had the man known about them—was he a local?

Too wired to drive straight home, he drove down the street by the river. Headlights followed him.

Probably someone going home. Elijah turned right at the next street which led towards the SES depot.

The car turned right as well.

OK. He was being totally paranoid. He knew that. Someone wasn't following him. There was no need to. Ask a few people around town and someone would be able to say where he lived. Still he turned right at the next intersection, maybe a little too fast on the wet road and then right again, back on to the main street through town.

The car did as well.

His skin prickled. So maybe he was being followed. Probably a scare tactic. He didn't dare call Adam or any of the other police officers. Morgan hadn't seemed worried about the gun. He'd stood up for himself and even appeared to know who he was talking to. The thought didn't ease Elijah's conscience.

And he didn't dare go straight home.

The distance between his driveway and the front door was far enough for him to be an easy target.

But Jamie would be arriving at six-thirty. He was supposed to get groceries for dinner. The store would have good lighting and people around. Maybe whoever was following him would get bored waiting.

He parked next to a white four-wheel drive and checked his mirrors again. No car followed him in. Nerves humming, he pushed open his door, kept his shoulders hunched and hurried into the supermarket. When the doors closed behind him, he sighed in relief.

Safe. For now.

He drew his phone out of his pocket and stared at it for a moment. Too public to call the police, but there was one other person he wanted to call. He picked up a basket and dialled the number. "Hey, Mum."

"Elijah. How are you? Did you finish writing your speech for Will's wedding?"

He smiled, soothed by her voice. "Sure did. What have you been up to?"

She sighed. "I'm trying to convince your stubborn father to go to Perth with me this weekend."

Elijah raised his eyebrows. Getting his parents out of town was a great idea. "What for?"

"There's a craft fair I want to go to."

OK. No wonder his father wasn't interested. "Is there a football game on?" Elijah asked. "You could go to the fair while he goes to a game."

"What a good idea. I'll check."

"If not a game, the maritime museum might have a new exhibition."

His mother chuckled. "You're such a smart boy. I'm going to search right now."

Elijah scanned the vegetable section as he heard her typing in the background. What was he going to cook?

The wind gusted inside as someone walked through the automatic doors and Elijah shivered. It was a hot soup and crusty bread kind of night. He had the perfect recipe. "Oh, there is a game!" his mother exclaimed. "I'm going to buy him a ticket and tell him we're going."

"Maybe you should spend a couple of nights with Donna while you're up there." His sister was not going to thank him for the suggestion, but at least they'd all be out of harm's way.

She laughed. "I will. Thanks, baby. I'll talk to you later." She hung up.

Elijah shook his head. His mother was easily distracted. She hadn't even asked why he'd called. It must be one hell of a craft fair. The tension leached out of his shoulders and he made his way around the store, adding the groceries he needed.

He'd meant to stop at Mai's bakery to get some bread but it would be closed, so the supermarket's options would have to do. By the time he reached the checkout, he'd half convinced himself he'd made up the whole thing at Morgan's.

The man with Morgan had probably waved a wrench or spanner and Elijah's eyes had deceived him in the dim light. Elijah had probably been face to face with a pipe. People didn't carry hand guns in Australia. And the car following him might have been a tourist who'd got lost. It happened.

He paid for the food and walked outside. He had a nice bottle of red wine at home which would go perfectly with the soup.

As he unlocked his car, he scanned the car park, smiling at a couple of people. No one tall and thick lurked in the shadows waiting for him.

He dumped his bags on the passenger seat and drove home. The minestrone wouldn't take long to prepare and they could have some wine while they waited for it to simmer. A bright flash of headlights in his rear-view mirror as he pulled into his street made him squint. The car was close behind, too close. He clenched the steering wheel.

Don't be paranoid.

Still he accelerated and the car fell behind. Faster than was probably safe, he pulled into his driveway and shut off the engine. He grabbed the bags, his hand fumbling on the handles and then ran to the front door.

The house key was stuck in the loop of the keyring. He couldn't get it out.

He glanced behind as the car slowed and turned into his driveway.

Shit.

He dropped the bags and fought with the key.

The car door slammed.

Elijah thrust the key into the lock and pushed the door open.

"Hey Elijah, what's the rush?"

Elijah squeezed his eyes closed at Jamie's voice and put a hand to his chest to slow his rapidly beating heart. Breathe.

Jamie bent to pick up the groceries and then looked up at him. His eyes widened. "What's wrong?"

Elijah couldn't speak. He shook his head and gestured him inside, then locked the door behind him.

In the kitchen, he busied himself getting the groceries out of the bag.

Jamie placed a hand on his arm. "Elijah, you look like you've seen a ghost and you're trembling."

"Give me a second." He poured a glass of water and swallowed it, feeling it move through his body. When he opened his eyes, he gazed straight out the kitchen window facing the backyard. It was dark outside. Anyone could hide in the shadows. Anyone could watch him. And the window had no curtains or blinds.

He shifted away, his skin crawling.

Jamie took his hand and pulled him towards the couches in the living room. He pressed him into one. "What's going on?"

He wasn't supposed to tell anyone. What if they were looking through the kitchen window and saw him talking to Jamie? Would he be in danger?

"Elijah." Jamie shook him. "You're starting to freak me out."

He drew in a long, shuddery breath. "You can't tell anyone."

Jamie frowned, but nodded.

"Promise!"

"I promise."

"Someone pulled a gun on me." As Jamie's mouth dropped open, Elijah explained what he'd seen. When he finished, Jamie wrapped his arms around Elijah and held him tight.

"It must have been terrifying."

Elijah closed his eyes. Being cocooned in the warmth of Jamie's arms made the fears fade. He could focus on this, on Jamie and pretend like the past hour hadn't happened.

Jamie pulled back. "You need to tell Lincoln."

The words made the fear flood back. "No! He threatened my family."

"The police can put protection in place," Jamie said. "Besides, chances are he only threatened them to keep you quiet, and he won't carry it out."

Still not odds Elijah wanted to take.

"Elijah, I know you're scared, but Morgan might be in trouble. Those two guys might be the same two who helped Henk kidnap Zamira. They need to be stopped."

Elijah bit his lip. The whole town had been shocked when Border Force had uncovered an illegal slavery ring in Blackbridge. And one of the reasons Elijah had been shot a few months back was because people had been too scared to speak up. He sighed.

"All right. But not tonight. They might still be watching me. I'll talk to Adam when he gets home." He checked the time. "You're here early."

Jamie ducked his head and grinned. "I saw you carrying groceries to your car and I figured I'd help you cook." He glanced up. "I've been looking forward to tonight."

The admission warmed Elijah. "Well if we're going to eat, we should start cooking." He stood and pulled

Jamie to his feet. They were chest to chest, only inches apart. One kiss wouldn't hurt.

He closed the distance and brushed his lips against Jamie's. Sweet heaven. He kissed him again, and again, small, brief kisses and then figured, what the hell, and pulled him closer, deepening the kiss. Jamie's moan of agreement sent thrills through Elijah's body.

This man was addictive.

Jamie ran his hands down Elijah's back, leaving a trail of tingles and then squeezed his butt. Elijah hardened. No. As much as he wanted Jamie, he'd promised himself no sex until they were open about their relationship. With a great deal of effort, he stepped away, the lust fogging his mind. "Dinner."

Jamie grinned. "Probably wise."

Elijah walked back to the kitchen and took out a cutting board.

"What are we having?" Jamie asked.

"Minestrone." He switched on the radio and Queen blasted from the speakers. He lowered the volume and retrieved the bottle of red wine from the pantry. "Can you pour us a glass?"

Jamie held up a bottle he must have brought with him. It was the same. "Great minds."

Elijah smiled as he handed Jamie a bottle opener and two glasses. Then he started to chop an onion. "How was your day?"

"Pretty casual." Jamie poured the wine. "With only a day to go until the holidays start, there's not much work for the kids. They've finished all their assignments and can't wait to go home."

Elijah remembered those days. "What about Lewis?"

"He's excited about starting work with you and Kit."

"That's great." He added some oil to the pot and when it was hot enough, he added the onion, garlic and other vegetables, loving the sizzle and fresh garlic smell. "What are your plans for the holidays?"

Jamie shrugged. "I'll probably help Mum and Dad at the cheese factory." He sipped his wine. "But there's also this cute farmhand I want to spend more time with." A smile played around his lips.

Elijah grinned. "This cute farmhand will put you to work if you hang out at the farm."

"Hard work never fazed me."

The image of Jamie sweaty and dirty from a day's work filled Elijah's mind and he hardened. Yeah, he'd like to see that. Plus there were plenty of isolated places on the farm where they could *work* together.

He finished adding the vegetables to the pot and stirred them. "How's Hannah's shed working out for you?"

"It's great. You should come and check it out. It's nice having my own space."

Elijah understood. When he'd moved back to Australia, he'd been itching to move out of his parents' place. He loved them, but they were hard work. Not so hard that he wanted them on the wrong side of a gun. He shivered and pushed the memory away, taking a deep breath. Finding this place and sharing with first Will and now Adam had been a Godsend. Speaking of which, "You coming to Will's bucks' party tomorrow night?"

"Yeah. What's the plan?"

Elijah chuckled. "Well considering Will would curl up and die if we took him to the strippers, I've opted for dinner at the Vale."

"Who's coming?"

"The usual plus Fleur's dad, and some of Will's family." A thoroughly chilled night was exactly what Will wanted.

Jamie smiled. "Will and Fleur are so perfect for each other."

Elijah nodded. "I remember Will stressing about his first date with her. You know he threw up on her shoes at the end of it." He added the stock.

Jamie laughed. "Yeah. Lucky Fleur's nursing had prepared her for such things."

"I knew she was a keeper when she brought him home and tucked him into bed."

"Fleur has always been the mothering type," Jamie said. "Whenever any of us got hurt, she'd take care of us."

Elijah turned the soup to simmer and picked up his wine. "And what was your role?"

Jamie avoided his gaze, sipped his drink. "I was the ring-in. Tagging along when they visited Kit."

Elijah raised an eyebrow. "That's not how Kit tells it. She says you were always welcome, but often hung out with the boys at school."

He shrugged. "I did. I had my reputation to maintain."

"And yet the musketeers are your closest friends now."

"I didn't say I was smart."

Elijah took the glass from him and placed it on the bench. "I understand your fear. We've all been there at some point in our lives."

"You never seemed scared to me."

Tonight's incident had put the fear he'd had as a kid into perspective. His skin prickled and he forced a laugh. "Honey, we moved so often when I was young, I was the perpetual new kid. Starting a new school terrified me, especially being gay." He'd learnt to fake confidence. "It wasn't until we moved here and I met Kit at the ag college, that I found my place."

"I'm glad you found it here."

The smile Jamie gave him made Elijah want to kiss him again. He stepped back, stirred the pot and then sipped his wine.

"Have you picked up your suit for the wedding?" Jamie asked.

"Will's picking them all up tomorrow." He sliced the loaf of bread and set the table. There was none of the awkwardness usually associated with a first date. Perhaps it was because he was at home and comfortable here, or maybe it was simply because they knew enough about each other already. The only way it could be better was if Jamie was comfortable acknowledging their fledgling relationship to others. "What are we going to do at the bucks' night?" Elijah asked. "No fraternising?"

Jamie screwed up his nose. "Well it's hardly fair. None of the others will have their partners with them."

Elijah raised his eyebrow. "Is that what we are?" On his way past Jamie to put the bread on the table, Jamie snagged him around the waist and pulled him close.

"I think we could be." He kissed Elijah lightly and Elijah leaned into him. "I'm enjoying being alone with you tonight. I'm comfortable with you, I just..." He sighed. "I'm trying to get over it. Logically I know it makes no sense..." The frustration on Jamie's face soothed Elijah's concerns.

Elijah kissed him. "I'll try not to push over the next fortnight."

Jamie brushed his thumb over Elijah's cheek. "Thank you."

Elijah's heart clenched and he continued to the table with the bread. This was Jamie not Alex. Jamie wasn't involved with anyone else. But part of him felt inferior. If Jamie was happy about the relationship, if he was pleased to be dating Elijah, wouldn't he want to tell everyone, not keep it a secret?

Elijah wanted to tell the whole world Jamie was his.

Patience. He only had to wait fourteen days to see where this was going.

Past the fortnight, all bets were off.

Chapter 9

Jamie caught himself checking the clock multiple times during last period. Finally he announced, "All right. You're free. Enjoy your holidays."

The reaction was instantaneous. Chairs squeaked, voices rose and a few kids cheered. Jamie said goodbye to them as they filed out of the room, high-fiving a couple who were totally pumped.

"Have fun in Bali," he called to the girl who had spoken about nothing but her first overseas holiday for weeks.

Finally the room was empty and silence reigned. He closed his eyes, savouring it.

"Mr Z?" Lewis stood at the door, twisting his hands together, a little uncertain.

"Hey, Lewis. You ready to go?" Jamie was taking him out to his parents' this afternoon.

"I've just got to get my bag."

"Do you want to wait until the rest of the kids clear out of the dorm?" He didn't want Lewis to suffer more teasing when they saw him getting into Jamie's car.

Lewis shrugged. "It doesn't matter what they think."

Huh. This seventeen-year-old was far more

confident than Jamie had been at that age. "All right. I need to stop by my office. I'll meet you at the front of the dorm."

Lewis nodded and hurried away.

Jamie went to the staff room to wish his colleagues a good holiday and to remind Noel he was taking Lewis with him.

"Taking him where?" Patricia asked.

Jamie turned to her. "He's staying with my parents during the holidays and doing work experience with Kit Zanetti."

"Why?"

"He has a few issues at home," he said.

Noel spoke up. "His parents don't approve of him being gay."

Patricia screwed up her nose as if she smelled something bad.

Better if he didn't engage with her. "I've got to go," Jamie said. "Enjoy drinks tonight."

By the time he reached the dorms, the bulk of the students had gone, already picked up by their parents who had made the journey to Blackbridge. Lewis waited inside the building, framed by the window, out of the cold.

Jamie popped his boot and when he turned around, Lewis was there. "Got everything?" He helped Lewis put his suitcase in the car.

"Yep. Thanks, Mr Z."

Jamie smiled. "It's no problem. Get in."

When they hit the highway, Lewis asked, "Are you sure your parents don't mind me staying? Do they know I'm gay?" Lewis tapped his foot.

"They're looking forward to it," Jamie said. "Mum loves cooking for people."

"And your Dad?"

"He'll probably want to take you fishing or surfing, but if you don't want to, tell him no. He won't mind." He glanced at the teen. "And neither of them care about your sexuality." He hesitated. It was the perfect opportunity to mention he was bi-sexual, help to soothe some of Lewis's concerns. The only people Lewis would see this holiday were his parents, Kit and Elijah, so he had no one to tell. And Jamie had promised Elijah he'd tell everyone by the time school went back. His stomach churned and he cleared his throat. "I told them I was bi when I was younger than you. It didn't faze them."

Lewis's eyes widened. "Seriously?"

Jamie nodded. "Yeah."

"I didn't realise."

Jamie shrugged. "It's no one's business but my own."

"Right. Sorry."

Jamie winced. Way to make the kid embarrassed, but he wasn't sure how to smooth it over. He pulled off the highway onto the drive which ran past the cheese factory. "If you want a tour of the factory, ask Dad. He'll be happy to show you how everything works." Jamie chuckled. "Though you might be sorry you asked by the end of it."

Lewis's lips edged up in a smile.

Jamie parked in front of the farmhouse. As they got out, Sasha ran around the side barking. She stopped in front of Lewis and almost collapsed in delight as Lewis rubbed behind her ears. Jamie hefted the suitcase out of the boot and said, "This way."

He opened the back door and inhaled as the scent of baked goodness wafted out. "You're in for a treat," he said. "Mum's been baking." He called, "Mum, we're here."

His mother hurried down the corridor, a large smile on her face. "Great timing. I just pulled the cake out of the oven." She beamed at Lewis. "You must be Lewis. We're so happy to have you here." She hugged the unsuspecting boy and his eyes widened.

Jamie grinned and continued down the corridor calling back, "Don't scare him off, Mum."

He heard her tut behind him. "Nonsense. There's nothing wrong with a hug. This way, Lewis. I'll show you to your room."

She hurried past Jamie, winking at him and Lewis followed her, slightly shell-shocked, his eyes glistening.

Poor kid hadn't expected such a warm welcome. He'd learn pretty quickly the Zanetti house was full of love and acceptance.

It was outside the house Jamie was worried about.

He followed his mother and Lewis through the house as she showed him to Lincoln's old room, pointing out the bathroom along the way, and explaining he was welcome to watch television whenever he wanted and to help himself to anything in the fridge and pantry. They ended up in the kitchen where the cassata was cooling on the bench top.

"Have a seat," his mother said. "Would you like a cuppa with your cake?"

"I'll have tea thanks, Mum," Jamie said.

She glanced at Lewis.

"Ah, tea please, Mrs Zanetti."

"Call me Rosa." She made a pot of tea and carried it to the table.

The back door slammed and Jamie's father came into the kitchen. He kissed his wife on the cheek and Jamie grinned. "I swear you have a sixth sense for when cake's on offer."

His father winked. "My girl lets me know." He held

out his hand to Lewis. "I'm Harold. Looking forward to having you stay a couple of weeks. Do you like to fish?"

Lewis shook his hand. "Ah, yes, I do, sir."

Harold winced. "Please don't call me sir. It makes me feel ancient." He grinned. "I'm going fishing at Old Man's Blowhole tomorrow if you want to come."

Lewis glanced at Jamie and nodded slowly. "OK."

His father cut the cake while his mother poured the tea.

"So tell me, Lewis, which area of farming are you most interested in?" Rosa asked, passing Jamie a jug of milk.

"Dairy."

Jamie relaxed. This was home. He hoped Lewis would be able to unwind here and find some comfort.

"You only think that because you haven't tried cheese making," Harold said. "It's better to see what happens to the milk after it's come out."

Lewis laughed. "I hadn't thought about that."

"We'll get you up to the factory. Bet I can change your mind."

Lewis grinned. "That would be great."

Jamie stood. Lewis would be fine. "I'm off. I've got to get ready for the bucks' night."

Lewis glanced at him, eyes wide.

Not quite so comfortable yet. "Lewis, want to walk me out?"

He got to his feet.

Jamie kissed his mum's cheek, squeezed his father's shoulder. "I'll see you at the wedding on Sunday."

He walked out the back door with Lewis and stopped on the verandah. "How are you feeling?"

Lewis shrugged. "Your parents are nice, but it's kind of weird."

Jamie nodded. "If you have any problems at all over

the next few weeks, call me any time." He handed over his number. "It's OK to tell Mum and Dad you don't want to do something. They'll understand."

Lewis cleared his throat. "I appreciate all your help, Mr Z."

He smiled. "It's fine. I understand what it's like being different."

The teenager frowned. "But your parents accepted you."

"They did, but I worried about the rest of the town."

Lewis shuffled his feet. "Do they count?" His face went red. "I…I mean, if you've got your family's support, does it matter?"

Shit. What should he say? The kid didn't even have his family. Jamie didn't want Lewis to think he had so many more hurdles to jump for acceptance, but the reality was, there would always be some. "We each have to make our own decisions," he said. "Don't forget you can call me any time."

Lewis nodded. "Thanks."

Jamie gave a wave and strode along the verandah, his mind replaying what Lewis had said. He was getting life lessons from a seventeen-year-old.

Maybe he should pay attention.

***

Jamie pulled into the Vale's gravel car park, stopping under one of the tall gum trees. The stilted restaurant was illuminated in the dark and patrons sat by the windows enjoying dinner. He hugged his leather jacket closer to his body as he got out and the wind instantly ruined the work he'd put into getting his hair right. The school bus Elijah had hired to bring those who wanted to drink was already there.

Nerves played in his stomach. This was his first time

in public with Elijah since they were officially dating. Could he hide his attraction? Should he even bother? Perhaps Lewis was right and it was time he stopped hiding.

The wind blew again, chilling his bones. He jogged up the stairs and paused at the restaurant entrance, allowing his eyes to adjust to the brighter light. Shirley Jameson, one of the town's biggest gossips, was having dinner with Hannah's grandparents who she worked for at one of the local caravan parks. A dragon statue peeked out from the rafters above them as if eavesdropping on the conversation. Jamie smiled. Richard's wife was responsible for all those quirky touches.

In the middle of the room, Will sat at the head of a long table, his white shirt contrasting against his dark skin. Will's father and brothers sat with him, as did Fleur's father, Adam, Kim, Lincoln and of course Elijah.

Elijah moved around the table. His hair was coiffed in the gravity-defying style he liked, and he wore a forest green shirt with the top button undone. The dark grey pants he wore fit snuggly over his butt, defining it in all its glory. There was only one word for him.

Hot.

Jamie ran a hand over his black shirt, tucked it into his slim-cut black pants and checked his hair in the glass. He looked good.

"You going to stand in the doorway all day?" A shoulder bump had Jamie taking a couple of steps forward as Jeremy and Nicholas walked past him.

"Impatient git." Jamie grinned and followed them to the main table. Elijah blew them all a kiss, though his eyes lingered on Jamie.

No one seemed to notice.

Jamie sat next to Kim, leaving the seat next to him empty. Maybe Elijah would sit there.

"How's the ankle?" Jeremy pulled out the empty chair and plonked himself down. Damn.

"Fine." It was his own fault. If he was willing to be open about their relationship, he could have saved Elijah the seat. "How's Zamira?"

Jeremy beamed. "She's great. Only eight days until she arrives."

Jamie smiled. "Do you chat to her much?"

"Every evening. Tonight she said she felt like she knew everyone in town already."

"The musketeers are likely to adopt her," Jamie said. "She'll have more friends than she knows what to do with."

"Yeah. At fire training the other day, Mai said she wants to organise a welcome party. I'll let you know the details."

"I'll be there."

"Just don't make it on a footy day," Kim said.

Jamie laughed. "You're worried we'll go to Jeremy's instead of the game."

"Yeah. You're all a bunch of slackers." He smirked and they settled into an easy conversation about football. They ordered food and drinks and Will was in his element, smiling and laughing with his family. Jamie grinned. When he'd first met Will, Will had been totally awkward in social situations. Living with Elijah and meeting Fleur had been good for him.

Elijah was out of reach, sitting on Will's right-hand side, but occasionally his eyes would meet Jamie's and he'd smile.

While they waited for dinner to be served, Jamie excused himself to go to the bathroom. He caught Elijah's eye as he stood up and winked. They could be alone, although getting together in the bathroom felt kind of sleazy.

He passed the door for the kitchen. Inside the head chef, Craig Patton, stood next to his father. "Dad, you can't stay in here. We've got a full house tonight and you're getting in the way."

"This is my restaurant," Richard replied, his deep voice booming through the room. "I can go wherever I want."

"Dad, you signed it over to me five years ago," Craig said, the helplessness on his face clear.

Jamie grimaced and kept walking. He hadn't had a lot to do with the Patton family. Craig was at least ten years older than Jamie, so they hadn't been at school at the same time. Everyone knew of them though. The Pattons were one of the wealthiest families in town, always donating money when it was needed. It must be hard that their patriarch's mind was faulty. Otherwise he appeared to be in perfect health, tall, slim, strong. He might live for decades yet.

But at some stage, his unreliable memory would become a hindrance and they'd have to manage it. At least they could afford the best health care.

He continued to the bathroom and was back at the table before he remembered he'd been hoping Elijah would follow him. Elijah was deep in discussion with Fleur's father about fishing.

Between dinner and dessert, Elijah stood up and cleared his throat. Talk around the table died. He inhaled deeply. "I want to make a toast," he said. "When I met Will a few months ago he'd just met Fleur and he was all a-tizz about what to do." Elijah blew Will a kiss. "But Fleur was just as smitten, even though he threw up on her shoes on the first date." Will groaned and ducked his head as his brothers teased him. Elijah waited for them to finish. "They'll need to make compromises—she'll have to deal with his pathological hate of plastic, and he'll have to sweet-talk her into letting him into her garden." He smiled. "But I know they'll manage. I want to wish Will all the best for his marriage." Elijah raised his glass. "So here's to Will."

"To Will," Jamie echoed with the others and sipped his wine.

Will glanced at his plate, his embarrassment clear and then stood. "I want to say something too." He shifted his feet, looking a little uncomfortable, but he picked up his glass. "Advertising for a roommate was one of the best decisions I've ever made." He smiled. "Elijah swept into my house like a rainbow willy-willy. Without his encouragement, I never would have met Fleur at the pub and walked her home. So my toast is to Elijah—the best friend a man could have."

Elijah dabbed at his eyes and stood and hugged Will. "You're the best."

The waitress came to take their dessert requests and after Elijah had ordered, he slipped away from the table. Jamie expected him to head to the toilet, but instead he went outside.

Where was he going? "Can you order me the chocolate mousse?" Jamie asked Kim and followed Elijah outside.

The night was bitterly cold and the wind was still biting. He moved to the top of the stairs and let his eyes adjust to the darkness. The fairy lights shone around the playground, and some brighter lights were at intervals along the fence separating the restaurant from the vineyard and processing buildings. Elijah stood by the fence, hugging himself, staring out over the vines.

Jamie trotted down the steps and over to him. "What are you doing out here?"

Elijah shrugged but didn't turn. In the pale garden light, tears glistened on Elijah's cheeks. Jamie's heart leapt and he checked they were alone before he pulled Elijah into his arms. "Hey, what's wrong?"

Elijah sniffed, wiped his face with one hand. "I'm fine. Really." His voice caught. "I didn't expect Will to say anything."

Jamie pulled back to look at him. "What he said was nice."

He nodded. "Will acknowledged me in front of all his family, in front of the whole restaurant."

"You deserve it."

"It took me by surprise."

Maybe Elijah wasn't as sure of himself as he pretended. Jamie brushed the remaining tears from Elijah's cheek with his thumb and kissed him gently. "It shouldn't. You're smart, caring and amazing."

Elijah sniffed again. "Thanks. Kiss me again."

Jamie pulled him close and their lips met. Jamie wanted to keep it light, but the moment Elijah kissed him back his good intentions vanished. Passion fired inside of him, his tongue teased Elijah's and his body went hard. Laughter echoed from the restaurant and Jamie opened one eye. They were too exposed here. He backed Elijah towards the wooden fort in the playground and pressed him up against the wall.

There was something deliciously different kissing a man from kissing a woman. Pressing against Elijah's hard body, feeling his arousal against his own and having his strong hands sweep across his back. He ached for more.

He shifted, letting his hand run down Elijah's body and cover his manhood. Elijah groaned and pushed him away.

"Not so fast," Elijah panted.

Damn it. "Are you sure?"

Elijah looked around. "We've moved where no one can see us." His voice held the hint of accusation.

Guilt tickled Jamie and he stepped back a little further. "What I want to do with you is R rated. There are kids upstairs."

"Right." Elijah's tone told him he didn't believe him.

Before Jamie could defend himself further, loud voices came from over by the processing sheds behind them.

"You idiot! Why didn't you stop him?" a male voice yelled.

"What did you expect…" The wind drowned out his next words. "…shoot him?" The other guy whined. "Then we'd… body to hide."

Jamie froze, and slowly turned around. Elijah stepped closer and his breath was warm on Jamie's ear as he whispered, "I recognise the second voice. He was the one who threatened me last night." He gripped Jamie's arm, his hand trembling and pulled him into the fort.

"If he… police, we're screwed," angry man continued.

"He… only Morgan."

"He lives with a fucking cop," the other man said, his furious tone carrying clearly.

"Shit…"

They had to be talking about Elijah. Jamie slipped his phone out of his pocket. The wind was blowing towards them, helping to carry the voices, but if Jamie called Lincoln, they might hear him. Instead he twisted, using Elijah's body to shield the light from the phone as he typed out a text message. Lincoln never ignored a message.

"We can't afford… cop's radar. They got to Henk…

our whole business is over."

"The boss has Henk covered."

What did that mean? Jamie peered around the opening of the fort. Two figures stood by a dark ute, but it was far too dark to make out any features.

"What do we do?" Elijah asked.

"Wait for Lincoln," Jamie whispered.

The angry man swore loudly. "I've got to get back. Watch the poofter… We want him scared." The man stalked away and a moment later the roar of a motorbike pierced the night and slowly faded.

"What's going on?" Lincoln's voice was hushed but Jamie jumped all the same and Elijah gasped, slapping his hand over his mouth at the noise.

It was crowded in the fort but it shielded them from being seen. Jamie put his fingers to his lips and Lincoln nodded. The ute nearby started and the headlights switched on, illuminating part of the playground. They all squatted as the car drove past.

"Get the number plate," Elijah hissed and Jamie squinted to make out the letters. "BB…"

"Three something," Lincoln said. "Now why the hell am I standing in the freezing cold taking number plates?"

Jamie glanced at Elijah. "Didn't you tell Adam?"

"I fell asleep before he got home." He shrugged. "Plus I wanted to wait until Mum and Dad went to Perth this afternoon."

"Tell Adam what?" Lincoln asked.

Elijah cleared his throat. "I saw something last night."

The first drop of rain hit Jamie's hand. The clouds hung low and dark. "We should get undercover."

Lincoln glanced around. "Under the restaurant."

They hurried past the steps they'd come down and

under the restaurant where during summer, tables were set up for guests to enjoy the fresh air and scenery.

"What did you see?" Lincoln asked.

The rain came down in earnest, heavy, noisy drops and they all huddled closer while Elijah explained. Jamie told his brother what they'd overheard.

Lincoln swore. "OK. Here's what we'll do. I'll call Albany and get them to run the partial plates. You're both going back inside and pretending you didn't see a thing. If anyone asks where you've been, you can tell them you were making out."

Jamie inhaled sharply. Kit must have said something.

Lincoln looked at him. "No one in there is going to care." He didn't give Jamie time to respond before continuing, "Tomorrow Elijah will tell Adam everything he just told me. Tell him to record it." He ran a hand through his hair. "How much wedding stuff have you got to do?"

"Mostly picking up things—decorations, that kind of thing."

"Can Adam go with you?" Lincoln asked.

"I guess."

Jamie wasn't leaving Elijah by himself. "I can."

"You're not a cop," Lincoln said. "Adam can keep an eye out for anyone following you and I'll get Albany working on it." He glanced to the side. "The rain's letting up. You two go back inside and I'll be in shortly. Go back in the way you left."

Elijah tugged Jamie's hand. "Come on, before I freeze my balls off."

Jamie hesitated. Was Lincoln right? Would no one care if he and Elijah were a couple? But it wouldn't take long before word spread. Especially if they walked back in there hand in hand.

Elijah tugged him. "Are you coming?"

"No one will question you keeping close to Elijah if you two are a couple," Lincoln said.

It was the best way to protect Elijah, keep him from being hurt. He had to do this.

"Ready?" Elijah asked.

No. He wasn't ready at all. Jamie's muscles tightened and his dinner threatened to make a reappearance. He breathed out.

He could do this.

He squeezed Elijah's hand, and together they ran up the steps back into the restaurant.

Chapter 10

Jamie's hold on Elijah's hand tightened as they entered the restaurant. The urge to drop it was strong, but Lincoln was right. None of his friends would care—not if they were true friends. And if it meant he could be close to Elijah to protect him, it was worth it. He'd worry about everyone else in the morning.

His pulse fluttered in panic as Elijah led him back to the table, hand in hand, both of them slightly damp from the rain. The waitress served the desserts and Jamie released Elijah's hand in order to take his seat at the other end of the table. No one in the restaurant was looking at him.

"Where did you two go?" Jeremy asked as Jamie sat.

Jamie glanced at Elijah. "Ah, we had some things to discuss."

"Wedding stuff?" Kim asked, digging into his crème brûlée.

His face warmed. "Not exactly." At the other end of the table, Fleur's father spoke to Will's dad about fishing, and Elijah made Will laugh as he sat.

Adam glanced up the table at Will and lowered his voice hissing, "You guys didn't get Will a stripper, did you?"

"No! We're not that cruel."

Jeremy frowned as Lincoln came back to the table. "Is something wrong? Lincoln was gone as well."

Trust Jeremy to notice. He'd been super observant since his fiancée, Zamira had been kidnapped. "No." At least nothing they could discuss here.

His three friends still waited for his answer. Shit. Just get the words out. "Well, see, the thing is… Elijah and I are kind of dating." His voice trailed off as each of his friends' eyes widened almost comically large.

Jeremy was the first to speak. "Didn't you have a girlfriend in Perth?"

Jamie cringed but before he explained, Kim said, "Congrats."

Jamie blinked. "You don't sound surprised."

Kim shrugged. "I overheard the musketeers mention you were bi back in high school when Mai had a sleepover. I had to look it up to understand what they meant. I couldn't ask them, because I wasn't supposed to be eavesdropping."

Jamie chuckled. He could imagine Mai's wrath if she'd known her younger brother had been listening in.

"So you're the reason Elijah spent so long in the bathroom last weekend," Adam said. "I knew he was primping for someone." He smiled as if pleased to be proven right.

Jeremy was still frowning. "Did I crash your date the other night?" He winced.

Jamie laughed. "Kind of. We were working things out."

"Sorry, mate. If I'd known I would have left you in peace." He ate some of his chocolate mousse. "This is damned good."

And just like that, the conversation switched to

food. Jamie's hand shook a little as he picked up his spoon and glanced up the table at Elijah. Elijah caught his gaze and grinned. He'd been right. None of their friends cared. A weight lifted from his chest.

He'd cleared the first hurdle.

But there would be more to come.

It was getting late when dinner ended and they all went downstairs to the car park. The drunk and not-so-drunk climbed into the bus Elijah had organised. Jamie pulled Elijah to the side. He wasn't ready to say good night yet. "Are you on the bus?"

Elijah nodded.

"I can give you a lift if you want," Jamie said. "We could stop at my place for a coffee."

"Honey, if we stop at your place, the last thing we're having is coffee." Elijah grinned at him. "And I've decided to make you work for this a bit harder."

Jamie deserved that. He shuffled his feet. They stood in the middle of the dimly lit car park and a few people looked out the bus window, probably wondering what the hold-up was. He pushed back the nerves, breathed deeply to loosen the tightness in his chest. "Well…" He pulled Elijah closer to him, his hands trembling a little. "At least let me kiss you goodnight."

He captured Elijah's smile with his mouth and kissed him hard. Elijah's arms snaked around Jamie pulling him closer and he gave back as good as he got. Someone on the bus gave a loud wolf whistle.

Jamie pulled back, held on to Elijah a moment longer, his hands steady. The heavy lust in Elijah's eyes made him grin.

Elijah smiled slowly. "Good start, Zanetti." He sashayed towards the bus.

"Hey, Elijah," Jamie called.

He turned, raised a sexy eyebrow.

"I'll see you tomorrow?"

He grinned. "If I'm not too busy." With an air of importance, he climbed onto the bus. "Home, James."

The bus doors closed behind him, but not before Jamie heard a few teasing comments from those on board.

Jamie adjusted himself and moved towards his car. He almost bumped into Shirley Jameson.

"My, my. That was some display of affection." She grinned at him and fanned herself. "I wish I had someone like that."

Jamie's chest tightened, but he smiled and kept walking. "'Night, Shirley."

He got into his car, a slight shake to his hands. She hadn't been perturbed, but she also wouldn't keep it quiet.

This was happening. He no longer had control of it. It felt like that moment on a rollercoaster when he was at the top of the peak and unable to get off before the uncontrolled plunge. His chest tightened again and he battled to keep his breath regular.

His phone beeped with a message.

Way to go, little brother.

The panic subsided and the pressure in his chest loosened. His family would support and shield him.

Jamie smiled and drove home.

***

The next morning Elijah glanced down the hallway to Adam's closed bedroom door. If he was going to get all the wedding errands done before he had to pick up Fleur's friend from the airport, he needed to wake Adam soon. But Adam had indulged the night before, and he wouldn't be happy about being woken at seven o'clock. Particularly because it was his day off.

Maybe he should go by himself, or call Jamie…

His muscles tightened as he remembered the gun pointing directly at him.

No, if someone was following him, the best way to catch them was to take Adam. Lincoln would be cross if he didn't and then Kit would be pissed and give him some truly awful job. So he'd spend the morning with Adam and then dump him to spend time with Jamie this afternoon.

That kiss last night in front of all those people… He did a celebratory booty shake. Jamie was coming out and Elijah didn't want to waste a minute.

After pouring a glass of water and tucking a packet of painkillers into his pocket, he strode along the hallway and knocked on Adam's door. "Time to get up, Sunshine."

Adam groaned and swore at him.

"Don't be like that, Adam. I've got sustenance. I hope you're decent, I'm coming in." Elijah opened the door and flicked on the light.

"What the hell, Elijah?" Adam pulled the bedcovers over his eyes.

"I'm sorry, honey, I'm under Lincoln's orders."

That made Adam lower the blankets. "What?" His eyes were bloodshot.

Elijah handed him the glass of water and the painkillers. "You know last night when Jamie and I left the restaurant?"

Adam frowned. "I don't want to hear about your love life."

"If only that's all I had to tell you." Elijah sighed. "We overheard something and Lincoln told me to tell you, and you have to come with me today to see if anyone is following me."

Adam sat up as he took the pills. "Slow down a second." He squeezed his eyes closed, rubbed his forehead and then reopened his eyes. "Why would someone be following you?"

"That's the story I've got to tell you. You might want to have a shower first."

"I'm not going back to sleep, am I?"

Elijah shook his head. "'Fraid not. Sorry I couldn't warn you last night not to overindulge."

Adam growled.

"Would bacon and eggs for breakfast make it up to you?"

"And coffee," Adam said. He rubbed a hand over his face. "I'll be out in ten."

"Take fifteen." Elijah left the room. Having Adam at home made Elijah feel a lot safer. He heated the pan and added the bacon and eggs, inhaling deeply when the bacon began to sizzle. True to his word, Adam was sitting at the kitchen table in ten minutes, dressed in jeans, green jumper and with his blond hair still wet and mussed.

"Here you go." Elijah placed the hot bacon and eggs in front of him and slid the biggest mug of coffee they had onto the table.

"Thanks." Adam took a deep sip of the coffee and sighed. "Where's your breakfast?"

"I already ate."

Adam frowned. "You didn't have to make this just for me."

"Yeah, I did. I'm going to be stealing your morning at least." Elijah slid into the chair next to Adam, nerves dancing in his belly. He placed his phone between them and hit record. "Lincoln said we should record this."

Adam raised his eyebrows, swallowed his mouthful as he checked his phone, then said, "It's Saturday, sixth of July. This is Constable Adam Marshall. You are not obligated to say anything unless you wish to do so, but whatever you do say will be recorded and may later be given in evidence. Will you state your full name?"

Elijah blinked at how quickly Adam switched gears. "Elijah Aaron Johnson."

Adam went through the rest of the legal information before saying, "Tell me about the event in question."

Elijah told him about stopping at Morgan's shop, the gun, the threat and the conversation he and Jamie had overheard last night. Adam interrupted on occasion to ask for clarification and when Elijah was finished, he switched off the recording and rubbed his hands over his face. He swore. "Blackbridge was supposed to be a quiet town, good for a first posting."

Elijah patted his hand. "If it's any consolation, this is the first time I've known it to have so much major crime."

"It's not," Adam grunted. "Let me call Lincoln and ask if he got any matches on the licence plate."

Elijah took the empty plate and mug to the sink and ran some water. Behind him, Adam spoke in quiet murmurs, not loud enough for him to overhear. Then Adam came into the kitchen and dried the dishes Elijah had washed.

"What did he say?"

"They got a couple of hits, so I know who to look out for." He put the dried plate back into the cupboard.

Elijah waited, but when Adam didn't say anything further, he asked, "Are you going to tell me who?"

Adam shook his head. "Not yet. We don't want to falsely accuse anyone. So what are our plans today?"

"We need to pick up the decorations and take them to the venue in Albany. The staff at Blue Yonder are going to put them up for us. One of the suits Will picked up yesterday had a mark on it, so I have to take it back and exchange it, and then we have to pick up a friend of Fleur's from uni."

"That's not too bad."

Elijah wiped down the sink. "Ready to go?"

"Yeah."

As Elijah locked the front door, Adam walked to his car and stretched his arms above his head, twisting from side to side as if loosening his muscles. But his gaze scanned the quiet street. "You drive," he said. "I'm too hungover."

No children played outside despite it being the first day of the school holidays. It was still wet from the rain they'd had overnight and cold enough to make Elijah's breath cloud. In the distance, a few cars drove along the main road and a high-pitched whistle shrieked from an early morning football game.

Peaceful.

Except Elijah's muscles were so tense he could barely move.

"Hurry up, Elijah. I'm freezing my tits off," Adam called.

His voice spurred Elijah into action and he hurried to the car and unlocked the doors.

As soon as he started the engine, Adam twisted the heater on. "Act normally today," he said. "No looking around trying to spot someone. You're not supposed to know they're there. Go about your tasks as if they're the most important thing you've got to do today. I'll be the lookout."

Elijah pulled on to the main road. "I can't help it. It's totally creepy to think someone is following me."

"Yeah, I get it, but they don't know we know. So it gives us a chance to catch them."

It made sense, though when Adam was in plain

clothes it was hard to remember he was a police officer.

"Are you doing a wedding rehearsal at some stage today?" Adam asked.

Elijah shook his head. "The celebrant will run through what we have to do in the morning."

"Is Will cool with that?"

"Yeah. He's remarkably relaxed about the whole thing. The wedding's relatively small—neither of them has much extended family."

"Great." Adam held up his phone to look behind them.

Elijah glanced in the rear-view mirror. A black ute was a few car lengths behind. "Do you think it's them?"

"Who knows?" Adam lowered the phone. "This is the main road out of Blackbridge so if they're headed for Albany they'll be behind us the whole time. We'll see what they do when we get to town."

Elijah's fingers tightened on the steering wheel. He was tempted to take the scenic route, but there was no guarantee the person behind them wouldn't also take that road.

Adam switched on the radio, but the upbeat song telling him to shake it off did nothing to soothe Elijah's nerves. When they reached the city limits, he exhaled. They hadn't been run off the road. He shook off the tension and focused. First stop, decorations. The shop should have just opened.

"Is the ute still there?" Adam asked after they'd turned down a few streets.

Elijah checked his mirror. A blue sedan was behind him and in the other lane a red hatchback. "I don't think so." He changed lanes and checked again. He swore. "It's there."

"OK, park and we'll go inside. I'll get the licence plate." As Elijah pulled into a parking bay, Adam placed his hand on Elijah's. "Remember, relax."

Elijah nodded. Easier said than done.

He strode to the entrance of the shop. His shoulders started to hunch and he drew them back down. Confidence, Queen.

The sliding doors swooshed open and Elijah walked inside, heading straight to the party and decorations department. The table arrangements had been specially ordered and Elijah had called the day before to ensure they had arrived. He grinned at the woman behind the counter. "I'm here to pick up the decorations for the Lockhart-Travers wedding." He handed her the receipt Fleur had given him.

The woman smiled. "They're out the back. I'll get them for you."

Adam leaned against the counter. "I've never been here before. There's so much stuff."

"Your family wasn't into crafts?" Elijah asked.

Adam shook his head. "I don't know one end of a needle from the other."

"Will could teach you to knit if you want," Elijah said. "And my sister's a wicked seamstress."

"Nah, I'm good." He lowered his voice. "The guy by the candle-making stuff looks familiar."

Elijah turned slowly and took in the tall, broad-shouldered dark-haired man on crutches. "It's Mark Patton. Arrogant son-of-a-bitch."

Adam nodded. "Lives with Alyse Wilson, right?"

"Yeah. His parents own the Vale winery." They exchanged a glance. Could he be the one Elijah had heard last night? He was the right build for the guy who'd held a gun to Morgan, but he hadn't been using crutches. Elijah had been too shaken up to notice if he was wearing a moonboot.

Mark had given him hell when he'd briefly worked at

the winery. Didn't take kindly to working with a poof. Elijah narrowed his eyes and sauntered over to him. "Hey, Mark, what brings you to this fine establishment?"

Mark glared at him. "I'd expect someone like you to be in here."

Elijah rolled his eyes. People like Mark weren't worth the effort. "I'm picking up decorations for the wedding tomorrow." Adam came and stood next him.

Mark's glare briefly darkened before he smiled, large and fake. "Constable Marshall."

Adam nodded. "What brings you here?"

Mark grunted and gestured to the shelf. "Alyse wanted me to get some more candle wicks while I was in town. Don't know why she can't order them on the internet."

As excuses went it was a good one. Alyse made her own beeswax candles, but by all accounts, Mark wasn't the doting partner who would run errands for her.

"How'd you get here?" Adam asked.

"Drove."

Adam raised his eyebrows. "Should you be driving with a broken leg?"

"It's an automatic."

"Here they are!" The sales woman had returned with a trolley full of decorations.

Hopefully they'd all fit in Adam's car. Elijah didn't bother saying goodbye to Mark. He checked the trolley contents against the receipt. "Thanks so much."

Adam helped him transfer the decorations into the boot of his car. Elijah waited until they were on their way to the venue to ask, "So, what do you think?"

"About?"

"Mark," Elijah replied.

"Doesn't he drive a four-wheel drive?"

Good point. "He might have borrowed a car, or sold it. He's constantly buying new stuff."

Adam made a sound which might have been in agreement. "The ute was still in the car park when we left, but no one was in it."

Elijah blinked. He hadn't even thought to look, but now he checked his rear-view mirror. No black ute. "When we were called out to Alyse's place the other night, there was a lot of cash in the office." He glanced at Adam. "I mean *a lot*—thousands. Alyse pulled me out of the room and shut the door behind me. She seemed scared."

"I'll tell Lincoln," Adam said.

Elijah pulled into Blue Yonder restaurant which would be both the ceremony and reception venue. It was situated on the edge of a cliff and had stunning views over the windswept ocean. The water was dark and angry today with white caps peaking, but it was still breathtakingly beautiful. Lush gardens closer to the restaurant added to the luxurious feel of the venue.

Elijah understood why they'd chosen it. He hurried inside to ask where to leave the decorations and after a short conversation, they carried them through to the function room.

"Can we stop and get another coffee?" Adam asked as they drove back towards town.

Elijah checked the time. Just enough to stop at the suit hire place before they had to be at the airport to pick up Olivia. "You can get one at the airport." He glanced in the rear-view mirror and jolted. "The black ute's back."

Adam shifted and looked out the side mirror. "Same plates."

"Are you going to run them?"

"No need. Lincoln has the list already." He typed a

message on his phone.

"When will you tell me who is following me?"

"Not until we're certain."

Elijah gritted his teeth as he parked outside the suit place. "I won't be a minute." He retrieved the suit from the back seat and hurried inside. A few minutes later he was back with a clean suit he'd examined himself.

Ten minutes until the plane landed. Hopefully it would be late. Fleur had given him a photo of Olivia and asked him to apologise profusely for not picking her up herself. But Kit had organised a surprise beauty session for all the musketeers.

"Who are we picking up?" Adam asked.

"A uni friend of Fleur's—Olivia Demidenko. She's staying at her aunt and uncle's place, but they're away this weekend."

"Ian's parents?" The flat tone in Adam's voice had Elijah glancing at him. He stared straight ahead, unseeing.

"Maybe." He mentally scrolled through the names of people he knew, to work out why Adam was so upset. The only Ian he knew of had been Foley's farmhand, and he'd been killed a few months ago… Oh. That would explain it.

"It might be better if you drop me off and I'll get my own way back to town."

"Nope. You're supposed to be protecting me. She won't blame you for what happened to Ian."

He grunted and said nothing. This wasn't good. It might be best if Elijah didn't mention Adam's job. Olivia would only be in town for the weekend and they would all be busy with the wedding.

People were already streaming out of the little airport building when they arrived. "Do you want to stay here?"

Adam reached for the door handle. "No, I need coffee."

At the entrance, Elijah scanned the crowd for a young blonde. Adam headed for the café and then stopped short, his gaze caught on someone by the luggage carousel. Elijah followed his line of sight and compared the person to the photo on his phone. Olivia.

She was tall and curvy, her blonde, wavy hair cut to just below her shoulders and her jeans hugged her legs like a second skin. She wore the cutest pink knitted jumper. Elijah stepped next to Adam, though Adam didn't notice. His eyes were all for the woman they were picking up. "Oh, you spotted Olivia, well done."

Adam blinked. "*That's* Olivia?"

Elijah nodded, grinning. "Glad you stayed?"

His friend swore. "I'm getting coffee." He stalked off.

Olivia already wore a backpack and she lifted a second bag from the carousel. Elijah hurried forward. "Let me help." He flashed her a grin. "You're Olivia, right?"

"Elijah?"

"Right, first guess."

She smiled, letting him take the barrel bag which didn't weigh much.

"How was your flight?"

"Uneventful." She scanned the area. "I'd kill for a coffee though."

"Adam's in line. What would you like?"

"An espresso."

He moved to where Adam was about to order. "Add an espresso for Olivia."

Adam nodded.

He was back in sullen mood. Not good.

Elijah returned to Olivia and she said, "I appreciate

you picking me up."

"It's my pleasure. Plus I was in town anyway." They waited while Adam got the coffees and then waited some more for a break in the rain to run out to the car. Adam got in the back seat.

"Fleur and Will are thrilled you could come to the wedding," Elijah said.

Olivia fiddled with her long, dangling silver earrings. "I wouldn't miss it. Fleur and Hannah were good friends at uni." She glanced at Elijah. "So how do you know Fleur?"

"I was Will's roommate when they met," Elijah said.

She grinned. "I can't wait to meet him. What do you do?"

"Farmhand. I work with Kit van Ross, sorry, Kit Zanetti."

Olivia beamed. "Fleur and Hannah used to talk about Kit and Mai so much, I feel like I know them." She twisted in her seat to look at Adam. "What do you do, Adam?"

Elijah checked his rear-view mirror, saw Adam's long look before he answered, "I'm a cop."

She sucked in a breath and Elijah quickly said, "So are you just staying for the weekend?"

"Yeah." She glanced back at Adam. "Were you involved when my cousin, Ian was shot?"

Adam gave a short nod.

"I never got a clear account of what happened."

"You should ask your aunt and uncle."

Elijah winced. Adam had never mentioned the day to him, but Kit had, and he understood why Adam didn't want to talk about it.

"They're still grieving. I don't want to bring up bad memories."

But she didn't consider they might also be bad for

Adam.

"Let's leave discussions of murder and mayhem for a weekend when there isn't a wedding." Elijah glanced out the windscreen. "I hope we get some clear weather tomorrow."

Olivia sighed. "I've heard it's supposed to be lucky for it to rain on your wedding day." She started chatting about other weddings she'd been to.

Elijah met Adam's gaze in the rear-view mirror and Adam gave him a nod of thanks.

That's what friends were for.

Chapter 11

Jamie checked the clock for the tenth time and dragged the quilt from his bed to the couch where he'd set up his laptop. Hannah hadn't been kidding when she'd said the shed was cold. Maybe he should go into town, hang out at Mai's bakery while he waited for Elijah to get back. His muscles tightened. How far would word have spread about him kissing Elijah? Shirley wouldn't have kept her mouth shut, but it depended on whether she'd been working this morning at the caravan park, or having brunch with a friend in town.

It didn't matter. There was no taking back what he'd done and he didn't want to. The kiss had been scorching. He couldn't wait to do it again.

Which meant he had to face any criticism, man up, stop letting others dictate what he did with his life.

He sighed and looked at the time again.

Lincoln had been useless when Jamie called to ask whether they'd got a hit on the partial plate. He'd been in cop mode, with his *I can't tell you* bullshit.

Jamie would rather be with Elijah than twiddling his thumbs here. If he'd agreed to tell people about their relationship sooner, it would have been the perfect reason for him to go into town with Elijah to run those errands. But it was better Elijah was with a trained police officer. Safer for him.

Jamie wanted Elijah to be safe.

Jamie glanced around the big open shed for something to do. He'd thought moving out would feel better than this, but it still felt as if he was in limbo with all the boxes piled in the corner. The shed was meant to be temporary so he needed to decide what to do next.

He had some savings, so he should be ready to buy a house, or go somewhere other than Bali on a holiday. Somehow he'd fallen into the rut of complacency—no, not complacency, of trying to please. Of doing what people expected of him, of making people happy so they'd like him.

He'd had lots of friends in Perth, university mates he'd gone drinking and dancing with, but no one he'd connected with the way he had with the musketeers. It was probably why he'd joined the SES in the first place. Sub-consciously he'd needed something to make him feel better about himself.

Who was he kidding? It was more pathetic than that.

He'd joined because Sandra's brother was a member and he'd wanted to please her.

Even that relationship had been superficial. She'd moved in when his roommate had moved out and he hadn't come up with a reasonable excuse to refuse. He'd wanted to believe their relationship was going somewhere, but she'd never been interested in visiting Blackbridge. The Swan Valley was the furthest country she'd go and it was only half an hour from the city. She'd liked to go to shows and out to dinner, and while Jamie enjoyed that too, he also loved a night spent curled up on the couch watching movies or reading a book. And that bored Sandra. She had to be seen out and about.

Jamie had stuck with it until last Christmas holidays when she'd been jealous of him spending time here with the musketeers and had given him an ultimatum—her or them. It hadn't been a contest. Mai, Kit, Hannah and Fleur had been his best friends forever, though he didn't deserve them. He'd transferred his lease to Sandra, packed up and come home.

Something he should have done sooner.

He groaned.

How had he not seen it before? He'd gone with the flow for most of his life, unwilling to risk upsetting people, unwilling to go after what he really wanted.

And what he really wanted was Elijah.

The town could go to hell if they didn't like it. His sexuality didn't define who he was, it was part of him.

Yeah, it was easy to be brave when he was alone in his shed. But what would the reality be like? Only one way to find out.

He called Elijah.

"Hey. You're on speaker and Adam and Olivia are in the car with me."

Jamie smiled at Elijah's perky voice. "It's Jamie. Will you be finished by lunch?"

"Yep."

"Want to meet at Mai's bakery?" Central and public. It was time to make a statement.

"I can meet you there in an hour." There was a smile in Elijah's voice as he hung up.

The short conversation was enough to lift Jamie's spirits. Outside the wind howled, but Elijah's voice had warmed him. Still the noise reminded him of how bare the shed was. In summer it would be a furnace. He picked up his laptop from the coffee table and shifted the quilt so its heavy layer settled around him. It was time he took charge of his life. Blackbridge was his home, he was happy here surrounded by friends and family, and he had a good job. So he had to find somewhere decent to live.

His skin prickled as he checked his bank balance. He'd never been a big spender, and living with his parents for the past six months meant he'd saved enough for a decent deposit on a house.

If he couldn't find a rental, he had to consider buying. He flicked through a real estate website.

He had options. A few empty blocks both in and out of town where he could build exactly what he wanted, or a number of houses around his price range. The idea of having a place of his own made his stomach churn in excitement. He could put down roots, take control of his life.

His gaze caught the time at the bottom of the screen and he slammed the laptop shut. Shit. He was supposed to be meeting Elijah.

He grabbed his wallet, checked his reflection in the mirror and hurried out the door.

***

Elijah walked into *On the Way* bakery and scanned the people seated at the wooden tables. No Jamie. He was a little later than he'd expected to be by the time he'd dropped everyone at their respective houses. Adam had warned him to keep a lookout for people following him and Elijah had been a little paranoid as he'd dropped off the suit at Will's place. Then Will had wanted to chat about the wedding, and Elijah had lost track of time.

Elijah raised a hand to Jody behind the counter and snagged the last two-person table in the middle of the room. The scent of freshly baked bread and coffee filled the room and he inhaled deeply.

A few familiar faces were at the bakery today. Shirley and Barbara were having coffee together; Lynette from the caravan park was with her husband and three boys; and Lawrence, the captain of the volunteer fire-brigade was there with his wife. Friends and families. No one looked like they were there on a date. Except him.

Shirley leaned over and asked, "Are you waiting for Jamie?"

Elijah blinked. How had she known? He nodded.

The bell over the door rang and Jamie rushed in, looking a little flustered. A smile lit up his face as he found Elijah and Elijah's heart skipped a beat. "I'm sorry I'm late." He slid into the chair opposite, his knee bumping Elijah's as he did so.

"I just got here."

"Good." Jamie let out a long breath. "I lost track of time looking at houses."

Elijah raised an eyebrow. "Are you thinking of buying?"

"Yeah. It's time I took my finger out and bought something."

Elijah's chest tightened. "In Blackbridge?" He hoped the question seemed casual.

Jamie nodded. "Have you ordered?"

"Not yet."

"What would you like? My shout."

Elijah pursed his lips. After last night he'd thought Jamie was ready to be open about their relationship, but there'd been no kiss on arrival. Patience. No matter what had happened last night, he'd promised Jamie two weeks of anonymity. "I'll have a cappuccino and a banh mi."

Jamie stood, leaning forward to kiss Elijah on the lips. "I missed you." With a smile that set Elijah's heart racing, he went to order.

Well, that answered *that* question. He fanned himself and glanced around to gauge people's reactions.

No one seemed to have noticed.

He smiled. Just the way it should be.

A few minutes later, Jamie was back. "Did you get all your errands done this morning?"

"Yeah."

Jamie slipped his hand into Elijah's and lowered his voice. "Were there any issues from last night?"

"I'll tell you about it later." He hadn't noticed the black ute after the airport. Maybe they'd got bored or changed cars. He'd stay alert just in case.

"Two cappuccinos." Jody stood at the table holding two steaming cups. Her eyebrows raised as Jamie let go of Elijah's hand so she had room to put the cups down.

"Thanks," Elijah said.

Jamie smiled, but his posture stiffened slightly. Or was Elijah imagining it?

Don't fret. This is new for him. He's not going to be comfortable one hundred percent of the time. Still after Jody left, he squeezed Jamie's hand. "What kind of house are you after?"

"I'm not sure yet. I looked at a bunch in my price range. I want a bit of backyard, maybe get a dog."

Elijah liked the idea of Jamie settling in Blackbridge.

"Maybe you could help me?"

Elijah's heart expanded. "I'd love to. Buying gives you so many more options than renting."

Jody brought their food and this time she grinned. "Enjoy."

As Elijah bit into his roll, his phone beeped and seconds later Jamie's did too. They exchanged glances.

Missing person call out.

Elijah swallowed. As much as he wanted to spend

the afternoon talking with Jamie, he had made a commitment to the SES. "We going?"

"We should."

Elijah skulled his coffee and Jamie picked up his plate. "I'll get Jody to wrap them for us."

Moments later they stood outside the bakery. "Can you follow me to my place?" Elijah asked. Adam had said he was going to have a nap, but Elijah didn't want to leave him without a car for the rest of the afternoon.

Jamie handed him his wrapped roll and nodded.

Elijah tapped his fingers on the steering wheel as he drove home to get his gear and then drove with Jamie to the depot. Another missing person. Who would it be this time?

Several cars were already there. "What have we got?" Elijah asked.

Morgan looked up from the desk. "Richard Patton's missing. He took the family four-wheel drive, and they found it by one of the beach lookouts. Richard's not there. Marine Rescue is also mobilising."

Elijah winced at the implication. Even with dementia, surely Richard wouldn't have fallen off the cliff.

When the others arrived, Morgan briefed them.

"The weather forecast isn't good." He handed around a photo of Richard. "Thunderstorm is coming in, should hit about three o'clock and temperature's dropping to about three degrees tonight. Richard's car was found by the inlet lookout. The police are checking the roads in the area, Marine Rescue are scanning the sea. The bush is thick and scrubby. If he's climbed the barriers into the bush, hopefully he's left us a trail of broken branches. Line of sight is going to be hard to maintain." Morgan glanced at the map on the table. "We'll have two groups. One will go east, the other west. We'll go from lookout to lookout first. Albany SES are coming and they'll search across the road further inland."

"How long has he been missing?" Jamie asked.

"A couple of days. Craig thought he'd gone home, and Kay thought he was with Craig. It wasn't until this morning they realised he was missing and the family searched all the usual places and found the car. Kay called it in, but her family have been going to each lookout along the coast. He may have been parked there for days."

"Do we know what he was wearing?" Elijah asked.

Morgan shook his head.

"Hey, Morgan." Jamie was frowning. "I saw Richard last night at the Vale talking to Craig. At best he's been missing overnight."

The SES didn't normally get involved until someone had been missing for much longer, except in particular cases like the child last week.

Morgan closed his eyes for a second and made an angry growl in his throat. "Right. Well, we're here now. Do you remember what he was wearing?"

"Black pants, royal blue knitted jumper," Jamie replied.

"Thanks."

Without a rain jacket, Richard was likely soaked, unless he'd found a limestone cave to hide in. But that would require him to climb down the cliffs and that was dangerous.

"These will be your groups." Morgan read out names. Elijah was with Morgan and Jamie was with Siobhan.

Damn it.

As they finished getting the gear together, Jamie pulled Elijah aside. "Take care of yourself. If you see someone strange, get one of the other volunteers' attention."

Elijah's heart jumped. He'd forgotten all about being followed in his focus on Richard. "I'll be within eyesight of everyone."

Jamie shook his head. "The bush is thick in this area." He hefted the torch in his hand before sliding it into his pocket. "The torch will make a good weapon."

Elijah nodded. "You take care too. Conditions are going to suck if we don't find him soon."

Jamie kissed him fast and walked over to his group. Elijah stared after him. Wow. Jamie had kissed him in front of people who weren't close friends. He smiled as he joined the other group and took another look at Jamie's retreating back. Siobhan frowned, confusion on her face.

They drove to the lookout where Richard's car was parked. Morgan gave an onsite rundown of the terrain. "All right. Line up," he said.

Elijah found himself at the end of the line, closest to the cliffs. Morgan handed him a radio. "You're in the best position to talk to Marine Rescue if necessary."

Before Elijah could ask to swap, Morgan walked off calling, "Let's go!"

The limestone rocks at the edge of the cliff had a few tufts of grass sticking out, but it was another couple of metres before the rock gave way to sand and higher shrubs. No need to get too close to the edge. Marine Rescue would spot anyone who had fallen or was stuck on a ledge on the rock face. The boat bobbed in the rough waves below and it looked like Kim was at the wheel.

Elijah scanned the ground and the bushes for traces someone had come this way. "Richard!" he yelled. To his side, others echoed his call.

The wind buffeted him back and he tripped on a loose rock, taking two unsteady steps towards the edge. He clenched his teeth and moved closer to the bushes. Focus.

"Richard!"

Rain spat and he pulled his hood up which blocked some of his peripheral vision. So much for the weather forecast. He kept his steps slow and steady, pacing himself with the other searchers he could hear, but not see, in the bush to his right.

Richard could have easily wandered this way without leaving any traces. The rock was bumpy but reasonably flat and Richard was still fit despite his dementia.

The spits of rain stopped and Elijah lowered his hood to see better. The Marine Rescue boat slowly made its way through the waves, not too close to the cliffs. The water foamed below which would make it difficult to spot anyone under the water. Elijah kept scanning just in case.

The Pattons would have a difficult decision to make when Richard was found. He was becoming a danger to himself and to others. Last month he'd blacked out while driving and almost driven someone off a lookout. When Kay had realised, she'd taken him to the police station to hand in his driver's licence. The ocean, or the lookouts, must have some significance to him.

Elijah stopped. He'd heard that people with dementia could remember clearly what happened decades ago and not remember yesterday. The Pattons had set up the winery more than thirty years ago. Richard would have seen the area before the developments, before all the strict safety fencing was in place. Had he come to the lookout to dream?

Would he have wandered away from the main area to get some privacy?

Were there unknown paths along here?

Elijah kept his gaze on the cliff edge, trying to discern a dip or path which would indicate a way down. The limestone caves were generally considered too crumbly to be safe, but occasionally a teenager on a dare or a tourist would ignore the signs and climb over the railings to explore.

"Richard," he yelled.

The other searchers' yells were faint, the wind blowing the sound away from him and the crash of the waves below was loud and continuous. The clouds darkened above, blocking more of the sun and the light faded to almost as dark as dusk.

He switched on his torch, sweeping its beam across the ground, hoping to catch a glint of something Richard might have dropped. Nothing.

Up ahead the scrub was closer to the cliff, the ground more sandy. The day lightened as the darker clouds passed by and Elijah squinted. One branch appeared broken.

He hurried over, heart beating faster.

Yes, definitely the edge of a thicker branch had been broken as if someone had pushed past it. But the gap between the cliff and the bush was only about a metre and the ocean was a long way below.

His stomach swirled and his head spun.

Get a grip. He could do this.

He slipped the torch back into his pocket. Where was the rescue boat? It had already got ahead of him, which probably meant Richard wasn't anywhere on the cliff face. Maybe he'd veered away from the cliff and headed inland. Or perhaps the bush receded around the bend he couldn't see beyond.

He had to continue.

Breathing out, he stepped forward, pressing his back

close to the thick bushes. The rocks here were loose, crumbly. If they broke away, the bushes weren't thick enough to hold him if he grabbed them. The whole plant would probably come out of the ground.

Elijah edged sideways keeping his gaze on the rock edge and not the ocean crashing below. He panted as he moved slowly, wanting to rush, to get beyond this narrow patch and back to open rock, but too scared to do more than shuffle. The point was right up ahead. Surely the path would widen there.

"Richard!" The wind whisked his call away.

Damn it.

His heart beating heavily, he pushed the branches back and saw a flash of blue below. "Richard!"

It might have been a blue wren or a bit of plastic. But at least here the rock had beaten the shrub back and there was an open area, almost a V-shape with the point towards the bush. Elijah stepped into it, away from the edge and examined the ground.

Mud. The dark reddish soil found on farms in the area. He lowered to his hands and knees and crawled to the edge, discovering another dollop of mud a step below, and then another. His eyes tracked a narrow path down along the cliff. At the bottom was a tiny patch of beach. His head spun and he moved back, reaching for his radio. No way he was climbing down there without a safety harness.

"I've found something," he called. "There's red mud on the rocks and it looks like there's a path down the cliff."

"Roger that," came the reply. "Where are you?"

"About a hundred metres east of the rescue boat. Kim, do you read?"

"Copy that, Elijah. We'll swing around and take another look."

In the distance, the boat made a large arc, heading back towards Elijah.

"Argh!"

Elijah jolted. The yell came from below. What the hell?

"Let go!" A female screamed.

Heart thumping, Elijah moved closer to the edge and peered down, his head dizzy as he took in the scene. About five metres below, Richard and Kay grappled on the edge of a ledge that jutted from the cliff face. Richard shoved his daughter towards the edge and her arms flailed as she tried to regain her balance.

"Richard, stop!" Elijah yelled.

Kay glanced up, fear in her eyes.

"She's trying to kill me," Richard roared and grabbed his daughter.

Shit. He had to stop them, had to help Kay. Elijah spoke into his radio as he picked his way along the path, ignoring the drop. "Richard and Kay are fighting on a ledge below me. Richard's delusional. I'm going down."

Steeling himself, he lowered onto the first ledge. He swallowed hard, keeping the nausea down. The waves crashed against the rocks louder now, more threatening. The rock was rough under his hand as he gripped it and forced himself to find the next step. There. He scooted down and held on to a rock which hung over what appeared to be a path. It was only about half a metre wide, but it was smooth. He could do this.

Kay and Richard still grappled, shouting and grunting as they fought close to the edge of the ledge. Richard's foot slipped and he fell to his knees, his feet dangling off the edge.

"Hold on. I'm coming!" Elijah yelled. His eyes glued to the rough path, he moved as fast as he dared, keeping his centre of gravity close to the rock beside him.

"No!" Richard yelled. He was on his knees, his grip tight around Kay's arm.

"I'm almost there."

Far below, the rescue boat bobbed in the waves. Someone shouted into the radio, but Elijah was too focused on the path to make out the words.

His head spun and he breathed out. You can do this. You will not fall to your death below.

He stepped onto the ledge as Kay wrenched her wrist free of her father's grasp. She stumbled, twisting as she did and she bumped Richard with her hip. The impact overbalanced Richard, and his arms flailed as his body shifted backwards out over the empty space. He bellowed.

"No!" Elijah lunged forward as Kay fell into him, sending them both to the ground.

Kay was first to her feet, stumbling to the ledge, hand over her mouth, eyes wide with shock as she stared down.

No. No, no, no. Elijah crawled to the edge, peering below as Richard's limp body was pulled off the rock below by a wave. The breath left his lungs and he wanted to vomit. He squeezed his eyes shut. When he opened them again, Marine Rescue were already working to recover Richard's body. He shifted back before getting to his feet.

He wrapped an arm around Kay's shoulder, pulled her away from the edge. "I'm so sorry, Kay."

She let him lead her back into a cave. She sat heavily on a rock.

Elijah's radio buzzed with conversation between Marine Rescue and the police. "He might still be alive."

Tears leaked from her eyes.

"Elijah, where are you?" Morgan demanded.

He turned his head, spoke into the radio. "I'm with Kay in a cave about five metres down the cliff face. We're both…" There was nothing fine about this situation. "…uninjured. We'll come up in a minute."

"We'll lower some rope," came the reply.

Thank God.

"I can't believe what just happened," Kay whispered, her body shaking.

What the hell was he supposed to say? "Your dad wasn't well."

Thunder rumbled across the sky and the light dimmed. Almost three o'clock. "Kay, I'm sorry, but we need to move. The forecast is for storms and heavy rain. If we don't go now, we might be stuck here all night."

She stood and pushed her hair off her face.

Elijah switched on his torch. "Give me a second to ask if the guys are in place." He gritted his teeth as he stepped further out on the ledge and looked up. A harness dangled about a metre above him and someone in orange peered down. "Lower it further," Elijah said into the radio.

The harness was lowered to him. "You go first," he said to Kay.

"I don't need a harness. I got down here in the first place."

"It's safer. If you slip, the guys up there will catch you."

She scowled but nodded. This was more the Kay he was used to. This would distract her if only for a short while. He checked the harness was on correctly and said, "She's coming up."

Kay climbed the path.

Lightning flashed. A couple of seconds later another

crack of thunder split the sky. Not good.

As if on cue, the heavens opened and big thick raindrops bucketed down.

Elijah ducked into the cave and his torch beam illuminated the area.

The cave was about three metres deep with a sandy floor. At the back of the cave a square hole had been chiselled out of the roof.

Odd. He moved closer, shone the torch up. The top of the hole was covered in wooden planks. That had to be close to the surface. A thick, rusted metal ring protruded from the wall just below the hole. It might date back to when the area was first settled, though why anyone would want to lift things up here was beyond him. He swung the torch around. The rest of the cave was empty.

"Elijah, you ready?" The radio crackled.

He glanced out of the cave where the empty harness dangled in the drenching rain. His gut clenched. It had been bad enough climbing down when the rocks hadn't been slick. After the incident at training, the harness didn't give him any measure of comfort at all.

"Elijah?"

"Should we wait until the rain lets up?" Elijah responded.

"You'd be there all night," Morgan said. "Hurry up. The rest of us want to get out of the rain."

He gritted his teeth. Man up. He tucked the torch back into his pocket and pulled the harness into the cave so he could get into it. He triple-checked the buckles and carabiner and swallowed hard. "Ready."

The slack in the rope decreased and he stepped out into the rain.

Instantly he was soaked. The water fell heavily through his hair and down his neck. The path he'd climbed down earlier had turned into a river of water pouring towards the ledge and over it.

There had to be another way up.

"Come on, E. There are three big strong men waiting at the top for you." Jamie's teasing voice was music to his ears.

"Does that include you?"

"Sure does."

The thought of Jamie holding the other end of his safety rope gave him strength. He stepped onto the narrow path, keeping his gaze glued forward and slowly moved up. His legs trembled. Not far to go. The overhang was right there. Once he got past it, it was two steps to the top. He stepped up, in a hurry for the ordeal to be over and his foot slipped. His palms scraped against the slippery rock and his whole body slammed against the rock face, tugging him down. Fuck. The rope kicked in, yanking him to a halt. Pulse racing, he grappled to get his feet under him again, his heart pumping hard. Finally he found purchase and stayed where he was, panting, his grip tight on the rope.

"Almost there." Jamie's voice was close.

He looked up, blinking through the rain dripping off his eyelashes and caught Jamie's concerned gaze. Jamie grinned and nodded.

Right. He could do this.

Keeping low to the ground, he half crawled, half scrabbled up the path until strong hands pulled him up and away from the cliff.

Jamie.

Elijah flung his arms around him.

"I've got you," Jamie murmured and kissed his cheek.

Elijah shook, the warmth of Jamie's body contrasting against the ice cold of the rain coating them both.

Morgan cleared his throat. "You ready to go?"

"Give me a second." He peeked over his shoulder. Two others stood in the small V-shaped clearing, Morgan and Brenton. Brenton wound up the safety rope and Elijah quickly unclasped the end from his harness. Kay must have already been taken back to the car park. "You go ahead."

Morgan motioned Brenton to leave and Elijah and Jamie were left together. He pulled Jamie close to him, and Jamie shifted so he was a beautiful barrier between Elijah and the cliff.

"You OK?"

Elijah shook his head. He could barely breathe. He let go and bent over, trying to draw air into his lungs. "Any news on Richard?"

"Marine Rescue hasn't said." Jamie made him stand straight. "Which probably means he was dead when they pulled him out of the water."

Elijah huffed out a breath. Poor Kay. She'd be devastated. He closed his eyes, but his whole body was shaky and rain slipped beneath his coat, adding to his discomfort. "Let's go."

Jamie helped Elijah out of the clearing, and they followed the others back to the car park. The volunteers milled around and Kay spoke with Lincoln and Ryan under the cover of a portable gazebo.

"The police want to talk to you," Morgan told Elijah.

"I'll stay with you," Jamie said.

"We'll need you to write up a report as well," Morgan said.

"Of course." His body was going numb.

"This way." Jamie led him under the gazebo and one of the volunteers handed him a towel.

"Thanks."

Kay twisted, saw Elijah and her eyes filled with pain and tears. "Thank you for saving me."

Elijah jolted. He'd never seen her so upset, so human. It ripped his heart. "I'm sorry I couldn't save your father."

She nodded. "He wasn't well. He didn't recognise me."

Lincoln spoke. "We've called your brothers. They're coming to pick you up. Go home, get warm and we'll come out and get a statement."

"Thank you."

Lincoln glanced at Elijah. "We'll need your statement too."

Elijah accepted a mug of hot coffee from Morgan. Most of the crew had already packed up and taken one of the land cruisers back to the station. All that remained was the gazebo, Morgan, Jamie and Elijah.

A car tore into the car park and Mark and Craig jumped out. Craig ran to his sister. "Are you all right?"

She nodded, sniffing. "Dad…"

"We know," Craig said. "We'll talk about it later. Right now, you have to get warm and dry." He asked Lincoln, "Can we take her home?"

"Yes. We'll be out in about an hour to get her statement."

Mark scowled. "Give me a break! Our father just died."

Elijah frowned. The whole Patton family was supposed to be out searching for Richard, so why had Mark been at the craft store in Albany? Perhaps Mark hadn't heard about it yet. It had been early.

"I'm sorry for your loss," Lincoln said. "But we need to record what happened while it's still fresh in Kay's mind."

"I don't think it's ever going to fade," Kay said. She placed a hand on her brother. "It's fine, Mark. I'd like to close this off."

Mark glared at Lincoln and then limped back to the car, his siblings following.

Morgan set to work dismantling the gazebo and Lincoln and Ryan turned to Elijah. "How are you?" Ryan asked.

"OK." The shaking was part cold, part residual fear.

"I'll take him home to change before I bring him to the station to give a statement," Jamie said.

Lincoln nodded. "Don't be long."

Jamie tucked his arm around Elijah and led him to the land cruiser.

And for the first time that day, Elijah felt truly safe.

Chapter 12

Elijah had much better colour in his face by the time he got out of the shower. Jamie had changed out of his SES gear while he'd waited, and had filled Adam in on what had happened.

Elijah's smile was a little fragile. "We should go to the station."

Jamie hugged him. "Feeling any better?" He handed Elijah a hot cup of coffee.

"I'm warmer."

It was a start.

He drove Elijah to the station. The police car was back in the yard and he and Elijah hurried up the steps. Inside, Ryan buzzed them through to the offices.

"How are you holding up?" Ryan asked.

"I'm a little shaky," Elijah said.

Lincoln moved over to them. "I can offer some fresh coffee."

Elijah held up the mug. "Jamie's got me covered."

Lincoln gestured them into his heated office and put the recorder on the desk. After going through the necessities, he said, "Elijah, tell me what happened today."

"Where should I start?"

"From when you left the car park."

Elijah spoke slowly, carefully going through every detail. Jamie had never heard him so thorough. He couldn't believe Elijah hadn't told Morgan about his fear of heights. Jamie wasn't going to sit through another incident like this, terrified for Elijah. He'd tell Morgan himself.

"I saw a flash of blue and then heard them arguing," Elijah said.

Jamie listened closely. Richard had been having another paranoid episode, thinking his own daughter wanted to kill him. It must have been so hard for the Patton family. When school went back, he'd have to take Don aside and chat to him, ask whether he needed any support, to talk to anyone.

When Elijah was finished, Lincoln and Ryan took turns asking questions, getting him to clarify information and repeat what he'd said. Elijah answered each question with patience and consideration. Jamie squeezed his hand and Elijah flashed him a smile.

"All right. I think we have everything." Lincoln glanced at Jamie. "Are you staying with him this afternoon?"

"Yes."

"Will's picking me up later," Elijah said. "We're staying in Albany tonight before the wedding."

Jamie swore. He'd forgotten about that.

Lincoln nodded. "You shouldn't be followed, but keep an eye out anyway."

Another damn thing to worry about. "Who was it?"

Ryan and Lincoln exchanged a glance. "Mark Patton owns the black ute."

Right. Mark being involved in something dodgy didn't surprise Jamie. The man believed he was entitled to everything.

Elijah exhaled. "I never liked him, but he doesn't deserve today's tragedy." He got to his feet and Ryan walked him out, telling him about the counselling available to him.

Lincoln gripped Jamie's arm and lowered his voice. "Keep an eye on him, all right? If you get a bad feeling about anything, call me."

Jamie's muscles tightened. "What are you worried about?"

Lincoln sighed. "Just promise me. More people might be involved."

Well that was vague. Jamie gritted his teeth, wanting to demand answers, but Lincoln had his police face on. Jamie would never get it out of him. Instead he simply nodded and left with Elijah.

"Where to?" he asked when they were in his car.

"I need to give Will a call. Find out when he's picking me up." Elijah got out his phone and chatted to Will. As they reached Elijah's place, he hung up. "We're leaving in an hour."

Jamie would stay with him until then. Elijah was too silent, too still. Jamie followed him inside. "Can I help you get ready?"

Elijah let out a long shaky breath. "I don't know." He ran a hand through his already dishevelled hair and flopped onto the couch. "I keep seeing them fighting on the edge, the fear in Richard's face before he fell." He squeezed his eyes shut and then they flashed open again.

Jamie sat next to him, took Elijah's ice-cold hand in his. He didn't know how to make it better. "You got there as fast as you could."

Elijah shook his head. "This stupid fear of heights. If I didn't have it, I would have been faster, would have reached them in time to drag them both back from the edge."

"Don't." Jamie turned Elijah's head towards him. "Don't you dare take the blame for this. Richard might have dragged you over too." It wasn't a thought Jamie wanted to pursue. "Richard was ill. He shouldn't have been out there in the first place. We don't even know how Kay found him." Or why she hadn't called the SES.

"I feel so helpless." Tears welled in Elijah's eyes. "I haven't felt this helpless since I was a child."

Jamie drew him in, kissed his cheek. "There's nothing any of us could have done." He kissed Elijah's lips, wanting to give him comfort.

Elijah gripped the back of Jamie's head, holding him there, deepening the kiss. Elijah's lips were like fire. Hot, scorching desire swept through Jamie and he tried to slow things but Elijah would have none of it. "Just kiss me," Elijah breathed and Jamie couldn't deny him. If this would help…

He shifted on the couch and ran his tongue along Elijah's bottom lip. Elijah hummed in appreciation and opened for him. His lips were so luscious, so kissable, so right.

Elijah's hands swept down Jamie's back and up under his jumper. Jamie's nipples peaked and he growled low in his throat. Elijah's hands were a little rough, calloused from farm work, but the slight scratch made it all the better.

Jamie slid his hand under Elijah's wool jumper and discovered Elijah wasn't wearing anything under it. His skin was warm and his muscles hard; Jamie's thumb brushed against his six-pack.

Hot.

He wanted to rip the jumper off Elijah and see him,

lick all those delicious muscles, but today he had to let Elijah set the pace. He was still coming to terms with what happened. And with that in mind, he softened his kisses, let his touch become more of a caress and Elijah moaned.

Jamie brushed kisses along his chin, down his neck and then up to nibble on his ear.

"I knew you'd be amazing with your mouth," Elijah sighed.

Jamie smiled. "Have you been thinking about my mouth a lot?"

"Every day, honey." The tease in his tone told Jamie Elijah was moving past the shock.

"Really?" He kissed back down Elijah's cheek. "What did you picture my mouth doing?" He teased Elijah's bottom lip, nibbling and sucking gently and brushing quick, soft kisses on his mouth.

"This," Elijah said.

"Anything else?" Jamie circled Elijah's nipple with his thumb. It was puckered and ripe for his tongue.

"I fantasised about you sucking my nipples."

Jamie smiled against Elijah's mouth, still peppering kisses on it. "Want it to become a reality?"

"Hell, yes." The reverence of the words made Jamie grin.

Slowly he pushed up Elijah's jumper and Elijah leaned back, stripping it off. Jamie took his time, taking in Elijah's tanned skin, his chiselled muscles which would make a model proud and the happy trail leading below his belt to places yet to be explored. His fingers traced the path he wanted his lips to go and he pressed Elijah back so he lay along the couch and started his journey.

He nibbled his way along Elijah's neck, finding a particularly sensitive spot which made Elijah's hips arch and press against Jamie's body. Oh, yeah.

Slowly he moved down Elijah's body, licking and sucking, discovering what Elijah liked, what made him groan and thrust. He licked the contours of Elijah's abs, loving the hardness under his tongue and fingers, grazing his teeth against Elijah's skin.

"Geez, Jamie," Elijah breathed.

"Does this measure up to your fantasy?" Jamie asked, glancing at Elijah's face.

Elijah opened his eyes, gazed at him with a raised eyebrow. "It surpasses it."

Jamie slid his thumb under Elijah's belt. "Anywhere else you pictured my mouth?" He brushed the tip of Elijah's warm erection and Elijah moaned.

A sudden banging on the door had them both flinching and Elijah swore violently. "What time is it?"

Jamie glanced at the clock. "Five."

Elijah scrambled to a seated position, grabbing his jumper as a voice called, "Elijah, are you there?"

Will.

Frustration flooded Jamie. "Do you have to go?"

Elijah hesitated. "Yeah."

"Let me answer the door while you get your things."

Elijah pouted but nodded.

Jamie adjusted himself and yelled, "Be right there," as Will knocked again.

He took a second to think of something other than Elijah's rock-hard body under him, and then opened the door. "Hey, Will."

Will blinked and smiled. "Jamie. I wasn't expecting you."

Should he mention the call out? Someone was likely to mention it at the wedding tomorrow, and he didn't want the news to ruin Will's day. "Richard Patton went missing and the SES was called to search for him."

"Did you find him?" Will walked into the living area.

"Yeah, but he was confused and thought his daughter wanted to kill him. He fell off the cliff in the struggle and died."

Will sat hard on the sofa. "How awful."

"Yeah." Jamie glanced down the empty hallway. "Elijah saw it all, so be gentle with him."

Will tapped his leg, concern on his face. "Should I get him to meet me at the venue tomorrow?"

Before Jamie answered, Elijah walked into the room carrying an overnight bag. "Not necessary. What I need right now is to be kept busy and the wedding is the perfect distraction." He ran a hand down Jamie's back. "Shall we go?"

After Elijah locked up, Jamie walked him to Will's car. "Call me if you need to chat," Jamie said.

Elijah placed his bag on the backseat and turned to him. "I will."

Jamie pulled Elijah close. "Maybe we can sneak off during the reception and finish what we started today."

Elijah's smile was wicked and it sent a shot of lust through Jamie. "I like the way you think."

Jamie kissed him. "I'll see you tomorrow."

He waited where he was as Will backed out and drove away. He scanned the empty street. The crappy weather was keeping everyone indoors. At least it meant no one was following Elijah.

One less thing he had to worry about.

He got in his car and hesitated. The idea of being alone didn't thrill him. Now he'd heard exactly what Elijah had seen, had discovered how close Elijah had been to falling off the cliff himself, he couldn't stop his mind playing a horrific what-if scenario. It didn't matter that Elijah was safe.

Most of his friends were getting ready for the

wedding. Kim would be going to Albany with Will and Elijah, the musketeers would be doing something together, so that left Jeremy. He dialled his friend's number. "Want to grab some dinner?"

It might distract him from the horrible day.

***

As guests arrived, Elijah adjusted his lavender tie, ignoring the nerves skittering along his skin. It was ridiculous. This wasn't his wedding. All he had to do was stand next to Will and pass him the rings at the right time.

He brushed the rings in his coat pocket for the fifth time to make sure they were still there.

In contrast, the normally anxious Will was a picture of serenity. He greeted guests and showed them to their seats.

At least Mother Nature had agreed to play nicely today. A few clouds hovered in the blue sky, but not dense enough to hold rain and there was even a touch of warmth in the air. Will had chosen to have the ceremony outside in the restaurant garden, so hopefully the weather wouldn't suddenly change.

"What's wrong with you today?" Kim asked.

Elijah glanced at his friend. "Nothing."

Kim laughed. "That's the third time you've adjusted your tie in as many minutes. What gives?"

Elijah shrugged. "It's my first wedding." It was a good excuse. But he'd barely slept last night. The strange bed combined with his mind not shutting off meant he was still gazing at the dark ceiling long after Kim had started snoring in the bed next to him.

How was he meant to sleep with everything going on? He was being followed, he'd watched a man die, he'd got hot and heavy with the very sexy Jamie Zanetti and he had to give a speech today. His brain had flittered from one event to the next, each ensuring his heart kept racing and scaring sleep off.

His speech.

He touched his jacket pockets and then his pant pockets. No paper.

Shit. What had he done with it? Had he left it back at the motel?

"What's wrong?" Adam asked, walking over to them looking gorgeous in a charcoal black suit.

"My speech. I don't have my speech."

"Don't worry about it. You know it off by heart anyway," Adam said.

"What if my mind goes blank?"

"I've heard it so many times, I can probably prompt you."

"Or we can go by the motel after the ceremony to pick it up," Kim said.

"They might have cleaned the room by then. They might have thrown it out." Though the accommodation wasn't far away, he was required to greet the guests and help Will. He was so screwed.

"Hi, handsome." Jamie's voice was enough to calm him a little.

Elijah turned and momentarily forgot all of his problems. The dark grey suit fitted Jamie to perfection. The jacket caressed his shoulders and hugged his waist and the pants clung to his thighs. The burgundy shirt he wore brought out the richness of his brown eyes and he was every bit as delectable as always. "Jamie." He sighed.

Jamie frowned. "Is everything all right?"

"He's stressing about the best man speech," Kim said. "He left his notes at the motel."

"You don't need your notes. You've got this."

Elijah shook his head. "My mind will blank. I know it will. I'll be standing in front of all those people, gaping like a fish." It would be a nightmare.

Jamie checked the time. "Do you want me to fetch them? I can probably be back before the ceremony starts."

"Oh my God, you're my hero." Hopefully housekeeping hadn't been yet. "It's room five-oh-one. I was reading it this morning, so it might be on the dressing table."

"Have you got your phone on you in case I have any issues?"

Elijah nodded.

Jamie stepped closer, brushed a kiss on his lips. "I'll find it. I'll be back soon."

As he walked off, Elijah sighed and his shoulders relaxed. Everything would be fine.

Jamie hadn't returned by the time Fleur and her bridesmaids arrived. Elijah met their limousine as Kit climbed out and he did a double-take. He wasn't used to seeing his boss in a dress, let alone a demure pale lavender outfit that fell all the way to her ankles. Her hair was a mass of curls, half tied up and the rest hanging loose like Mai and Hannah's. Fleur's father helped his daughter out of the car and Elijah knew Will would swallow his tongue.

Her hair was also curled and piled up on top of her head to leave her neck bare. The wide lace straps of her gown plunged to form a V-neck which was both modest and seductive and the A-line skirt had a slit allowing her leg to peek out. It was simple and sexy.

"Honey, you look stunning."

Fleur beamed at him. "Thanks, Elijah. Is everything ready for us? How's Will? I thought he'd call me more than he did."

"He's totally calm," Elijah assured her. "I've never seen him so together. He's so confident about this."

Fleur placed a hand over her heart briefly and took the lush red roses Mai handed her. "Let's get this show on the road."

Elijah glanced towards the main road. He didn't want Jamie to miss Fleur's wedding because of him.

"Is something wrong?" Kit asked.

"No. Not really. I forgot my speech and Jamie went to get it. He's not back yet." Elijah dug his mobile out of his pocket. "He can't be far away." He dialled and as the phone rang, Jamie pulled into the car park. Elijah grinned and hung up.

Jamie hurried over, kissed Fleur on the cheek and said, "You look beautiful, Flower." He handed Elijah his speech.

"Thanks."

Jamie kissed him hard and murmured, "You can thank me later." With a grin, he hurried towards the ceremony.

Elijah's heart raced and he waved his hand to cool himself. That man...

Someone cleared their throat and he turned to find the musketeers all grinning at him. Fleur raised her eyebrows. "Can you tell the harpist we're ready?"

"Right. Of course. Sorry." His face heated and he strode down the path to Will. A quick word to the musician and the beautiful strains of the notes lifted into the air. Mai, Hannah and Kit walked down the aisle and after a tiny pause, Fleur walked into view arm-in-arm with her father.

Will's eyes were wide as if not wanting to miss a thing and his smile covered his face, happiness radiating from him.

Tears pricked Elijah's eyes as he saw the same joy reflected on Fleur's face. That's what he wanted. Love, happiness, acceptance.

He scanned the audience and found Jamie sitting next to his family and Lewis. Jamie smiled and Elijah's heart expanded even further.

In the front row, Will's mother was already dabbing her eyes with a tissue.

Fleur reached Will and Elijah paid attention to the ceremony, handing over the rings at the right moment and after the celebrant pronounced them married, he cheered along with the others. While Will and Fleur signed the marriage certificate and greeted the guests, he helped to pack up the chairs. The guests would go inside to the function room for drinks while the bridal party photos were being taken. He glanced at the gathering clouds. Hopefully they'd have time before it rained.

"Need a hand?" Jamie asked.

"You can stand there and look pretty for me," Elijah joked. Thanks to the bridal party, the chairs were almost packed away.

"You're looking handsome enough for the both of us." Jamie brushed Elijah's back.

A thrill shot through him. It was hard to keep his emotions in check when Jamie was looking so damned hot and saying nice things. To keep things light, he blew Jamie a kiss. The sunlight dimmed and Elijah glanced up. Darker clouds were blowing in. He moved over to the photographer. "Do you want me to hurry the receiving line along?"

She pursed her lips. "Can you round up the bridal party?" she asked. "I can get a few photos of the bridesmaids and groomsmen first and by then Fleur and Will should be finished."

Elijah nodded and a few minutes later he was posing for photos. The photographer was friendly, encouraging them to smile and making jokes. Will and Fleur joined them and they laughed together as they took photos around the garden with the wild ocean as a backdrop.

"We should get a photo with all the guys," Will said. "Since we all look pretty good."

"I'll find them," Elijah said and ran off to round them up. The clouds were definitely gathering and lowering.

A few minutes later he was posing next to his friends with the bridesmaids and Olivia watching.

"Come on, Adam, smile," Olivia called.

Elijah glanced at the scowl on Adam's face. Oh. Having her there had to be difficult for him, had to remind him of a day he never talked about. "I know it's hard," Elijah whispered in his ear. "But try to smile for Fleur and Will's sake."

Adam let out a shaky breath.

"Imagine Olivia naked," Elijah suggested. "Pretend she's the one you want to hook up with."

"Not helping," Adam growled.

Kim laughed. "I'd smile before Kit makes you."

Elijah grinned. Kit's bark was worse than her bite but Adam was always wary around her. Probably because she was also married to his boss.

Jamie tugged him closer and murmured, "When photos are done, think I can get a few minutes with you?"

"I think we can work something out." He brushed a kiss against Jamie's lips, keeping it light. The clouds opened and rain fell in thick waves.

They all ran inside, laughing and shrieking. Now maybe he could have a minute with Jamie, thank him properly for fetching the speech. He grabbed Jamie's hand as Fleur said, "I guess that means the photos are done. Let's get everyone seated for lunch."

Damn. Jamie was MC which meant he needed to make the announcement.

"Later," Jamie whispered and strode up to the lectern to do his thing.

Chapter 13

From where Elijah sat at the bridal table, he could see everyone. Empty plates and half-filled wine glasses littered the tables and people mingled, catching up before dessert was served. He could relax now that his speech was done. Rosa and Harold were introducing Lewis to Mai's sisters and Hannah's grandparents were chatting to Fleur's father. Jeremy and Kim were deep in conversation, probably about the football. The only person who didn't look happy was Adam. He sat next to Olivia scowling deeply while she spoke to him. That wouldn't do. Elijah placed his cloth napkin on the table and stood. "I'll be right back," he told Will.

He made his way towards Adam and arrived as Olivia said, "But you must know what happened to Ian."

Elijah winced and put a hand on the back of both their chairs. "Did you enjoy lunch?"

The relief on Adam's face was evident.

Olivia frowned briefly before smiling. "Yes, it was lovely."

"Great. Can I have a word, Olivia?" He gestured for her to follow him.

Elijah walked away from the tables so they wouldn't be overheard. What was the best way to address this?

"No one seems to want to talk about what happened to my cousin," Olivia said.

Right, so being direct would work. "Cut Adam some slack. He's still dealing with what happened that day."

She narrowed her eyes. "And my family and I aren't?"

He held out a placating hand. "I understand you're grieving, but so is Adam. He killed someone."

Her face paled. "Ian?"

Elijah shook his head quickly. "No, honey. He killed the man who shot Ian."

"Good." She glanced to where Adam stared off into space.

Elijah took a deep breath. "Listen, I understand you want answers, but I don't know if there are any easy ones. Lincoln might be able to help." He pointed the sergeant out to her. "But everyone would be grateful if you left your questions for another day, so we can enjoy our friends getting married."

Her face fell. "You're right. I'm sorry." She swallowed. "It's just Ian was like a brother to me, and no one can explain how he got mixed up with drugs in the first place."

Elijah squeezed her hand. "Sometimes there are no easy explanations."

"All right. I won't ask any more questions today," she promised. "But you said Lincoln can help?"

"He's the sergeant in charge at the police station. He was there the day Ian was shot. He was shot as well."

Olivia placed a hand over her mouth. "Oh. OK. Thanks for telling me something."

"It's fine, honey. Enjoy the rest of the wedding."

Elijah returned to the bridal table. "Is everything all

right?" Will asked.

Olivia leaned towards Adam and his face no longer looked like it was carved in stone. He glanced to Elijah and nodded his thanks.

"Yeah, it's fine," Elijah answered. He would have to stage an intervention with Adam. He hated seeing his friend so miserable.

Jamie announced dessert was about to be served and he settled back to enjoy it.

But he'd keep an eye on Adam.

After the meal and the speeches, it was time for dancing. Elijah made the rounds of the function room, making sure everyone was having a good time. A few people, like Olivia, didn't know many others, and he didn't want them to feel left out. He needn't have worried about Olivia. She was tearing up the dance floor with the musketeers. Adam was across the other side of the room talking with Jeremy and Nicholas, but his gaze often drifted to her. It was a shame what happened to Ian stood between them.

Elijah kept his eye on Jamie, looking for an opportunity for them to sneak off. Jamie was currently chatting to Will and Kim so maybe Elijah could interrupt him.

"Elijah!" A hand grabbed his arm. Will's mother pulled out the seat next to her. "Can you tell me some more stories about Will?"

The hopeful expression on her face had him taking a seat. "Sure." He was happy to assuage the worries of a woman who lived thousands of kilometres away from her youngest child. He started with the story about the day he answered Will's ad for a roommate and finally finished with the story of Will's nickname. "He came home from the motocross to tell me Kit had given him the nickname 'Captain' shortened from Captain Planet. He was so chuffed."

Will's mother smiled. "I can see how happy he is," she said. "He was so shy, I never imagined he would have so many friends." She brushed away a tear. "Thank you for being such a good friend to my Will."

Elijah's heart expanded and he hugged her. "It's my pleasure. He's been good to me as well."

Mai's mother came and introduced herself to Will's mum. "I wanted you to know we consider Will part of the family. He married one of my daughter's best friends, and we'll be here for him if he needs us."

Will's mother dabbed her eyes again as Elijah stood up to let Bian take his seat. This town was so supportive, why didn't Jamie see it?

Someone tapped his shoulder and he found Jamie behind him. "May I have this dance?"

The music had slowed, playing a dreamy love song. Elijah slid his hand into Jamie's. "With pleasure."

On the dance floor, Jamie pulled him close and they swayed to the tune.

"You've been busy," Jamie said. "I didn't think I'd get a chance to dance with you." His fingers brushed Elijah's side.

"I wanted to make sure people were having a good time. It can be lonely if you don't know many people."

Jamie pulled him closer and brushed a kiss against his lips. "It sounds like you know from experience."

Elijah shrugged. "I've been the new guy almost my whole life. In Europe it was a little easier. Staying in backpacker hostels meant everyone was open to meeting new people, but at some schools I was the kid eating his lunch on the bench alone." Not a time he liked to remember.

Jamie pulled back to look at Elijah. "It's hard to

imagine you not being the gregarious, gorgeous man you are today."

"It wasn't until high school that I found my groove." He placed his cheek against Jamie's. "I'd watched a show with a gay couple in it and I finally felt connected, like I understood who I was. I wanted to have no fear, have their take-me-as-I-am attitude, so that's what I became."

"Are you happy?"

"Right now I am, honey." He ran his hand over Jamie's back, pulled him a little closer.

"Let's find a quiet corner," Jamie murmured.

Part of his anatomy perked up as Elijah mentally scanned the restaurant for somewhere secluded. It was raining outside and the main restaurant was full of diners. Nowhere he could get his hands on Jamie the way he wanted to. Not unless they sneaked out to his car and necked on the back seat.

The idea had merit.

The music changed to an upbeat pop song and he stepped back. "Let's go outside."

Before he'd taken more than two steps off the dance floor, Fleur stopped Jamie. "We're going to do the bouquet toss," she said. "Can you announce it?"

Damn it.

To Jamie's credit he smiled and said, "Sure, Flower." He squeezed Elijah's hand and headed to the lectern.

Finally Fleur and Will left and the guests went home. Elijah worked with the bridal party to gather the leftover flowers, decorations and cake to take home. The tension in his chest eased. The wedding was over, Will and Fleur were happy, his job was done.

As Elijah took a last look around the venue to ensure he had everything, Jamie said, "Need a lift?"

Adam had been his backup plan, but this was much, much better. "Yes, please."

"I won't wait up," Adam said, his tone dry.

Elijah grinned and followed Jamie, running out into the rain that had settled in for the afternoon, and to his car.

The second the doors closed, and they were cocooned in the small space, Elijah pulled Jamie towards him. Their lips met.

Passion ignited and his fatigue dropped away, energised by the spark of Jamie's heat.

A car horn beeped behind them and Elijah drew back. "I've been wanting to do that all day."

Jamie let out a breath. "Me too. Want to go to my place?"

"Yeah." Better than combusting in the car park— and less likely to be arrested for indecent exposure.

On the drive back to Blackbridge, Elijah checked the side mirrors for a black ute. Being at the wedding had protected him, but he was out in the open again.

No cars were behind them.

Jamie said, "Your speech was great."

The fields outside the window were green and damp and the light was slowly fading. "Thanks. I appreciate you fetching it." He brought Jamie's hand up to his mouth and kissed it.

"My pleasure."

He was hoping for all sorts of pleasure with Jamie, not all of them carnal. "Do you want to go out to lunch tomorrow?"

"Sure. Where?"

"The River Café." It was a small café on the river foreshore.

"All right. Don't you have to work?"

"Not until milking in the afternoon. Kit's given us

both the day off. She wants a day to bask in the glow of Fleur getting married." Which meant he had almost twenty-four hours free to do whatever he wanted with Jamie. And he wanted to do a lot. No need to wait for the fortnight to be over. They'd kissed publicly, their friends and the SES volunteers knew they were a couple and hell, if Shirley and Barbara knew, then the whole town probably did. Tonight wasn't for holding back.

Jamie turned into Hideaway Retreat and finally parked in front of a large silver shed. "Here we are."

Huh. He knew Jamie was living in a shed, but he'd been expecting a little more than this. He should have suggested they go back to his place—though at least here they would be alone and not have to worry about making Adam blush.

Jamie unlocked the small door next to the huge roller door and pushed it open. He flicked on a light switch and bright, fluorescent lights flooded the area. A tiny kitchenette was on the right-hand side and next to it was a round dining table. The open-plan feel continued to the double couch, coffee table and television, with a couple of bookshelves partitioning the bedroom from the main area. A ride-on lawn mower along with a bunch of gardening and painting gear was located on the far side of the shed and the whole place had a dusty, grassy, oily smell to it.

No photos or knick-knacks, and boxes were piled to one side. He'd stayed in dingier places than this though, and at least the bed was queensize.

"It's not much but it's home for now," Jamie said, walking to the kitchen. "Do you want a drink?"

Elijah shook his head. "How long are you planning to stay here?"

Jamie shrugged. "Depends on how long it takes to find a place." He strode over and slipped his arms around Elijah's waist. "You look incredible in your suit, but all day I've been thinking about the ways I can get you out of it." He ran his hands up Elijah's chest and eased the jacket off his shoulders.

A sentiment Elijah could get behind. He smiled and unbuttoned Jamie's shirt. "We were interrupted last time."

"No one should disturb us out here." He threw Elijah's jacket over the back of the sofa.

Yeah, it was an advantage being this far out of town. Elijah tugged Jamie's shirt out of his pants and finished unbuttoning it, spreading it open and sliding his hands over Jamie's warm skin. For a teacher who didn't work out, he was still in fine shape. He pushed the shirt and jacket onto the floor, and pulled Jamie closer so he could taste him.

Lips and tongues met, clashing, battling. He'd waited a decade for this. There would be time for slow, but not this first time. He was too desperate to wait, too desperate to taste Jamie and make him moan. He pushed Jamie back, walking them both towards the bed as Jamie unbuckled Elijah's belt.

A second later Jamie gripped Elijah's cock. Elijah groaned, closing his eyes to take in the sensation of Jamie's strong hand around him. Better than his fantasies.

"You're so hot," Jamie growled in his ear.

Elijah closed his eyes as shivers rippled up and down his body. He fumbled for Jamie's belt, his fingers not working the way they were supposed to. His brain couldn't function while Jamie stroked him. He pushed Jamie's hand away, finally managing to undo Jamie's pants. He shoved them to the floor and pushed Jamie back onto the bed. Quickly he rid himself of his own clothes as Jamie kicked off his shoes.

He took a moment to admire the man lying naked in front of him.

Sensational.

So many hard lines and all that smooth skin. Jamie's cock stood to attention, prominent and begging to be sucked. Elijah licked his lips as he climbed onto the bed over Jamie. "Did you ever fantasise about my lips on you?"

"Yes."

"Where?" He gazed at Jamie's erection. "There?"

"Yes."

Keeping his eyes on Jamie's, he licked the length of Jamie's warm, hard cock. Jamie's eyes rolled back. "Oh, yes."

Elijah wrapped his hand around it and pumped as he tasted and licked and sucked. This was his fantasy come to life. Jamie had always been in the starring role. Now though, Jamie was all man, and there were no fumbling or awkward moments. Just hot, fast sex.

"Stop." Jamie pulled him up the bed and then flipped them. Suddenly Elijah was on the bottom and Jamie's hand was on him. "I need to taste you." Jamie moved down the bed and his mouth covered Elijah's cock.

Elijah moaned. Sweet heaven above, the things he did with his mouth. Elijah clenched his muscles to avoid thrusting. He wasn't going to last. He'd been waiting for this for too long.

"Jamie," he gasped. "Together."

Jamie slid back up the bed and kissed him hard. They gripped each other's cocks and stroked them hard.

Oh, this was bliss. Elijah threw his head back as both of them came.

***

It took a moment for Jamie's heart rate to decrease, his breathing to normalise. He'd known it would be good. Elijah's groan sent a shot of lust through him again.

"Oh, honey, why did we wait so long?" Elijah asked.

A twinge of guilt swept through him. "That's on me." He brushed a kiss against Elijah's cheek and stood to clean up.

Elijah sat up. "I didn't mean it like that."

Jamie smiled at him. "I know." But it was true nonetheless. He handed Elijah the tissues. "Are you hungry?"

Elijah studied him. "Depends on what you're offering." He smirked.

"Food before other things." Jamie pulled on some track pants, grinning. "I can whip up some pasta."

"Sounds great. I was too distracted to eat much at the wedding." He pulled a jumper and another pair of track pants from the bookshelf doubling as Jamie's wardrobe, and dressed.

Elijah's easy comfort, making himself at home hit Jamie right in the heart. He remembered feeling slightly uneasy the first time Sandra had slipped on one of his jumpers but not now.

As if he'd heard Jamie's thoughts, Elijah froze. "Is this all right?" He indicated the clothes.

"Yeah. Help yourself."

"Why are you looking at me so weirdly?"

"I'm not."

"Yes, you are, but I can't tell if it's a good weird or a bad weird."

Jamie chuckled. "It's a good weird then. I like that you're comfortable here." He took Elijah's hand and led him into the kitchen.

Elijah tilted his head. "It's funny, isn't it? I feel as if we've been together for more than a few days."

"Maybe because we've been watching each other for months." Jamie got a few things out of the fridge for the pasta sauce.

"And we were friends first." Elijah picked up the knife. "What should I chop?"

Jamie explained the recipe and they worked side-by-side, preparing the meal.

"I think Will's mum feels a lot better about Will moving here," Elijah said. "Bian chatted to her, told her he was part of the musketeer family."

Jamie smiled. "I saw you talking to her." And pretty much every other guest at the wedding.

"She wanted the inside scoop on what Will's been up to." Elijah laughed. "She's lovely."

"What about Adam and Olivia?"

Elijah raised his eyebrows. "Were you watching me, Mr Zanetti?"

"I couldn't keep my eyes off you." No matter where he was, his focus kept coming back to Elijah. He'd been too far away.

Elijah sighed and placed a hand on his heart.

Jamie slid his hand around Elijah's waist, turned him so they faced each other. "You've always captured my attention." His lips brushed Elijah's, tasting him.

"You are such a smooth talker," Elijah murmured, kissing him back.

"Only to you." He'd never felt such an urge, a gut deep need for anyone before. He slid his hand lower, cupped Elijah's butt, pulling him closer.

"Careful, or we'll never end up eating."

"I have an appetite for something else."

Elijah chuckled wickedly. "I like the way your mind works, but I'm going to need a few minutes." He kissed Jamie deeply, his tongue teasing and Jamie groaned as Elijah turned back to the bench. "You were asking about Adam and Olivia?"

Jamie cleared his throat and adjusted himself, a smile playing on his lips. "Yeah. Adam didn't look very happy sitting next to her, but stared at her the whole time she was dancing."

"She's Ian Demidenko's cousin."

It took Jamie a second to make the connection. "Oh. How's Adam dealing with that?"

"He's not," Elijah said. "I'm going to stage an intervention. He has to address what happened because it's eating him up."

It was nice Elijah cared. "Do you need a hand?"

"Maybe. I want to talk to Lincoln first, find out what counselling Adam's had."

Jamie nodded. "Lincoln would have offered it all, probably would have forced him to go to at least one session. He's been taking Adam to the shooting range." He switched on the stove and heated a pot.

"Do you think I should visit the Pattons?" Elijah asked.

The change of subject and Elijah's switch in tone made Jamie look up. "Why?"

"To express my sympathies, ask if they need help with anything." His voice was low and his focus stayed on the food he chopped.

Jamie took the knife from him. "What happened to Richard wasn't your fault."

Elijah nodded. "But it can't be easy for them. They'll need to keep the winery running and plan the funeral and deal with everything."

"You are the kindest man I know." Jamie kissed him. "If it will make you feel better, you should ask, but don't be surprised if they say no."

"Yeah." Elijah sighed. "I don't think they'll welcome help from me."

"From anyone," Jamie corrected. "What was it like working for them?" He put the pasta on to boil.

Elijah shrugged. "It was a job. Mark was obnoxious whenever he was there and Kay was pretty abrupt, but as long as I did my work they were happy."

"I'm glad Kit gave you a job."

"Me too."

Jamie stirred the sauce. "What made you come back to Blackbridge?" he asked. "You could have settled anywhere."

Elijah opened the fridge and got out a bottle of white wine. He held it up and Jamie nodded, handing him a bottle opener. "Blackbridge was where I embraced who I was." He opened the bottle. "I discovered my love of farming and I decided to hell with what people thought of me, I was going to be myself." He handed Jamie a glass. "I wanted to come back, figure out if I still felt the same way, and with my parents still living here, it was easy." He sipped his wine and smirked. "Then I noticed you were still here and it made it a much more attractive option to stay."

Jamie smiled. "I remember you watching the cricket and joining us at the pub afterwards. I asked Will about you."

Elijah groaned. "I know. Will told me and I couldn't decide if it was a good thing or a bad thing that you remembered me."

"Why wouldn't it be a good thing?"

"I wasn't at my best in high school."

"You were pretty amazing to me." Jamie tested the pasta and Elijah ran a hand down his back with a sigh.

"Such a wasted opportunity."

Jamie pulled him close. "We won't waste any more time." Need throbbed through him, not just sexual, but emotional as well. Something as simple as making dinner together filled a hole in Jamie he hadn't known he'd had. He'd been stupid to let his fear rule him.

Elijah kissed him long and hard and stepped back. "We should eat before dinner burns."

Yeah. Good idea. He dished up and they sat next to each other at the small round table. Elijah sipped his wine. "So are you really OK with public displays of affection now?" he asked. "I mean around town and not only with our friends."

Jamie's stomach still clenched, but it was easier to ignore. He covered Elijah's hand with his. "I can't guarantee something won't trigger my anxiety, but I want to be with you, E. I'm so damned happy you seem to like me."

"No seem about it, honey. I like you a lot." Elijah kissed his hand. "Let's go to dinner at Kim's restaurant on Thursday. Celebrate properly."

Jamie nodded. "I'd like that." And the more they went out in public together, the more he'd get used to it, and hopefully his anxiety would disappear for good.

They finished dinner and Elijah cleared the plates turned on the taps and started to fill the sink. Jamie turned off the taps, slipped his hand under the waistband of Elijah's pants and squeezed his butt. "How about we leave the dishes for the morning?"

Elijah grinned. "I can deal with that."

Good. Jamie dragged him back to the bedroom.

Chapter 14

The heavy feeling of satisfaction suffused Elijah's body after he'd orgasmed again. This connection between him and Jamie made sex so much better than it ever had been before. "I might never move again."

Jamie laughed, propping himself on his elbow, deliciously naked. Outside, thunder rumbled across the sky. He glanced up. "You should stay the night," he said. "It's far too stormy to go out." As he spoke, rain pinged on the metal roof.

Elijah grinned. "You've convinced me." He climbed under the thick quilt on Jamie's bed, his body cooling already. Jamie joined him and they sat next to each other with the quilt pulled up around their chins.

Jamie laughed. "I feel like a kid on a sleepover."

Elijah's heart squeezed. "I never did that."

"What, never?"

Elijah shrugged. "Perpetual new kid, remember?" Even at the ag college he hadn't been invited to secret after dark get-togethers.

"If I could go back to high school, I'd invite you over."

Elijah grinned. "I can imagine what our sleepovers

would entail."

"I think we'd have blown both of our minds."

"It's not our minds that would have been blown," Elijah said.

Jamie's laugh was full of delight and it warmed Elijah, made him feel good about himself.

"Tell me about your time in Europe." Jamie curled into him, stroking his chest.

Elijah closed his eyes, enjoying the touch. "What do you want to know?"

"Where did you go? What did you see? Why did you go?"

"Oh, the why is easy. I wanted to see what the world could offer me." He shifted, wrapping an arm around Jamie's shoulders. "I'd lived in so many small towns, I wanted to experience city life and wanted to spread my wings. Australia felt so confining, as if I'd never get out."

Jamie's touch stopped. "But you came back."

"Yeah. Turns out, there's no place like home." He kissed Jamie's head. "I started in London which was a no brainer. We speak the same language and because Dad's originally from the UK it meant I could get an English passport. Made travelling in Europe a hell of a lot easier."

"So, you worked in London?"

He nodded. "Got a job in a bar, met some people, found an apartment."

"Were you happy?"

"For a while." It had been such an adventure. "I worked pretty solidly for about a year, saved money, got to know my regulars. When I wasn't working, I went to matinees at West End, but the bar hours weren't conducive to a social life. I'd work most of the night and sleep during the day. That's when I switched to retail, selling clothes in a boutique."

"Is that where you got your sense of style from?"

"In part. My boss took me under his wing, introduced me to the gay scene. I met Alex through him."

Jamie shifted to look at him. "Alex?"

"My bastard ex, who turned out to be married."

"Oh. Want to talk about it?"

Elijah sighed. He wanted Jamie to know everything about him, which included the bad and embarrassing bits. "Alex was about five years older than me. He worked in finance, always wore a suit and was just so into me—it was amazing. He called me the day after we met. I guess my boss gave him my number, because aside from a few intense looks at dinner, he hadn't said anything to me." That should have been a sign. "We met for coffee in my neighbourhood and within an hour we were at my place fucking."

Jamie stiffened and Elijah stroked his hair. "I was so young, so desperate for affection. Despite having a bunch of people I went out with, I didn't have any close friends and Alex became a regular part of my life. He'd come over every Wednesday night for dinner and we'd talk and have sex. Looking back on it, I realise it was more sex, less talking as we went on, but the pretence of a relationship was what I needed."

"Didn't you ever go out together?"

"Alex was adamant that he didn't do public displays of affection. He never knew when he might run into someone at work, and they couldn't know he was gay. So we'd go to the movies or out to dinner but it was a rare occasion." He shrugged. "It felt so secretive and I loved it. Loved having something special that only we knew about."

Jamie relaxed. "So what happened?"

Elijah told him about the night at the theatre.

Jamie sat up. "You fell off a balcony?"

Elijah nodded, feeling the familiar nausea in his stomach. "Luckily I only broke my arm, but I've been crap with heights ever since."

Jamie pulled him into his arms, kissed him slowly. "You are incredibly brave."

Elijah's heart expanded but he shook his head. "Not really. I'm going to tell Morgan not to put me on roofs in future."

"That's sensible. I'll help you with it, if you want. We could do some trust exercises. I'll catch you always." He brushed the hair from Elijah's forehead, his expression so earnest.

Elijah's heart softened and fell. It was impossible not to love Jamie with that declaration. He ran his thumb over Jamie's bottom lip and kissed him, pouring all his love into the kiss. They were both breathless when Elijah pulled away. "Thanks, honey."

"Any time, especially if it gets me thanked like that." Jamie kissed him again and asked, "So what happened to Alex?"

Elijah rolled his eyes. "The bastard visited me the next Wednesday as if nothing had changed. Swore he thought I realised he was married, said I could never be more than a hookup because I was too much of a Twink."

Jamie growled. "Bastard. You're perfect the way you are."

Elijah closed his eyes briefly. Yeah, Jamie said all the right things. "It took me a while to realise that. I left London, spent some time in Edinburgh, Cardiff and Dublin before heading to the continent." He smiled. "My last job was on a hops farm in Germany and I remembered how much I loved farming. When I decided to come home, I had to come here."

"I'm so glad you did."

"Me too. So tell me what you've been up to in the last eight years."

Jamie smiled. "I guess we've got all night."

***

Jamie rolled over and bumped into a warm body. His eyes flashed open and in the dim light he recognised Elijah's sleeping form. He smiled. They hadn't gone to sleep until way past midnight.

Their conversation had ranged from places they wanted to visit, to tales of their childhoods, to their deepest hopes and dreams. After Elijah had told him about Alex, he'd vowed right then not to be an asshole anymore. He was proud to be dating Elijah. He'd never had deep and meaningful conversations with Sandra, ever. But last night, in the dark, he and Elijah had shared their souls. He wanted the world to know they were together, and he cared for a man. He wouldn't let his fear of judgement stop him from claiming Elijah as his. He wouldn't give Elijah any reason to doubt he wanted him and only him.

He slid his hand over Elijah's waist, pulling him closer.

Elijah yawned. "Is it morning already?"

"Looks like it." He kissed the back of Elijah's neck. It had been months since he'd last woken next to someone. It was nice to snuggle in and feel comforted. "Are you hungry?"

"Mmm." Elijah turned to face him. "We could do brunch rather than lunch."

Unwanted nerves attacked him and he pushed them aside. He was bound to run into people he knew, so he'd just have to suck it up. His fears were irrational.

He ran his hand down Elijah's body and stroked his cock. "We might have a bit of time before the café opens."

Elijah pressed his hips into Jamie's hand. "I think you might be right."

Then Elijah kissed him and Jamie forgot about his worries.

An hour later however, brunch was firmly on his mind. He drove into Blackbridge and scanned the river foreshore for a parking spot. Every man and his dog were out today, probably because the bureau had forecast no rain for the morning. "Will we get a table?" The River Café was the most popular eating place after Mai's bakery.

"Let's try."

Jamie found a carpark and together they walked inside. The noise of people chatting and the scent of freshly ground coffee assaulted his senses. The dark interior was all wood, from the floors to the tables and chairs and the counter. Even the wallpaper looked like planks of wood.

Elijah smiled at the waitress. "Have you got a table for two?"

She scanned the café. "Yes. Give me a second to clear it."

"Perfect."

Jamie glanced around. Barbara sat with her mother Gladys, Mark Patton was flirting with a woman who was clearly not Alyse, and Patricia sat with a couple of female friends.

The waitress led them to a table on the far side of the café and he made a conscious effort to relax his muscles. No one cared what he was up to.

As soon as the waitress left, Elijah said, "I can't

believe Mark is here with another woman. He doesn't appear upset about his father dying."

"No." Though people grieved in different ways. "Maybe she's the funeral director."

Elijah raised an eyebrow as he perused the menu. "At least he's not following me."

Jamie had forgotten about that with the joy of the wedding and being with Elijah. "We'll keep a look out today."

Elijah scowled and nodded.

Jamie slipped his hand into Elijah's. "I'll keep you safe."

"Hi, Jamie." The bright greeting made him jump. Patricia stood next to their table, smiling at him. "It's a shame you missed drinks on Friday night. It was a lot of fun."

Shit. He'd forgotten about Patricia's suggestion they see each other over the holiday. "I was at a bucks' party," Jamie said. "How's your holiday going?" Elijah ran a soothing thumb across the back of his hand, but Patricia didn't seem to notice, her eyes on Jamie.

"It's great. I thought maybe we could go for coffee some time." She tucked her hair behind her ear, hope in her eyes.

Crap.

Elijah cleared his throat and when Patricia glanced at him, he made a show of looking at their joined hands.

Subtle.

Jamie had to say something. "Patricia, this is Elijah, my…"

"Boyfriend," Elijah supplied.

Patricia stepped back, her face turning red. "Oh." Her hand fluttered around her chest. "You never said…" Then she frowned. "Isn't Lewis staying with you this holiday?"

Huh? What did that have to do with anything? "No, he's staying with my parents."

"But you live with them too." Horror crossed her face. "Lewis was crying when he left your office." Her voice had raised and a couple of people looked over. "You were touching him."

Jamie lost his breath. What the hell? His mind whirled. "What? When did you see that?"

"Before school ended. He was in your arms."

Crap. She must have walked past at the wrong moment. "Lewis hugged me when I found him a place to stay."

"That's what you say." She hesitated and then shook her head, determination on her face. "I can't let this lie. Not now I know you're gay."

More of the café had grown silent. Anger simmered in his belly and he kept his voice low. "What the hell are you insinuating, Patricia?"

She waved her hands. "You have a gay student staying with you and I saw him crying when he left your office. I have to call Noel."

Jamie gritted his teeth. "Noel knows everything. He approved it. And Lewis isn't staying with me, he's staying with my parents. I don't live with them any longer."

"Does Noel know you're gay?"

This could not be happening. Nausea stirred the anger around his stomach. "My sexuality is no one's business but my own."

Elijah growled low in his throat. "Noel already knows Lewis is working with me during the day. I don't think he'll have a problem with Jamie's sexuality."

Horror filled Patricia's face. "I have to go."

Jamie swore under his breath as she walked away, dread filling his stomach. It wouldn't take much for her suspicion to spread. It wouldn't matter what the truth was.

"She can't be serious," Elijah said.

Jamie snatched his hand away. "She is." He got to his feet, feeling all eyes on him, his reputation, his career crumbling before him. He strode after Patricia, who had stopped to speak with her friends. "Patricia, wait." The bell rang above the door as someone walked in, loud in the otherwise silence.

She stopped, her lips pinched together. "What?"

"Nothing is going on between Lewis and me. I was helping him out."

One of her friends coughed and it sounded a lot like she said, "With sex."

He ignored her.

Patricia shook her head. "Noel never would have approved a female student staying with a male teacher."

He couldn't get through to her. "Lewis is staying with my parents."

"And working with your boyfriend."

Jamie inhaled to contain his anger. "Do you go around fantasising about your male students? I sure as hell don't."

She sniffed. "They're children."

"Exactly."

"But homosexuals don't have the same morals."

His breath left him as the café went silent. Elijah leapt to his feet, his face red with fury, and right next to him were Kit and Lincoln. Lincoln's expression was dark, but Kit was primed for explosion.

Jamie wanted to duck for cover. This was not going to end well. "Kit—"

"Who the hell do you think you are?" Kit demanded, storming over to the table. "How dare you say Jamie and Elijah have no morals? They are two of the most generous, thoughtful and loving men I know."

Patricia's face screwed up. "Who are you?"

"I'm the person Lewis is working for over the holiday. Nothing bad will happen to him."

"How can you guarantee it?"

"Because I know both of these men," Kit retorted.

Patricia opened her mouth to speak as Lincoln placed a hand on Kit's shoulder.

"Those are very serious insinuations you're making," he said. "I would suggest you have firm proof before you go around repeating them and ruining the lives of two men." The stare he gave her could have frozen a lake.

The tension in Jamie's chest loosened a little.

"Well you'd say that about your brother," Patricia said.

She wasn't going to drop it. She had a defiant expression on her face he'd seen before.

A chair scraped back and Barbara stood. "I don't understand exactly what's going on here, but I'll speak for both Jamie and Elijah's characters. I've never known nicer young men."

Elijah turned to her and shaped his hands into a love heart.

"They're poofs, they're probably all fucking like rabbits." Of course Mark had to have his say.

Elijah whirled on him. "We all see you here with your new floozy rather than being at home supporting your grieving family, so you can shut the fuck up."

Mark growled. "You'll get yours."

Jamie flinched, but his attention was on the woman in front of him.

Patricia glanced around the café and realised she had very little support. "I'm still calling Noel." She walked out.

Jamie exhaled as Lincoln said, "Show's over, people."

Slowly the buzz of conversation returned to the room.

"What was that all about?" Lincoln asked.

Jamie's head throbbed and his limbs shook. "Can we go outside?" He didn't wait for an answer. He strode outside, stopping to take a deep breath of the cool air. Patricia was across the car park getting into her car.

Elijah slipped his hand around Jamie's waist and Jamie resisted the urge to step away from him. It wasn't his fault.

"Are you OK?" Elijah asked.

Jamie shook his head. How many people in town would side with Patricia, believe what she said? How would this affect Lewis? Rumours spread fast. Would he be trusted as a teacher any longer? Would they fire him?

"Who was that bitch?" Kit asked.

"Patricia's a teacher at the ag college," Jamie told her.

"What happened?" Lincoln asked, already in cop mode.

Jamie didn't want to talk about it. Not while his head was still spinning. He motioned for Elijah to tell them and closed his eyes. This was bad. It would only take a couple of days before the whole town would be talking about it. It didn't matter what the truth was, people wouldn't look at him the same way. He needed to call Noel, speak to him before Patricia got into his ear.

He walked away from the others and dialled his boss.

"Jamie, is something wrong?"

Jamie swallowed hard. "You're going to get a phone call from Patricia."

"What about?"

"Me." He explained what had happened.

Noel sighed. "I have to ask whether there's something between you and Lewis."

"There's nothing. I dropped him off at my parents' house on Friday and I saw him yesterday at Fleur's wedding, but that's it. I wasn't planning to see him on the holidays except when I went to my parents' for dinner."

"Thanks for letting me know. I'll talk to Patricia."

Jamie hung up. At least his principal was a reasonable man.

"How are you coping?"

He turned to his brother. "I'll deal." Kit and Elijah still heatedly discussed Patricia.

"People will forget about it," Lincoln said.

Jamie raised his eyebrows. "You know they won't." A taint like this never went away.

With all his concerns about how the town would react, he'd never once considered this scenario.

And it was far worse than he'd ever imagined. His chest squeezed even tighter, he couldn't breathe. "I need to go." He couldn't fight the urge to run. "Can you take Elijah home?"

He ran for his car.

Chapter 15

Tension vibrated through Elijah's body. The nerve of the woman! She obviously had no idea who Jamie was. To even think such a horrific thing, let alone say it out loud… This was Jamie's nightmare come true. Lincoln walked over to him.

"Where's Jamie?" Elijah glanced behind him as Jamie backed out of the car park. His stomach dropped. Jamie had left without him. Hurt stabbed him hard. He took two steps towards the road, but he was too late. Jamie was gone.

"He needs some space," Lincoln said. "We'll give you a lift home."

Kit squeezed his arm. "Don't feel bad. He likes to work through issues on his own—he always has."

Of course he felt bad. Jamie was upset and he didn't want Elijah's help. After last night, after all the things they'd shared, he'd thought he would be the one Jamie would turn to. Maybe it hadn't meant as much to Jamie as it had to Elijah. "I'll walk home." Clear his head too.

Lincoln stopped him. "You still shouldn't be alone."

Elijah glared at him. "Mark's in the café and Henk's guy isn't likely to show his face in town. I need air, so unless you want to follow me, I'm going." In his current mood, if anyone tried to mess with him, they'd see a much different side of Elijah.

Lincoln gritted his teeth, glanced at Kit to back him. "I don't like it, Elijah."

"Kit, go and enjoy having lunch with your husband for a change. I can take care of myself."

"They have guns, Elijah," Kit hissed.

His skin crawled and he exhaled. "Fine. If Mark leaves, call me and I'll hide somewhere until you can pick me up."

Kit sighed. "All right." She hugged him. "Don't let Jamie stew for long and text me when you get home."

"OK." He nodded to Lincoln and walked away from the foreshore.

He hugged his jacket around him, glad they'd stopped at his place so he could change before they'd gone to the café. The air was cool but fresh, and he inhaled the scent of wood smoke from people's chimneys. He cut through an alley and past the shops along the main streets. Normally on a day like today, when he had the whole day off, he would enjoy window shopping.

Jamie had left him there.

He pushed through the hurt to see it from Jamie's point of view. He'd feared coming out to the town, feared ridicule and disgust, but he'd never once mentioned fearing for his job. It had to have hit him hard. From their conversation last night, he knew how much Jamie loved teaching. This had to have shaken him to his core.

Elijah shook his head. So Jamie had gone back to what he did best—hiding.

The whole situation was messed up. Jamie had done everything to help Lewis, and he was being punished for it. And the irony was, if he'd been straight, this wouldn't have been an issue.

How could Patricia have been working with Jamie all year and seriously consider him to be a paedophile? Perhaps she was sore about being rejected. She'd come over to ask Jamie out, so maybe her embarrassment had stopped her from thinking things through. Not that it mattered. She'd said what she'd said, and enough people had heard for it to be all over town by tomorrow.

Some people would ignore it as gossip. But there'd be some who would feel cheated, some who would believe Jamie had lied to them and believe if he'd hidden his sexuality, he could be hiding other things as well.

Guilt swirled around his stomach, an unpleasant, nauseous feeling. He should have listened to Jamie's concerns and not been so defensive about their relationship.

No. That was bullshit. Anyone who believed the rumours could go to hell, but he wouldn't let them take Jamie with them. There had to be some way to stop the gossip before it took a hold.

But his mind was blank.

He strode past Mai's bakery as someone walked out, wafting delicious baked goodness smells with them.

They hadn't even had a chance to eat. Both dates had been interrupted before they'd even begun.

Was it a sign?

No. He wasn't superstitious.

He walked along the street where the SES depot was situated. The gates to the yard stood wide open, but the doors to the building were shut. Odd. The gates were only open when there was an incident or training. He checked his phone. No messages.

He entered the yard and tried the door to the office. Locked.

He walked around the building and came to a standstill. Huh. His blue hatchback was parked there, bonnet up, tyres missing and the number plate gone.

He peered in the window to find his thick red puffer jacket was still on the back seat. Swearing, he dialled the police station. Probably should put it on speed dial, since he'd called it so many times lately.

Under the bonnet he saw the ground below where bits of the engine had been removed. He scanned the yard but nothing moved. He was alone, whoever had done this was long gone. Still his skin crawled as he waited for someone to answer, and he kept scanning the area.

"I've found my car," he told Ryan.

"Where?"

"Behind the SES depot."

Ryan sighed. "We'll be right there."

Elijah hung up. At least whoever had stolen it had the courtesy to return it to where they'd taken it from. He frowned. But how had they got in? The gate should have been locked. He strode to the back door of the building and tested the handle.

Unlocked.

Hell no.

He backed away, running around the front to the gate. He should have listened to Lincoln's warnings. Then he wouldn't be here alone. This street wasn't used very often and it was silent, no one in sight at all.

The chain which normally closed the gate hung down, the padlock open, not cut. He didn't touch it in case the police wanted to fingerprint it, but he could use the chain as a weapon if he had to.

Not many people had a key; Morgan, Siobhan,

maybe a couple of the other section leaders.

But none were thieves. Siobhan had been on the callout with him and Morgan had been busy with his own house.

Maybe someone was framing Morgan. Whatever had been going on the night Elijah had stopped for a headlight globe couldn't be legal.

His phone rang, making him jump. Shit. Kit. "Hello?"

"Where are you? Why didn't you text me?"

He winced. "Sorry. I stopped at the SES depot because the gate was open. I found my car around the back."

"What?" She repeated the information to Lincoln.

"Ryan's on his way." As he said it a police car came down the street. "He and Adam have just arrived."

"Next time I'm not letting you go alone," Kit said.

Her willingness to protect him settled some of the tension in his muscles. "All right. You win. I've gotta go." He hung up as Ryan pulled in.

"Where is it?"

"Around the back," Elijah said. "The gate's been unlocked."

Ryan glanced at it. "Have you touched it?"

"No."

"We'll examine it in a minute." He parked outside the building and Elijah walked over to them.

"The back door of the building is unlocked as well," Elijah told Adam. "I tried both doors. When I saw the gate open, I thought we must have a call out."

"Stay here," Ryan said. "We'll check it out."

They went around the back and time slipped by slowly. Elijah stayed close to the car, not wanting to be an easy target in case someone burst out the front door, gun blazing.

He'd watched too many action films.

About five minutes later, footsteps crunched on the bitumen and Adam rounded the corner. "No one's inside, but someone's made a mess. Ryan's calling Morgan." This was Adam in cop mode. No smile, no emotion in his tone.

"Should I stick around?"

He nodded. "I need to take your statement." He gestured for Elijah to follow him and they walked around to where Ryan examined the car. He glanced up. "Are you sure it's yours?"

"I think so. My jacket's in the back."

"We'll run the vehicle identification number and go over it for evidence."

"What were you doing here?" Adam asked. "I thought you were with Jamie."

Elijah groaned as he remembered that mess. "I was." He told them about Patricia, and Jamie driving off.

"That sucks," Adam said.

Morgan arrived, pulling up next to the hatchback. "You found your car?"

"Yeah."

"Someone broke into the depot," Ryan told him. "We'll dust for prints and then you might want to call a few people in to help clean."

Morgan's face went dark. "They break anything?"

"I'm not sure. We'll need to take a closer look, but equipment is strewn everywhere."

Elijah's spirits dropped further. They were a volunteer organisation, existing only to help the public in times of need. Why would anyone want to destroy equipment they struggled to raise funds for?

"Can I go in?" Morgan asked.

Adam nodded. "Just don't touch anything."

Elijah followed them inside. The land cruisers sat in

their spot, but some of the heavy-duty shelving that lined the walls of the shed was empty, the tarps and ropes spread out over the concrete floor. The trailers that contained much of the equipment were still closed.

Not too bad.

Morgan shook his head and sighed. "I've got better things to do with my day than clean this mess."

"I'll do it," Elijah offered. "As soon as Ryan and Adam have finished investigating." By then hopefully Jamie had called and they could do it together.

Morgan studied him. "That would be great. Thanks."

They went back outside and Adam got the equipment out of the police car while Ryan spoke with Morgan. Then he turned to Elijah. "We'll be about an hour if you want to come back."

"All right." It wasn't far to walk home.

"I'll give you a lift," Morgan said.

"Thanks."

As they left the depot, Elijah bit his lip. This was his first chance to speak to Morgan alone since he'd seen the incident at his workshop. Maybe Morgan needed help. He cleared his throat. "Listen, Morgan it's none of my business, but you might want to talk to the police about what's going on."

Morgan glanced at him. "What are you talking about?"

This was awkward. "I stopped at your shop on Thursday night to get a new headlight globe. I saw a guy pointing a gun at you."

Silence.

Quickly he hurried on. "He might be behind this destruction."

Morgan pulled into Elijah's drive. "You saw that?"

He nodded, nerves jiggling in his chest. "I was going

to call the police, but the guy's accomplice pulled a gun on me. Threatened to harm my family if I told anyone."

"So you said nothing."

Elijah couldn't read his tone, but his senses were on high alert. "No. The guy scared the bejeezus out of me."

"Did you mention your theory to the police?"

"No. It's not my place," he lied. "I don't know what's going on."

"You're right. You don't. Those guys were drifters. They're long gone." Morgan stared at him as if daring him to disagree.

No way was Elijah mentioning the conversation he'd overheard at the winery. "Right. Good. I'm glad." He fumbled with the door handle. "Thanks for the lift. I'll see you at training."

He hurried to the front door as Morgan drove off. When he shut the door behind him, he sighed in relief.

Perhaps Morgan was in this deeper than he'd thought. He was definitely lying about the men being drifters.

Elijah groaned. He shouldn't have said anything.

Adam wouldn't be happy he'd opened his big mouth, but Elijah would tell him when he returned to the depot.

He wasn't in any rush to have another gun pointed at him.

***

Jamie drove with no real destination in mind. He had to get away from the café, away from Elijah, away from the whole situation.

What a clusterfuck.

What the hell was he going to do?

Should he wait until the town reacted or should he

make a statement? Either way people would read what they wanted from it.

He hit the steering wheel with his palm, frustration surging through him.

He loved being a teacher, loved educating students, learning about their lives, helping them navigate the world and hopefully setting them up so when they finished school, they had better skills to deal with what life threw at them.

Shit like he was dealing with now.

He turned towards the cheese factory and huffed out a breath. Without realising it, he'd headed home. But he shouldn't be here, not if Lewis was around. It would look like he'd run straight to him.

Crap.

He pulled up next to the garden shed which was a little distance from the house. His parents were probably at the factory today and Lewis might be with them. He hadn't been with Kit or Elijah.

He dialled his mother's number.

"Hi, love. What do you need?"

The warmth in her tone made him smile. "Can I borrow the bike? I need to go for a ride."

"Sure. What's wrong?"

He inhaled deeply. "I'll fill you in when I get back. Is Lewis with you?"

"Yes. He was interested in the cheese factory, so we pinched him from Kit for the day." She paused. "I'm here if you need to talk." Her concern was clear. "I love you."

Tears pricked his eyes. No matter what happened, he'd have her support. It comforted him.

He got the farm motorbike out of the shed. It was old, but his father kept it well-maintained. They didn't have a lot of property to ride it on, but Kit always let them use her place.

With that in mind, he started the engine, allowing the loud growl to shock his thoughts away. There was only one place he wanted to go.

His spot on the river.

He rode through the gate that separated Kit's place from his parents' and opened the throttle. The bike bumped along the damp ground, gaining speed. The wind was sharp and he squinted, his sunglasses not enough to protect his eyes. Part of him wanted to ride as far as possible until the petrol ran out and then keep walking. But hiding wouldn't solve a damned thing.

He slowed as he approached the fence line along the river and lowered the bike stand. Some of the tension left his shoulders as he slipped through the fence and walked the narrow, less defined path to the river. His jeans grew damp as he brushed past the grasses that crowded the path.

The burble of the river was a soothing melody as he reached its banks. More grass and a nearby gum tree had been cut down to provide somewhere to sit. Kit must still come down. He inhaled deeply, taking in the rich eucalyptus scent, and closed his eyes. It had been far too long since he'd been here.

He and Kit used to spend their afternoons after school here on hot summer days. Back then there'd been a rope swing in the tree and they'd spent hours splashing and playing, chatting about school and friends. Kit would complain about her family, he'd confide to her the boys and girls he liked and she'd tell him everyone had long forgotten about him wanting to be a hairdresser.

But he hadn't been brave enough then.

Just like now.

The last time he'd been to the river was right before

he'd left for university. The musketeers had ordered him to attend a ceremony where they'd vowed to keep in touch, to not let the distance get in the way of their friendship.

They'd swum in the river, drunk beer Kit had sourced from somewhere, and talked about what the future would bring. He'd left the next morning confident his friends would always have his back, no matter what happened.

They would stand by him with this as well.

The tightness in his chest eased. Whatever happened, he would get through this. He had support and he had Elijah. Jamie winced. If Elijah would talk to him after Jamie had left him behind.

That had been a douche move.

He shouldn't have let Patricia rattle him. He shouldn't have panicked.

But all of a sudden, the unfamiliar road he'd been going down had been filled with potholes and unexpected obstacles. Instead of stopping and figuring out a way through, he'd fled back down the road he knew.

Picking up a gum nut, he rubbed his thumb over the slightly rough shell and tossed it into the water.

Had his life become an endless cycle of taking the easy road because he was too scared of potholes? Thinking about it critically wasn't pretty.

He'd kept his head down as a teenager and when he'd moved to Perth, it had been much of the same. Sure he'd gone to gay bars and joined the community, but when it had come to a choice of who to date, he'd gone with Sandra. She'd been safe, non-threatening to his way of life and willing to do all the work in the relationship.

He frowned, picking up another gum nut. He'd

always considered himself a nice guy, but looking back at his relationship with Sandra he realised his heart had never quite been in it. She deserved better than him. She deserved to find a guy whose heart rate increased every time she entered the room. The way his did with Elijah.

He sighed. He wanted to be with Elijah. No more running away. Jamie needed to show his lover he wanted him in his life.

That he loved him.

Warmth settled over Jamie's shoulders like a blanket. He loved everything about Elijah; his kindness, his willingness to stick up for others, his sense of humour. He wanted so many more nights like last night, being together, talking about life, their hopes and dreams.

His phone dinged in his pocket. A group message from the musketeers. *We've got your back, always.*

He swallowed hard as his chest squeezed.

What was he doing hiding out here, moping, when he had people who cared about him?

He had to stop running, stop shielding himself from everything. It was time to fight back.

Chapter 16

Before Jamie got back on his bike, he pulled out his phone. Should he send Elijah a text to apologise? No, face to face was better. Instead, he phoned his mother again.

"Is everything all right, love?"

"It will be." He had to believe it. "I have to speak with you. Can you meet me at the house?"

A pause. "Sure. What's going on?"

Jamie sighed. "Something happened in town today which affects Lewis."

"We'll be there shortly."

He tucked the phone back into his pocket and rode back to the house. By the time he'd returned the bike to the shed, his parents and Lewis were walking up the drive.

Oh. He should have told his mother to come without Lewis. Too late.

"Hey, Mr Z. Harold's been teaching me how to make cheese. It's so cool." Lewis's enthusiasm was palpable.

Jamie hated he was going to ruin his day. "Yeah. You going to get into cheese-making instead of farming?"

He pursed his lips as they climbed the steps to the verandah. "Maybe."

Jamie's dad cheered, though his worried expression followed Jamie.

Inside the house, Jamie filled the kettle and his mother made sandwiches for lunch.

"I'll go change." Lewis winced. "I got a little enthusiastic stirring the milk. Got it over my boots."

Jamie placed a hand out to stop him. "Wait a second. I need to talk to you."

Lewis's face paled. "Has something happened to Mum?"

"As far as I know your family is fine." Noel would have to tell them about Patricia's accusations though. "You should hear about something that happened in town today."

His father poured a pot of tea and his mother pressed Lewis into a chair, placed a sandwich in front of him and sat next to him. "Whatever it is, we'll deal with it together."

Lewis nodded.

After only a couple of days with Jamie's parents and Lewis was already a more confident person. His parents were special.

Jamie cleared his throat but didn't sit. The anger and frustration coursing through him wouldn't be still. He paced the kitchen. "Elijah and I went to the River Café for brunch," he began.

His mother smiled. "You'll have to bring him to dinner next weekend."

Jamie shook his head. He had to focus. "We ran into Patricia Evans. She's the maths teacher at the college."

"She comes into the shop sometimes," his father said.

"She asked me out but Elijah made it clear we're dating, and she didn't take it so well."

Lewis's shoulders slumped as he paused between bites. "She doesn't like gays," he said. "I swear if she could figure out a way to fail me, she would."

Jamie raised his eyebrows. He'd known Patricia was conservative, but hadn't realised it had gone so deep. "You should have said something."

He laughed. "Like anyone would have believed me."

"I would have."

Lewis stopped chewing and nodded. "I know that now."

"So what did Patricia say?" Harold asked.

Jamie took a deep breath. "She implied it wasn't proper for Lewis to be staying with me and working with Elijah during the holidays. Insinuated a few things." He didn't need to clarify. They all understood.

His mother's mouth dropped open and his father's face went red.

"That's bullshit!" Lewis said. "No offence Mr Z, but you don't do it for me."

Jamie couldn't help laughing. "Glad to hear it."

His mother shook her head. "But he's not staying with you, he's staying with us," she said. "And he's working for Kit."

Jamie sobered. "She saw Lewis crying in my office, and saw him hugging me." He shrugged. "But it doesn't matter what the truth is. People are going to believe what they want to believe."

"I'm so sorry, Mr Z. This is my fault. If I hadn't come to you for help—"

Jamie interrupted him. "It's *not* your fault. This is all on Patricia, but you'll have to deal with this too. People might make nasty comments."

"I'm used to it." He scowled.

"So what happens now?" Harold asked.

"I've spoken to the principal, told him to expect Patricia's call. He'll want to come out here and talk to Lewis."

"I'll tell him Miss Evans is wrong."

Jamie glanced at him. "He'll ask you questions which might seem invasive, but he's got your best interest at heart."

"Will he take me away?"

Jamie hoped not. Lewis needed someone to support him. "I don't know. He'll need to talk to your parents as well."

Lewis swore and slumped in his chair. "Then I'm screwed."

"No, you're not," Rosa said. "You have a place here with us—always. We'll finish paying your tuition and you'll have somewhere safe to live."

Tears welled in Lewis's eyes. "But you hardly know me."

"We know enough. You're a good kid, who deserves better," Harold told him. "We'll be here for you."

Jamie's chest squeezed. He couldn't have asked for better parents.

"Thank you," Lewis said.

The phone rang and Harold answered it. His sigh was all Jamie needed to know Noel was on the other end. A minute later he hung up. "He's on his way out and said you shouldn't be here while he talks to Lewis. He'll call you later."

"Will you be all right?" Jamie directed the question at Lewis.

"Yeah. Thanks, Mr Z."

"I'll talk to you later." He stood, gave his mother a kiss on the cheek and left.

Noel was a reasonable man who wouldn't listen to

gossip. He'd talk to everyone involved, probably even go to the café and chat to whoever was there. Hopefully he'd understand Patricia had come to the wrong conclusion.

And if Barbara's response was any indication, Jamie would have some support. If he was lucky it would die down and become a non-issue. There was nothing more he could do about it though.

He headed for Elijah's place. He had an apology to make.

***

The rain had settled in for the afternoon. Elijah stood at the kitchen sink, drinking a coffee and staring out at the backyard. He really should weed it. Will had always managed the garden when they'd lived together, and Elijah had been happy for him to do so. Maybe he could convince Adam that gardening was therapeutic.

He sighed. The garden was the least of his worries. Talking to Jamie was at the top of his list. Had he given Jamie enough time? The idea of Jamie brooding, stressing over what would happen made him tense. Jamie's anxiety had been real.

His phone rang and he fumbled with it in his rush to answer.

"We're done at the depot," Adam said. "Are you still willing to clean?"

His hope deflated. "Yeah." When he was finished he'd call Jamie. Elijah placed his mug in the sink.

"Ryan and I will pick you up. See you in five." He hung up before Elijah agreed.

Well at least he wouldn't get soaked walking to the depot. He grabbed his rain jacket, phone and keys and when the police car pulled in, he ran out and slid into the back seat. "Thanks for the lift."

"We confirmed the car is yours," Adam said as Ryan drove. "We've had it towed to the station so we can examine it."

"Is much missing?"

"A few parts," Ryan said.

"Do you think Morgan's involved?" It was the only thing that made sense, though it was strange Morgan would dump the car at the depot.

"What makes you ask?"

He shrugged. "He's the only mechanic in town, and all the cars have been missing parts. When his roof lifted in the storm, I saw a bunch of greasy spare parts on his office desk."

"When?" Ryan asked, suddenly more alert.

"Monday night. I didn't think anything of it at the time, but now… I told Morgan I saw what happened the other night."

Adam swore. "Why?"

"I thought maybe someone was trying to frame him. I said he should talk to you about what's going on."

"What did he say?" Ryan asked.

"Told me the guys were drifters and long gone."

Ryan and Adam exchanged a glance.

"Yeah, he's got to be lying. Doesn't make me feel great."

They pulled up at the depot and went inside.

"Have you got someone you can call to help you with this?" Ryan asked.

"I can do it myself. I could do with some heavy lifting." The work might help him forget about the shit day.

"It would be better if you're not alone."

Elijah's skin crawled. "Do you still think I'm in danger?"

"I don't know, but we don't have the manpower to

have one of us stay with you." Ryan was apologetic.

"I'll call Kit."

"All right. We've let Morgan know we're done and he said you should call him when you're finished so he can lock up." Ryan hesitated. "Come and lock the door after us and make sure you check it's Kit when she arrives."

Ryan wasn't making him feel any better about this. Elijah followed them to the backdoor and locked it behind them. Then he went through the whole depot, checking rooms and cupboards and the windows and front door. He was alone and secure.

When he was done he'd call one of the other section leaders who had a key so he wouldn't have to see Morgan again.

Elijah called Kit. When she answered, it sounded like she was in her car. "Are you still in town?"

"No. I'm on my way to Albany for an appointment. What's wrong? Did the police find something?"

"It's fine. They took fingerprints and left."

"What do you need then?"

He hesitated. No need to worry her unnecessarily. "I was going to get a lift out to your place. My car's out of action for a while longer. Don't worry about it. Hopefully Jamie can take me."

"He hasn't called yet?"

"Not yet. I'll call him soon. Drive safely. I'll see you later." He hung up before she could argue further and looked at his phone, his finger hovering above Jamie's number.

Maybe he should give Jamie a bit more time. He was secure in here.

He flicked on more lights and took stock of the situation. So much was covered in fingerprint dust. This would keep him busy for the next couple of hours.

He'd wait another half an hour before calling Jamie.

It didn't take long to refold the tarps and stack them back on the shelves. The ropes took a little longer, tangling as he tried to separate them. He was so focused on the work that the deep base of his ringtone made him jump and he dropped the rope he was curling. Heart racing, he answered.

"I'm sorry, I freaked out."

Relief filled him at Jamie's voice and he smiled. "I don't blame you. Patricia was way out of line."

"Yeah. Can we talk?"

Elijah frowned. He couldn't read Jamie's tone. Would it be a bad talk or a good talk? "I'm at the depot cleaning. Someone broke in and made a mess."

Jamie swore. "Who else is there?"

"No one. It's not much work."

Jamie growled in disapproval. "I'll meet you there in twenty."

"Knock on the back door and I'll let you in." He slid his phone back into his pocket, acknowledging the nerves humming through his veins. Jamie had apologised, but it didn't mean he was OK. Maybe he'd already lost his job, or perhaps he'd decided his job was more important than Elijah. This could be an ending not a beginning.

He gritted his teeth. This was Patricia's fault. He wouldn't let her ruin Jamie's life.

His anger stirred his speed and it didn't take him long to finish tidying the ropes. A click echoed along the corridor, followed by footsteps. Elijah turned. "Jamie, is that you?"

As soon as the words left his mouth he remembered he'd locked the doors. No one should be inside. His gut clenched and a large man stepped out from behind a land cruiser, wearing a black balaclava and with a gun pointed at Elijah.

Fuck.

Elijah raised both hands, heart pounding in his chest.

The gunman strode towards him and Elijah backed up until he hit the shelving. He was so dead. The gunman reached him and smashed his fist into Elijah's face.

Then there was darkness.

***

Elijah woke, a strange pressure around his neck as if he was being strangled. He lifted his hands to his throat, blinking to clear his vision and trying to force his mind to work. His fingers encountered thick rope, wrapped around his neck, choking off his air supply.

Fear pierced through the remaining haziness and he clenched the rope, dragging it away from his neck, but it barely moved.

"Shit, you're awake." The voice came from the side and Elijah spotted a man holding the end of the rope that was currently strangling him. He glanced up. Not strangling, hanging him. Though Elijah's feet still touched the ground, the rope looped through the rafters of the SES depot.

"What—" His voice rasped against the rough rope and he swallowed.

"You know too much, Elijah."

Elijah managed to curl his fingers around the rope, inserting them so the rope wasn't pressing into his neck. "I don't know anything!"

"Morgan told me what you said. You should have kept it to yourself."

"No one's going to believe I hanged myself." The

gunman had no moon boot so he probably wasn't Mark, but he had to be the guy he'd seen on the motorbike. At least he'd put the gun down somewhere.

He pulled the rope and Elijah's heels left the ground, so he was balanced on his toes. He clenched his teeth, lifted his face to the roof to relieve the pressure.

"After the scene in the café they will," he said. "You're full of guilt about seducing that poor kid and ruining your lover's career. I've got the note right here." He held up a folded piece of paper in his gloved hand. "You should be more careful who you piss off."

Elijah's mouth dropped open. Mark had to be behind this. What had he said? "You'll get yours".

"You don't know my handwriting." He panted, his fingers frantically trying to loosen the rope, his chest tight. There had to be some way to convince the guy this wouldn't work.

"There's this great new invention called computers," the man said.

Elijah almost laughed. "You should try using one," he gasped. "The coroner will be able to tell I was strangled slowly, rather than jumping to my death." He rolled his eyes. "They'll be searching for you in a matter of days."

The man swore. "Bullshit."

"Google it," Elijah suggested.

The man tied the rope to the post and got out his phone.

The rope around Elijah's neck loosened a little and his heels scraped the ground. Elijah slid his hands to the slip knot to loosen it further. This was his chance. The gun was nowhere in sight, so if he was fast, he could overpower the man and run. He was concentrating on his phone, scrolling through entries. Elijah widened the loop and pushed it up.

"What the hell!"

Both Elijah and the gunman jumped. Morgan strode towards them both, horror on his face.

"Stay out of this, Morgan," the gunman said, untying the rope again.

The rope tightened around Elijah's jaw and lifted him off the ground. His feet flailed trying to find ground to take the pressure off his head.

"Put him down. I won't let you kill him."

Elijah's feet hit the ground and Elijah yanked the rope down instead of up. Shit. Right back around his neck. His grip tightened on the rope but it was too late to loosen it.

"You don't get a say in this, Morgan," the gunman said. "Your job is to do what you're told."

"I'll call the police."

"You'll go to gaol too."

Morgan's shoulders slumped. "I can't do this anymore."

He was on Elijah's side. Elijah had to convince the gunman. "The police are looking for you. You made a mistake when you sent Mark Patton to watch me. He's way too conspicuous."

The gunman swore.

"Killing me isn't going to help you," Elijah continued. "They know about the chop shop and that you've been using Foley's place. Murder's a far longer sentence than car theft."

"That's not all he's done," Morgan said.

"Shut up!"

Elijah tugged at the rope. "Give yourself in."

Pain crossed Morgan's face. "My family needs me. Julia requires so much help."

Elijah's heart went out to him. "How did you get messed up in this?"

"These bastards blackmailed me." He pointed to the other man. "I helped a kid out one time, used some parts on his car that he'd supplied even though I was pretty sure they were stolen. They were in on it. Kept evidence."

"Like I haven't been forced into this just as much as you," the gunman said. "You know what they did to Henk."

"They're trying to frame me. Why else would they leave Elijah's car here?" Morgan demanded.

"Because he's got a stupid sense of humour."

The rope gave a little, but the two men were too busy glaring at each other to notice. Elijah shifted it a little more. Not much further to go. Then the name registered in his consciousness. Henk had been in charge of the illegal migrant racket and had been arrested a couple of weeks ago. Before he could stop himself, he asked, "What happened to Henk?"

"He had an *accident* in gaol," Morgan spat. "Beaten to a pulp and is on life support. They don't think he'll live."

Elijah's blood ran cold. Is that what Mark had meant the other night when he'd said the boss had Henk covered? "It sounds like you both want out. I'm sure the police can protect you."

The man shook his head. "Not from these guys."

A movement behind Morgan caught Elijah's attention. Someone else was in the depot. Was it someone working with the gunman, ensuring they finished the job?

The head popped above the bonnet of the land cruiser and his heart froze. Jamie.

"Maybe Elijah's right," Morgan said. "Maybe we can bring them down."

The gunman shook his head. "Don't be stupid. Too

many people owe them favours. It would never work. You'd only end up like Henk."

Elijah kept his gaze on Morgan, but behind Morgan, Jamie crept towards them, the body of the land cruiser shielding him from the gunman's view.

"Not if we call the police now. Confess everything." Morgan's fingers twitched towards his pocket where his mobile probably was.

The other man swore and drew out his gun. "Don't even think about it."

Elijah froze. They'd shoot Jamie if they saw him. That couldn't happen. He had to distract them.

Had to save Jamie's life.

He fumbled desperately at the knot around his neck. The man yanked the rope and Elijah's feet left the ground.

Chapter 17

Jamie tapped his fingers on the steering wheel and resisted the urge to accelerate. He didn't like the idea of Elijah being alone. Especially at the depot. It was surrounded by the river and bush on three sides, and on a road not many people travelled.

He slowed further at the town limits and crawled into Blackbridge, making his way to the SES building. He hadn't noticed anyone following them today, but that didn't mean no one had.

He parked next to the building and walked around the back. As he rounded the corner, he halted.

A black ute was parked there. The car that had followed Elijah on Saturday.

His skin crawled and he dug his phone out and called Lincoln.

"You feeling any better?" Lincoln asked.

"I'm at the SES depot," Jamie said, his voice low. "There's a black ute parked outside. Elijah's inside."

Lincoln swore. "Stay on the phone. Don't go in. We'll be right there."

He wasn't waiting for the police. Elijah could be in trouble. "I'll put you on speaker."

"Don't go in there, Jamie," Lincoln growled.

"I'm not leaving Elijah in there alone."

"Jamie, it's too dangerous."

He had to put his feelings into words Lincoln would understand. "Elijah's my Kit." No way would Lincoln wait for backup if Kit was inside.

Lincoln swore. "Be careful. I'm right behind you."

Jamie tucked his phone in his jacket pocket, careful not to hang up, but left it off speaker. He couldn't risk whoever was inside hearing Lincoln. Slowly he rotated the back door handle and slipped inside the darkened corridor. He closed the door behind him and paused, listening. Nothing. His heart pounded. Was he already too late?

He moved swiftly down the corridor to where it branched. The left corridor led to the offices and meeting rooms, the right led to the equipment. He headed right. As he got closer he heard voices. Elijah's voice was clear and loud and some of his panic decreased. Elijah was alive.

He crept closer, staying low, using the vehicles as a shield. The voices came from behind the second land cruiser, next to the shelving. Jamie risked a glance above the bonnet of the car. His heart stopped. Elijah had a noose around his neck and a man held the other end, ready to pull him off his feet. In front of them was Morgan.

He ducked again. The man with the rope had to be his first target. Morgan was already talking about going to the police. He moved to the next land cruiser. Still a lot of open space to cover before he could tackle the other man. He might have some element of surprise. Or maybe he should wait where he was for Lincoln to arrive.

He peeked again, and this time the man held a gun

and was pointing it at Morgan.

OK, so tackling him probably wouldn't work.

Not without a bullet proof vest. He shuffled back while the two men yelled at each other and he murmured into his phone, "Morgan's here with someone else. The other guy has a gun. They're by the equipment shelving."

"We're right outside. Hold tight."

"Are you going to shoot me?" Morgan asked as Jamie tucked his phone back into his pocket.

"If it keeps you from talking. I'm not ending up like Henk."

"We don't have to. The police will help us."

Bang.

Jamie flinched as the gunshot echoed around the room and there was a thud. He peered under the land cruiser and immediately retched. Morgan lay there, eyes open, bleeding profusely from a bullet hole in his chest, gasping for breath.

"Please, you don't want to do this," Elijah begged. "The police are on their way. Adam was going to pick me up in an hour."

The man swore.

"They'll be here—" Elijah's voice was cut off and garbled noises came from him.

Jamie peered around the vehicle.

Elijah hung, his legs flailing and hands grappling around his neck. The man tied the rope off on the shelving, keeping Elijah hanging there. Elijah's face was turning red. Jamie didn't have time to wait for Lincoln.

He lunged for the man, knocking him forward against the shelving. He grabbed the rope, pulling at the knot.

The man roared and elbowed Jamie hard in the ribs. The air left his lungs at the impact and he stumbled back, unable to untie the rope. Voices shouted all around him, but his focus was on Elijah. His legs weren't moving anymore.

Panic shunted him forward. He had to get to Elijah. Had to take the pressure off the rope.

Another gun shot and he stumbled, holding onto Elijah's legs, pushing him up, to take the weight off the rope. Elijah's eyes were closed, his head floppy. No.

Fear flooded him. Elijah couldn't be dead. He wouldn't let him die.

He hooked a nearby chair with one leg and dragged it closer, standing on it and lifting Elijah at the same time. It was no use. He couldn't hold Elijah with one arm and loosen the noose with the other. Lincoln and Sue had disarmed the gunman and Sue applied pressure to the gunshot wound in the gunman's chest.

"Lincoln!" Jamie yelled.

Lincoln glanced over and in two steps was there and undid the knot. Jamie cushioned Elijah's fall and laid him on the ground. His hands shook as he tugged at the rope, undoing it and slipping it over Elijah's head. "Elijah." He shook him, and checked his breathing. Elijah's chest rose and fell.

Relief flooded Jamie and he moved Elijah into the recovery position.

"How is he?" Lincoln called from where he was checking Morgan.

"Alive."

Sirens wailed as an ambulance approached. Jamie clutched Elijah's hand. "Elijah, wake up for me. You're safe."

Elijah's eyelids fluttered.

Jamie kissed his hand. "That's it, E. Open your eyes."

Elijah opened his eyes. "Jamie?" he croaked.

"Don't talk. The ambulance is almost here. They'll check you." He pulled him close hugging him, his heartbeat slowing.

Elijah would be all right.

***

Elijah had been prodded and scanned and was sick of the antiseptic scent of the hospital. All he wanted was to curl up in bed and pretend the day hadn't happened. The one highlight was Jamie had stayed by his side the whole time, except for when he'd gone for his scan.

The doctor cleared her throat. "It's looking good, Elijah. Although there's severe bruising, there's no long-term damage to your throat. You'll be sore for a few days and should keep talking to a minimum." She smiled at him. "If anything gets worse, come back, and I want you to go for a check-up with your GP at the end of the week."

Elijah nodded. "Can I go?"

"Yeah. I'll get the paperwork sorted for you."

Jamie turned to him as the doctor left. "You should call your parents."

Elijah shook his head. "Not until I talk to the police." His parents were still in Perth and until he heard they wouldn't be targeted, he didn't want them coming home.

Jamie frowned but when the nurse returned with the discharge paperwork, he helped Elijah to his feet.

Elijah leaned against him for a moment, drawing comfort and warmth. Then they walked out to Jamie's car.

"Do you want to go home?" Jamie asked.

Elijah nodded. The less speaking he did the better. His phone rang as he got into the passenger seat. He put it on speaker so Jamie could talk.

"Hey, Lincoln," Jamie said. "We're leaving the hospital and I'm taking Elijah to his place."

"How is he?"

"Bruised, but whole. How's Morgan?"

"Alive. Both men are under police guard at Albany Hospital. We need to interview Elijah. Is he up for it?"

"Yeah," Elijah croaked and winced at the pain.

"All right. We'll meet you at Elijah's place."

Elijah hung up and Jamie asked, "Are you OK to talk?"

Elijah nodded. He wanted to put this behind him so he could finally haul Jamie into his arms and hold him all night. He gingerly touched his neck. A dark bruise had already started to form, but hopefully it wouldn't last for long.

They arrived at his place and once inside, Jamie pulled him towards the couch. "Sit, I'll make you a cuppa." He brushed the hair off Elijah's face. "Do you want lemon and ginger, or honey?" He turned to head to the kitchen.

Elijah stopped him, pulled him into his arms. "I want you." The emotion he'd been suppressing raised up and rattled his body. Elijah breathed deeply and clenched his teeth to keep from blubbering all over the place.

Jamie sighed and held him tightly. "I've never been so scared," he whispered. "When you were hanging there, not moving..." His voice broke.

Elijah flinched. It wasn't an image he wanted in his head. He kissed Jamie and then rested his forehead against his. "I was terrified the gunman would shoot you." He winced at the rasp.

"Don't speak. We're safe." Jamie ran his hands over Elijah's back, soothing them both.

Elijah didn't want to let go. While he held Jamie he

knew he was safe, but he kept reliving the explosion of the gun, the blood appearing on Morgan's chest and thinking Jamie could be next. He'd never felt such red-hot terror before and in that moment he would have done anything to save the man he loved.

He opened his mouth to say the words as someone knocked on the door.

Jamie reluctantly pulled away. "I'll get it. You sit down."

Elijah watched him go. He would tell Jamie how he felt soon, but first he had to get through the interview. And that would hurt his throat. He flicked on the kettle and chose the kitchen table for the interview. Better to have the hard dining room chair at his back, not something he could sink into and let his emotions take control.

Lincoln and Sue walked in and greeted Elijah while Jamie made the drinks.

"Jamie, you can't stay here while we interview Elijah," Lincoln said.

Elijah glanced at Jamie. He wanted him there, wanted to hold his hand and have his support.

"Why not?" Jamie demanded.

"Because we need to interview you as well. We can't have Elijah's statement potentially contaminating yours."

Jamie scowled.

"He shouldn't be alone," Elijah rasped. "There might be others who want to get him."

Lincoln's eyebrows raised. "Who?"

"Don't know." It would take a long time to explain everything.

"Jamie can wait in your room, put some music on or something."

Elijah nodded and Jamie placed a mug of tea on the

table for him. "If you need me, I'm not far." He kissed Elijah far too briefly and walked down the hallway.

Lincoln ran through the formalities of recording the interview and Elijah began his tale. It was difficult to speak and he had to take long pauses to rest his throat. But eventually he managed to tell the whole story. Lincoln didn't seem too surprised when Elijah mentioned he thought someone above both Morgan and the gunman was pulling the strings.

"Who was the gunman?" Elijah asked.

"The man who worked for Henk," Lincoln said. "We're not certain where he's been hiding the past couple of weeks."

"Foley's?"

Sue shook her head. "We checked all the buildings on the property after you found the cars there. No sign of anyone living there."

"Mark's?" Elijah guessed.

The officers exchanged a glance. "We're not sure," Lincoln said. "We're watching him. You should avoid him as much as you can."

He had no problem with that.

"Is there anything else you want to say?" Sue said.

Elijah shook his head and then remembered his response needed to be recorded. "No," he rasped, wincing at the scratchiness.

"We'll talk to Jamie," Lincoln said. "Why don't you rest for an hour?"

Elijah smiled at him. He might come across as officious at times, but Lincoln had a big heart.

Elijah opened his bedroom door. Jamie was lying on his bed, playing with his phone, as if he was meant to be there. Elijah's heart squeezed.

Jamie sprang off the bed. "Hey, E. Are you done?"

He nodded.

"You should rest," Jamie said, pulling him to the bed and pressing him to sit on it. He bent to untie Elijah's shoelaces.

Elijah's heart expanded further. How could he not love this man who was so concerned for his wellbeing? At Jamie's prompting he lay down and Jamie covered him with the quilt.

"Get some rest. I'll wake you when I'm done." He brushed a kiss on Elijah's forehead and Elijah smiled.

He closed his eyes and sleep pulled him under.

***

"How is he?" Lincoln asked as Jamie returned to the living room.

Jamie frowned. "I'm not sure." He wanted to talk it through with Elijah but with the damage to his throat, it wasn't advisable. Jamie sat at the table.

"How are you?"

He shrugged. "Shaken. Angry. I want to hit something or someone."

"I've got a punching bag you can borrow," his brother said.

It was better than a real person—unless that person was Morgan or the gunman and then it would be a real pleasure to hit them repeatedly.

Sue cleared her throat and did the introductions for the interview. Jamie relived what had happened moment by moment from when he'd first seen the black ute.

"What did the men say?" Lincoln asked.

"Morgan was trying to convince the gunman to give up, go to the police, but the gunman said he didn't want to end up like Henk."

Lincoln's eye twitched but it was the only sign he was upset.

"What happened to Henk? Isn't he behind bars?"

Sue glanced at Lincoln and he nodded. "He was attacked in gaol and he's in intensive care in a coma. The doctors don't think he'll make it."

Jamie whistled. "Did he say anything before the attack?"

Lincoln shook his head. "He refused to answer any questions about the migrants or who else he was working with."

Which meant someone else had to be involved and Morgan and the gunman were both scared of them. Not good. "Is Elijah in danger?"

"I don't think so," Lincoln said. "He's told us everything he knows. Morgan and Henk's guy are more likely to be the target. They can point a finger directly at the guy at the top."

Good.

"Do you have anything more you can add?" Sue asked.

"No."

Lincoln finished the interview details and switched off the recorder. Sue packed up their things.

"I'll meet you in the car. I need a quick word with my brother," Lincoln said.

Sue shot Jamie a sympathetic look as she left.

Jamie frowned. "What's up?"

Lincoln waited until the front door closed before he turned to him, eyes dark. "If you *ever* do anything that stupid again, I will kill you."

Jamie held up his hands and backed away, heart pounding. He'd seen Lincoln pissed before, but this was a whole other level. "What did I do?"

Lincoln growled, fists clenched. "You attacked an armed man," he bit out. "And then you were stupid enough to turn your back on him without disarming him." A vein in his forehead pulsed. "He was pointing the gun at you. If I hadn't shot him first, you'd be dead."

The blood drained from Jamie's head. "I had to save Elijah."

The sound of frustration in Lincoln's throat had Jamie flinching but he didn't have time to react further before Lincoln hugged him tightly. "You scared the living daylights out of me. I thought I'd have to tell Mum and Dad you were dead." The emotion in Lincoln's voice had tears welling in Jamie's eyes.

"I'm sorry." He patted Lincoln on the back and felt the tremor in his body. Jamie's heart clenched. He'd never seen his brother this upset.

"I told you to wait." Lincoln stepped back, glared at him.

"Elijah was being strangled to death. I couldn't wait. You were right behind me."

Lincoln shook his head. "I might have been too late."

"But you weren't," Jamie said. "Don't play the what if game, Slinky. It will only do your head in." He hugged him again. "I'm fine, Elijah's going to be fine. How are you?"

Lincoln took a shaky breath. "I'll be better when we catch the bastard behind all this."

"You'll see a counsellor about shooting the guy?" Jamie asked.

"Yes, Mum." Lincoln smiled. "They've already taken away my gun."

Jamie put his arm around Lincoln's shoulder and walked him to the front door. "Take care of yourself."

"You too. I don't like the idea of you out in the shed by yourself. Maybe you could stay with Elijah for a few days."

"Sure." He wasn't planning on leaving Elijah's side.

Lincoln pulled him close in a final hug. "I'm telling Mum on you."

Jamie laughed and winced at the same time. "She'll make sure you go to the counsellor multiple times."

Lincoln grinned and nodded. "See you later, JJ."

Jamie closed the door after him and locked it. Then he walked down the hallway to Elijah's bedroom. A peek inside showed Elijah was fast asleep. Good. He needed rest after his ordeal. Jamie entered the room and closed the door. He took off his shoes and jeans and slid into the bed next to Elijah, pulling him close.

"Jamie?"

"Yeah, it's me. Go back to sleep, love. I'm here."

Elijah shuffled back so he was nestled into Jamie's front and Jamie closed his eyes.

This was how he wanted to spend his life. Ending every day with Elijah curled up against him.

Content, he drifted off to sleep.

EPILOGUE

Jamie woke the next morning with Elijah still curled up in front of him. Memories flooded him of the day before and he pulled Elijah towards him, reassuring himself Elijah was fine. Elijah murmured in his sleep and Jamie smiled.

It was already nine o'clock. Adam would be at work which meant they had the house to themselves. Jamie could bring Elijah breakfast in bed. Before he could get up, his phone rang, the tone piercing the silence and Elijah flinched awake.

"Sorry." Jamie picked up his phone. His heart lurched. It was Noel. He'd forgotten all about Patricia's accusations.

He swallowed hard and answered, "Hi, Noel."

Elijah sat up and ran one hand over his face, blinking to clear the sleep from his eyes while the other reached for Jamie's hand.

Jamie smiled.

"I wanted to give you an update," Noel said. "I've spoken to both Lewis and Patricia. Patricia admits she might have jumped to conclusions in her shock at discovering you with Elijah."

"Might have?" He couldn't leave the incredulity out of his voice.

"Yeah. If it helps any, she did sound sorry."

It didn't matter. The words couldn't be unsaid.

"Lewis confirmed nothing untoward happened between you two, but I need to remind you of your fiduciary relationship with the students," Noel said. "And I'll send a report to the standards unit in case one of the parents gets wind of it and goes to them."

Jamie winced, but it was probably a good way of covering all bases. "Did you call Lewis's parents?"

"I couldn't get hold of them. I'll call again today."

Which might not be great for Lewis. Jamie would call his parents later and find out how it went. "Does this mean I still have a job?"

"You do."

Relief filled him. He hadn't known what he would do if he couldn't teach.

"I've warned Patricia about speaking out in public," Noel continued. "She should have come to me first." He sighed. "This may harm your reputation," he said. "So many people heard her accusations and that's going to be difficult to deal with."

"I'll manage." After almost losing Elijah, his reputation didn't seem so important anymore.

"I'll speak to Barbara," Noel said. "I understand she was at the café."

"She was. Will you tell her about your investigation?"

"If you're happy for me to."

"Please do." Barbara would spread the word about his innocence, and she would deal with anyone who said anything to the contrary.

"Enjoy the rest of your holidays, Jamie." Noel hung up.

"What did he say?" Elijah asked.

Jamie let out a deep breath. "I still have a job. Patricia admitted she might have jumped to conclusions."

"Well duh." Elijah hugged Jamie. "That's great. Why don't we go to Mai's bakery to celebrate?"

"Are you up for going out?" Jamie brushed the bruising around Elijah's neck.

"Yeah. Can't let the bastards keep me down." He stretched and yawned, wincing a little. "Let's have a shower." He got out of bed and headed for the bathroom.

Jamie followed him. "After we're done, do you want to come out to my parents' place?" He'd spoken to them last night after he and Elijah had woken from their nap, but he wanted to see them, and make sure Lewis was OK.

Elijah looked concerned. "Sure. As long as you don't think you should go alone?"

"I'm not letting you out of my sight for the foreseeable future." Jamie pulled Elijah into his arms. If he closed his eyes, he still saw Elijah hanging there, his face changing colour. He shivered.

"They might want to see you without me there."

Jamie shook his head. "Too bad. They'll learn you're the most important person in the world to me." When Elijah's eyes widened, Jamie realised he hadn't told Elijah how he felt. He'd been so relieved Elijah was alive, so busy taking care of him, that he hadn't said the words in his heart. Jamie kissed him. "I never told you what I did when I ran off." He ran a hand through his hair. "I'm sorry for freaking out. I should have stayed with you, talked it over."

Elijah nodded. "Yeah, you should have."

Jamie grinned, kissed him again. "While I was by the

river, feeling sorry for myself, I realised I'd been a douche leaving you behind. I wanted you there with me, by my side." Jamie cupped Elijah's face. "I love you, E."

Elijah's mouth formed an O but no words came out.

Nerves tickled his stomach. "Every time I think of you, my heart skips a beat."

"Maybe you should see a doctor." Elijah pulled him closer.

Jamie laughed. "You're my first thought when I wake, and the only one I think of when I'm lying in bed at night." He kissed Elijah slowly, sinking into the kiss, tasting the man he loved. When he pulled back, tears were in Elijah's eyes.

His heart stopped and he gently wiped them away. "Are you OK? Did I say the wrong thing?"

"Honey…" Elijah swallowed, brushed away the tears. "You said everything right." His smile was tremulous. "I love you, too."

***

It was another hour before Jamie and Elijah made it to Mai's bakery. Mai raced out from the kitchen and flung her arms around Jamie. "How are you? Kit told us what happened yesterday. I was about to call you."

Jamie hugged his small friend back. "Everything is fine. Elijah will be sore for a few days though."

Mai hugged Elijah as well. "If you need anything, you give me a call."

Elijah smiled at her. "Thanks, honey."

Mai stepped back, straightened her apron. "What can I get you two? It's on the house."

"Mayday, it's not necessary."

She raised an eyebrow. "I insist. It's not every day my JJ is almost killed."

"What?" Elijah whirled on him.

Jamie winced. Lincoln had obviously told Kit everything. Tell-tale. "Lincoln said the gunman turned his gun on me while I was rescuing you, but Lincoln shot him before he shot me."

Elijah dragged Jamie into his arms. "Oh my God. If I didn't love you so much, I'd be furious."

Jamie's chest filled with warmth. He wouldn't ever get tired of hearing it. "We'll both take care of each other."

Mai grinned at them. "Good. Now what do you want?"

They ordered and found a table in the middle of the bakery.

"The doctor gave you two days off work, didn't she?" Jamie asked. Two days he could spend completely with Elijah. Maybe they could look at houses together.

"Yeah, but Kit told me not to come back until Monday," he said. "She's got Lewis to help her over the next few days."

A smile spread across Jamie's face. "So does that mean I have you to myself for almost a week?"

"If you want me."

"I do." Jamie kissed Elijah's hand and Elijah fanned himself.

Someone cleared their throat next to the table. "Excuse me for interrupting."

Jamie flinched at Patricia's voice. He hadn't even noticed her in the bakery. Hadn't paid attention to anyone but Elijah. He breathed out. "Yes?"

She twisted her hands together. "I'm sorry about yesterday. I made some terrible accusations." She glanced around. The bakery was quiet. Her cheeks stained red and she straightened her posture. "Noel told me what you did for Lewis and it's commendable. I'm sorry."

Jamie studied her. She did look apologetic, although she studiously ignored Elijah and the way they held hands. "I appreciate you admitting your mistake, and in public too. It takes guts." Everyone was watching. Word had spread quickly.

"I'll see you next term." She walked out of the bakery.

Elijah squeezed his hand and Jamie smiled. It was a start. There were bound to be nasty comments to deal with, but maybe it wouldn't be too bad.

"Back to your food, people," Mai said as she carried their coffees to the table.

"Thanks, Mayday."

"You all right?" Elijah asked, his eyes full of concern.

Jamie nodded. "Yeah, I've got you."

That's what really mattered. He had his family, his friends, Elijah and a job he loved.

He didn't need anything else.

***

The nerves in Elijah's stomach grooved to a disco beat as they drove out to Jamie's parents' place that evening. They'd been invited to dinner, but he wasn't certain of his welcome. He'd put their youngest son in danger... The very thought of Jamie getting shot sent chills through him.

Elijah gritted his teeth. Don't think about it. "They know I'm coming, right?"

Jamie glanced at him. "Yeah. They invited you."

"Who else is going to be there?" Elijah asked.

"Just Lincoln, Kit and Lewis."

Hopefully Lewis would be all right. It wouldn't be easy dealing with Patricia's accusations.

Jamie parked in front of the farmhouse next to Kit's ute. Elijah exhaled and greeted Sasha as she wagged her tail in excitement. Why was he so nervous? At the stairs, Jamie took his hand and Elijah couldn't stop the slight tremor.

"Hey, are you OK?" Jamie turned to him.

He nodded. "Just a few nerves."

Jamie frowned. "But you know everyone."

He ran a hand over his throat, wishing the pain away. "This is the first time I've been to dinner at my partner's parents'," he said. "What if they don't like that we're together?"

Jamie pulled him close. "Mum is ecstatic I've found someone and Dad is pleased I'm happy. They will love you, because I love you." He kissed Elijah softly. "You don't have to worry about Kit or Lincoln."

Elijah chuckled. Yeah, Kit had been over the moon when he'd spoken to her.

"I'll be by your side the whole time," Jamie murmured. "I'll shield you from them if necessary, but if needed, it will be from an excess of love." He kissed him again and stepped back. "Ready?"

Elijah nodded. With this man by his side, he could do anything. "Let's go."

They walked in the back door and were greeted by the meaty scent of a roast. Elijah's stomach rumbled. In the kitchen, Harold carved the meat while Rosa dished roast vegetables into serving bowls. Kit and Lincoln chatted to Lewis at the table.

"Hi everyone," Jamie said.

Rosa spun around, dumped the hot tray she held on the bench and swept Jamie into her arms. "You're OK?" She held him at a distance to check and then hugged him again. "Lincoln was so upset, I thought you'd be more injured."

"Hey, I said he was fine," Lincoln protested.

She rolled her eyes. "I can tell when my baby is scared." She turned to Elijah, gently drawing down the scarf he wore around his neck and tutted. "Oh, honey. How are you?" She held him tightly.

Elijah could barely breathe.

"Will there be any lasting damage? Can you talk?"

Jamie chuckled. "If you let him get a word in, he can."

Elijah swallowed hard. "I'll be all right when the bruising fades."

"Good. Take a seat, both of you. Dinner's almost ready." She dashed back to her hot pan as Harold took his turn to hug Jamie and Elijah.

"Glad you're both here," he said.

Elijah had no words. He let Jamie pull him to the table and sat next to Lewis.

"How's things, Lewis?" Jamie asked.

Lewis shrugged. "Mum called this afternoon. The principal called them and Dad's disowned me."

Elijah's heart sank. "Oh, honey. I'm so sorry."

Rosa placed the bowl of roast potatoes on the table. "We agreed Lewis will stay with us. Harold and I will pay for his last semester at the ag college and after Lewis finishes, he can stay as long as he wants. He's family now."

Lewis nodded. "Real family sticks together." He said it defiantly, but Elijah saw the devastation in his eyes.

"We're all here for you, honey." Elijah squeezed his hand and Lewis's smile was shaky.

"The best family is the one you make," Kit declared.

Harold placed the meat on the table and they dished up.

"Speaking of family, and of Lewis staying around." Lincoln took hold of Kit's hand. "We might be needing some extra help at the dairy in about eight months' time."

Rosa froze, fork halfway to her lips, eyes wide.

"We're having a baby," Kit said.

Rosa's scream almost pierced Elijah's eardrums, but he grinned at the joy that enveloped the table as Rosa hauled Kit and Lincoln to their feet to hug them.

When she was finished with them, Elijah hugged Kit.

"I'm going to research what a pregnant woman can do around the farm," he said.

"You and Lincoln both," she growled.

"It's only because we love you."

She hugged him. "How's your neck really?"

"Sore, but the doctor says it will heal." He touched it.

"I'm glad."

He stepped back so Jamie could hug her and next to him, Lewis shook his head.

"It's some family, hey?" Elijah said.

Lewis nodded and Rosa grabbed his hands and spun Lewis around the kitchen singing, "I'm going to be a nonna!"

Jamie wrapped an arm around Elijah's waist. "It's your family now too." He searched Elijah's eyes. "If you want it to be."

Elijah grinned. "I want you, and everything that comes with it."

Jamie kissed him hard and fast. "Good."

Elijah's heart sang. It was better than good, it was amazing.

State Emergency Services

The state emergency services do a lot for the community. They're the ones who go out to help on days and nights when most of us would rather be rugged up inside. They're also the ones who search for missing people, help reunite you with loved ones. Though I only really mentioned the operations team in this book, there are many support roles as well. The SES runs on volunteers and they are always looking for more volunteers. If you're interested in discovering how you can help, go to http://www.ses-wa.asn.au/node/1603 or contact your local SES branch.

Acknowledgements

I must thank the Rockingham State Emergency Services and in particular Mark who answered all my questions about what they do and loaned me a uniform so I could arrange a photo shoot for the cover. A big thank you also to Daniel de Lorne who agreed to pose as Jamie for the original cover shoot. Dan is a romance author as well and you can find his books at https://danieldelorne.com/. Thank you to my sister-in-law, Shelly who took the photos for the original cover. You can find more information about her amazing photography at https://smilephotography.com.au/

As always a big thank you to my production team, Ann, Ida and Teena. You always make my novels shine.

Others who helped with my research include Noel Woodley and Libby Corson who answered questions about teaching and the agricultural college respectively. Thank you!

I really appreciate everyone giving their time to help me make this book as good as it can be.

Harbour

The Blackbridge Series #7

She doesn't love him anymore. But if she leaves him, she might pay the ultimate price…

Alyse Wilson can't remember the last time she felt safe in her own home. And after years of her abusive partner laundering money through her business, she doesn't see any way out. But when rough seas threaten to sink her small craft, she's stunned when she's plucked from the waves by an old high-school friend.

Marine Rescue Officer Kim On will never forget the day he lost Alyse. And when he unexpectedly finds himself pulling her into his arms from the depths, he can tell she needs saving from more than just choppy waters. So he vows to do whatever it takes to help her escape, unaware his rival is willing to employ deadly force to keep her in his power.

Gaining a glimpse of a life outside a toxic relationship, Alyse prepares a case to ensure her cruel partner's arrest. And though he realizes he's falling for his former crush all over again, Kim worries the closer they get, the more peril she's in.

Can Alyse and Kim break the hold of a controlling man without it costing their lives?

Harbour is the seventh standalone novel in the page-turning Blackbridge romantic suspense series. If you like breathtaking drama, high-stakes tension, and unexpected twists and turns, then you'll adore Claire Boston's tale of love and danger.

Buy *Harbour* to fight for freedom today!